Golden Orchid

SUSAN STRADIOTTO

BRONZEWOOD books

Eden Prairie, MN

Golden Orchid

© 2023 Susan Stradiotto

Published by:
Bronzewood Books
14920 Ironwood Ct.
Eden Prairie, MN 55346

Cover Design: Bronzewood Books

Interior Design: Bronzewood Books

Edited by: Owl Pro Editing.

Paperback ISBN-13: 978-1-949357-39-4

eBook ISBN-13: 978-1-949357-14-1

Publication history: A prior version of this book was published under the pen name Julia O. Green in 2019

For my girlfriends who need a
happy ending . . .
You know who you are!

Love to you all!

Susan

One

$\mathcal{T}$HIS IS IT.

Tonight.

The. End.

Callista Stockton slid the vodka back into the upper cabinet and flipped off the light switch. With her second martini in hand, she rounded the pristine white marble peninsula and went to the table where, once her eyes adjusted, she would still be able to see the entirety of the freshly remodeled kitchen, as well as the front door. A haunting glow emitted from the only remaining light in the house—an outrageously priced crystal pendant over the sink, the one Bennett had demanded they spend nearly six thousand dollars to have as a centerpiece in the kitchen. Shards of light created tiny rainbows on the far wall, but Calli wondered if there really was anything as bright as a rainbow that could cut through her current darkness.

The second martini had less of a bite than the first, but she still sighed loudly after the first sip, then chewed an olive to chase away the burn. She reached for the pack of Marlboro Lights and tapped it hard several times into her palm. She didn't smoke, at least she hadn't since she found out she was pregnant with her first son seventeen years prior. Her oh-so-loving husband, Bennett, had rejoiced when she'd given him the news of the pregnancy, and his first words after swinging her off the ground in a big hug were, I guess this means you'll give up those nasty cigarettes. He'd urged her to quit throughout college and into their first year of marriage. She had chalked it up to his love and concern over her, then over the baby. Quitting was tough, but her baby had been the motivation she'd needed.

She pulled the gold tab, feeling a little evil satisfaction and sweet revenge as she slid the first cigarette from the pack. This would eat Bennett alive—not only the fact that she was smoking, but that she dared to do so in his house, in his brand spanking new kitchen. Strike that, Calli. This house is about to be yours. She glared at the stack of papers sitting to her right, curved from how they'd been folded and stuffed into the envelope she'd signed for with the postman that afternoon.

As soon as she'd finished reading it the first time, she called Sue to ask if her older son, Jax, could spend the night with his friend. Then she did the same for Kent. Thank God that Jill loved having Kent over to keep Colton entertained— no matter that it was a school night.

It had been two hours since Bennett's plane from Tucson had landed. She'd checked with the airline; the flight had been on time. Since they lived twenty minutes from the airport, he should have been home long ago . . . or at any minute now. Reaching for the lighter, she watched the door and waited, hoping that he'd come in just as she lit the thing. He didn't.

She pressed the button—no roller or actual flame, just

a click and a little burning glow. That was one more thing that was no longer the same. Bringing the glow to the end of the cigarette, she pulled the smoke into her mouth as the end sizzled, then inhaled. Immediately, her throat and lungs constricted, spasming against the burning infiltration. Calli coughed, hard. Her eyes watered, but she didn't extinguish the thing. Instead, she stared at the smoke licking from the end, at the paper burning back and creating ash. She smelled the air. That freshly lit smell was already turning into rancid, old-smoke stench. It was gross. She wasn't about to become a smoker again, but she hoped to make a point tonight.

She tried again, taking a small drag on the butt. The taste wasn't any better, so she laid it down in the bowl sitting by her martini glass and smirked at the sight. Bennett's grandmother's fine china bowl with the gold-inlaid ring became her ashtray. He'd just love that part too. Good.

Calli let the cigarette burn to a stump, then stabbed it out and stirred the ashes in hopes that it'd look like she'd actually smoked it. She read through the first paper in the stack again, an unnecessary action as she'd already memorized the important parts and rehearsed what she'd say to her philandering husband. She waited. A fight for the ages was in store for the evening.

An hour and a half later, the security system beeped, announcing that a door had been opened. Calli, still seated at the dining room table, looked up to see Bennett sneaking inside as quietly as possible. He lifted the rolling suitcase and gently placed it beside the front door and hung his shoulder bag over the stair rail, careful not to make much sound. Of course, he thought the house was asleep. It normally would have been at eleven on a weekday.

Calli had lost much of her gusto as her two drinks settled

and she had waited. She'd let several more cigarettes burn and had ripped the envelope to shreds. The evidence of her fidgety wait sat in a pile next to the fine china turned ashtray. Mildly, she said, "I expected you'd have been here hours ago."

Despite her resigned and quiet tone, Bennett startled, just about jumping out of his skin. He wore a suit, but the shirt was already half unbuttoned, and the tie hung loose. He stammered, "I . . . uh . . . "

Calli held up a hand and rolled her eyes. She didn't want to hear any excuses about how traffic was bad or he got a call from the office or whatever he wanted to make up this time. She would have thought he'd been more practiced at lying to her since he'd been doing it for nearly sixteen years that she could reckon.

She didn't look away from him though. She wanted to see the shock and surprise as he took in the sight of her at the table, the empty martini in hand, the cigarette box and lighter scattered beside the delicate bowl with extinguished butts. In his reaction, he didn't let her down. With every step he took toward the dinette, his jaw dropped a little further open and his hands spread as if to ask, What the fuck? Though she wanted to celebrate the fact that she'd stabbed him and drawn a reaction, Calli schooled her expression to neutral and reached for the papers.

"Are you smoking?" Bennett asked. "Where are the boys?"

She ignored his questions. Her voice dry and husky from the smoking attempt, she summarized the key pieces of the summons in her hand: "Wallace County District Court. Jolene Hodge, plaintiff, has filed a claim for child support against Bennett Stockton, defendant."

Bennett shifted out of his cautious approach, rushed to the table, and snatched the papers from Calli's hand. "How dare she?" he said, outraged.

"I presume that means you know this Jolene Hodge person."

"It's impossible that the kid is mine!"

" . . . and you knew she was pregnant."

"What?" He snapped his head up from the documents. "Oh, no."

Calli didn't try to hide how exasperated she felt as she let out a heavy sigh and shook her head. "I thought we were past your affairs. I thought you had listened to the therapist. I thought we were getting back to being partners in this marriage." She fell back against the chair with her arms crossed. "Obviously, I thought wrong."

"No. Cal . . . " His voice slipped into that soothing tone he'd used on her too many times before. Actually, placating was probably the better description.

His attempt to calm her wasn't going to work now. She simply glared at him. Heedless of everything she thought her look would say to him, he continued. "Jolene is old news. Before we started seeing a therapist."

"Really, Ben? Her name isn't familiar." Calli shook her head. She'd done the math. "The papers say the baby is two months old." She raised a questioning brow at her husband. They had been going to the therapist for nearly eighteen months, and one of the conditions in redeveloping their trust was that everything was put on the table. Clearly, he'd assumed he was exempt from yet another rule.

He said nothing, which, in Calli's mind, only further confirmed his latest lie of omission.

"Listen, Ben. It's over. We are over. You can sleep in the guest room downstairs tonight." She stood. "Tomorrow, you should pack your things and go to your mother's."

"What? No, Cal. I'm not leaving. We're doing good, trying to work things out. For the boys' sakes."

She leaned forward, hands on the table supporting her weight, and looked squarely into his eyes. "Let me make this very clear. Our marriage is over. I can't handle any more affairs." Truly, one was too many, but her mother had always said, Marriage is tough, it requires work. You have to keep forgiving each other. Hell, their therapist had said as much. Calli had forgiven Bennett for far too long and for far too many indiscretions. For that matter, how many did she still not know about? Their separation had been coming for years. Calli would just have to deal with her mother's judgment over the broken marriage. It wouldn't be the first time she didn't live up to Isabelle Lindley's expectations. She sighed away the errant thoughts. "Tomorrow, I will find a divorce attorney and file the appropriate papers."

In that instant, his pleading eyes turned hard and all business. He dropped a fist onto the table, causing the bowl to clatter and ashes to spill. "This is my house and my family, and I will fight for what is mine. I am not leaving."

He reached for her, but she backed away. "Very well, then I'll pack myself and the boys and we'll go to Lindleyi Manor to stay with my parents. I'd hoped that you'd make this easy and the boys could finish out high school. But I guess I'll have to enroll them down there."

Bennett kicked a chair out of his way.

Calli jumped.

He yelled, "I said we are going to work this out. I'm not going anywhere, and you are not taking my boys away either."

Prepared for this reaction, Calli nodded and evenly asked, "Are you going to take time off work to see to Kent's special needs at school? Or make sure that he takes his meds every day? Or to make sure he gets to the psychologist for his appointments? You're gone before he even wakes up and half the time, you're gone when he goes to bed. Are you going to sacrifice your business travel or time at your precious office in favor of your kids?"

Bennett remained quiet.

"I didn't think so." She stood a bit taller. Her voice was firm and final when she continued, "One way or another, I won't be staying here with you. I am the boys' caretaker, and if you won't leave, we must." After a moment, she softened. "Ben, it'll be easiest if you go to your mother's while we figure out our next steps."

"Cal, we can't just call it quits, we have twenty-one years invested." He reached out again.

She'd said her piece and silently picked up the glass and walked around the peninsula to the sink. She was done giving into his reasons and logic. They all made sense for him, but not for her.

"Calli!" Quite mercurial, his volume rose a notch. "This is ridiculous. I made you. I made this home. I've funded everything from the remodels to the cars to Kent's therapy to the insanity of a marriage counselor. Everything you have is because of me. Where would you be if it wasn't for me?"

She slammed the glass down on the marble counter. "I'd

hopefully have a husband who didn't jump into the sack with every piece of ass he could find."

"What did you expect when you shriveled up like a prune after Kent?"

Calli's jaw hung open in silence. She couldn't believe that he'd find a way to make his cheating her fault or that he'd call her something so repulsive.

"Well?"

"Ya know what? Fuck you, Bennett! That's where this all started . . . when you showed me who you really and truly are. Kent was a hard baby and I had an eighteen-month-old to take care of too. You didn't help out at all, and I was exhausted. Any man worth his salt would have supported his wife."

"You knew when you married me that I had strong sexual needs."

"Yeah, but I didn't think a month off would have caused you to hop in bed with the nearest set of tits on legs."

"It was way more than a month, and you know it!"

"It's not like you tried much once I was back on my feet. It was always my responsibility to initiate sex, and that just got old. Who wants to feel like their partner thinks making love is a chore?" She'd tried several more times over the years to break the frigid gap between them. He'd gone through the motions, but they never really connected again as they had before Kent. She hadn't known why at the time, and she had blamed herself. Years had passed before she finally pieced together his patterns, and when she did recognize the signs, she knew exactly when it had all started.

Bennett started to say something else, but Calli took in a deep breath and released a long cleansing exhale. Holding up a hand, she said, "Listen, that's all in the past. We are where we are because we haven't really been a couple since Kent was born. We tried. Give us a fucking E for effort, but I just can't anymore. It's time to move on. I'll have the papers delivered to your office. What's your new secretary's name? I'll call her and have her watch for them."

Bennett's face turned bright red . . . so much so that it glowed even in the dim light. His eyes shifted down and away as he quietly said, "Zoe."

Calli stared at his reaction for a minute, a reaction that could only mean one thing. Her jaw fell and her brows rose in astonished disgust. Her hands flew in wild gesticulation as she launched into a full-on tirade. "Un-fucking-believable. You're fucking her! That's where you were tonight, why you're late. You ran right over to your newest little mistress to get your rocks off before you had to come home to the old ball and chain. You are fucking disgusting, do you know that? And you know what else? I have never once cheated on you, though I've had good reason to. It's been years since I've had sex, and you were off banging some ho-bag. Do you even care a little about my feelings anymore? Just a stitch?"

"No. I don't." Bennett ran a hand over his thinning hair and went to the basement door. With his hand on the knob, poised to go downstairs, he looked back and said, "There. Are you fucking happy? I've admitted it."

Two

Fourteen months later

CALLI STOCKTON SWUNG OPEN THE front door of Moffitt & Hall Financial Services and stepped onto 9th Avenue to a serenade of taxi horns and air perfumed with eau d'exhaust. She worked amid the high-rises on 9th Avenue in the downtown financial district, nicknamed Cloud 9 after the significant wealth managed there. She'd blocked her calendar and turned on her auto-reply in case any of her investors e-mailed, and she had left work early for her appointment at the county courthouse. Outside, a line of limos, the business person's taxis, waited for whichever notable executive or investor happened to be inside the building, drivers milling about or reading at the wheel. Fortunately, she didn't need a taxi; the courthouse was just around the corner.

Her breath fogged up in the crisp autumn air, and she buttoned her jacket. Winter was on the breeze, a fact for which she was thankful as she currently carried around excess weight that made her slim-fit suits tight in all the wrong places. She had to get to the gym, but God only knew how that was going to happen in her new life as a single mother.

Divorce wasn't something she'd asked for; for certain, she'd never dreamed of sitting in this boat alone. As taught by her mother, marriage was supposed to have been a lifelong commitment. She had tried so hard to make things work—man, had she tried. And he'd made so many promises that things would be better. It had even been his idea to enroll in counseling, and she had thought things were getting better—at least they'd resolved things enough to get back to a state of being partners if not lovers. She'd tried like hell to get past his infidelity, tried to reclaim the trust she'd once invested in their marriage, but when the court papers arrived demanding child support for his mistress's newborn, the proverbial camel's back buckled. Now, it had been fourteen months since she filed the divorce papers, and the day had finally arrived. She shouldered her bag a little higher, tucked the scarf around her neck, and strode purposefully for the courthouse, feeling a sense of relief after the long months of negotiation.

Her divorce attorney, Kristi, met her at the foot of the steps. "Are you ready?"

Calli answered, "My stomach is in knots, and I can't tell if it's from excitement or nerves."

In a weak attempt at offering comfort, Kristi rested a hand on Calli's shoulder and smiled warmly, professionally—a patronizing look that Calli had grown increasingly disenchanted with over the course of their attorney-client relationship.

Kristi said, "I'm certain it's a little of both. You have been through an ordeal with this." Eyeing Calli sideways, the lawyer tilted her head toward the door and added, "The meeting should be straightforward. Let's get it over with. They're already inside." The lawyer climbed the steps in her stilettos.

Calli watched her, wondering about the last time she'd worn stilettos. Of late, she'd opted for flats to accompany her more comfortable pant suits. Just as she was moving to follow, her phone beeped—a text message. She needed to silence that anyway, so she pulled it from her bag and glanced at the screen and the group chat.

JORDAN:	YOU GOT THIS GIRL!
JORDAN:	🎉 🎉 🎉
ME:	YEAH. I DO.
ME:	🙂
TORY:	HAPPY DIVORCE DAY!!! SO GOOD TO SEE DB GO!!!
JORDAN:	🍷 🍷 🍷
JORDAN:	REMEMBER EVERYONE, DRINKS TONIGHT AT MORETTI'S...

"Calli?" Kristi called.

Calli hit mute on the group message and slowly climbed the steps to follow her lawyer. Her friends were maybe too supportive of her divorce. Calli had tried to make the best of her marriage for the boys' sakes. That effort had proven difficult, and she'd been pretending for too long that things were okay. Then, everything had exploded once she'd filed for divorce. Calli kept trying to return to a state of civility with her soon-to-be ex-husband, but she had often vented to her close group of girlfriends. They were mad on her behalf.

Her lawyer waited at the top of the steps, holding the door. "This can be the hardest part of the entire process. Long, deep breaths," the lawyer said.

They entered the courthouse and walked down the long stone hallway. Paintings of current and former black-robed officials lined the walls; each pair of dutiful eyes seemed to judge her situation as she passed. Kristi turned into a suite to the left and Calli followed. In the arbitration room's waiting area, a young blonde girl behind the desk held out her hand toward the conference room. She and Kristi exchanged pleasantries, and Calli tried to smile but said nothing.

Calli's separation and now divorce had been a grueling process, but they'd managed to work everything out through arbitration, so there was no need for a courtroom. Inside, Bennett and his lawyer sat at the far side of the table in identical staunch black suits. Bennett also wore his smug look—the one filled with arguments that he'd adopted over the years—the one that told Calli how inconsequential she was to him and made her feel small. It hadn't helped when he finally admitted during one of their more epic arguments that she didn't matter to him. She raised her chin to show she no longer felt little around him. This was a business deal, and she'd act the part.

The tall and lanky arbitrator, Mr. Freeman, shook hands with Calli's attorney, then repositioned his glasses on his hooked nose and opened a folder. He extracted two packets from the folder and placed one in front of the men and one in front the empty chairs where Calli and her lawyer would sit.

Calli shrugged out of her coat and took a chair. Kristi had already walked her through the list of agreements, arrangements, and legalese so many times that the information was almost rote. Today was simply a review to allow for any final disputes or disagreements. It was excruciating.

Bennett's mask of solemnity never wavered. And Calli schooled her face to remain as serene as his through techniques she'd practiced with her therapist time and time again. It was like Lamaze for the to-be-divorcée. Today's meeting reminded Calli of when they'd closed on their first house in the perfect upscale and desirable neighborhood—a legal arrangement in which they had had to initial every page individually and then sign at the bottom.

Closing legal deals like this is an everyday ordeal for Bennett, Calli thought. He closed corporate deals in his job as VP of Mergers and Acquisitions at least once a week. She, on the other hand, had only done it a handful of times in her life. She steadied her pen in her lap before raising it to the tabletop to sign. She exhaled slowly as she inked the final signature.

When all was said and done, Bennett stood with his lawyer, buttoned his coat, and extended his hand toward Calli. His lawyer extended a hand in a mirror image toward Kristi. The lawyers shook hands. Calli stared at her ex's, then raised her gaze to his icy blue eyes and lifted a brow. As tempting as it was to brush him off, she slowly accepted the gesture. To her surprise, it did seem like sealing the deal and moving on to her next chapter. Her ex-husband left, but Kristi and the arbitrator kept chattering.

Calli grabbed her coat and bag and walked out the door. She crossed the waiting room and sank into one of the empty chairs, letting her bag fall to the floor. The chipper blonde receptionist asked if she could get her something to drink.

"Not unless you have a nice peppery Zinfandel," she answered and dropped her head back to the wall, closing her eyes.

When she sensed someone taking the seat beside her, the bitter almond and vanilla scent of the Tom Ford Fucking Fabulous perfume wafted toward her. Calli squeezed her eyes tighter, thinking, That's the smell of tens of thousands of dollars out the window. Callie opened her eyes to Kristi's patient stare.

"One more stop. Almost there," the expensive attorney said.

Out the reception area and down the hall, past the entrance to the courthouse, Calli and Kristi approached the county clerk seated behind a long counter with glass dividing the office from the customers. Kristi produced the papers Calli had signed and slid them through, then looked at Calli expectantly. After rummaging through her bag, Calli produced a check for $180, a minor drop in the bucket of debt she'd incurred to fund the divorce. The paper trembled as she laid it on the counter.

The clerk collected the documents and payment, made some copies, stapled the receipt to the papers and stamped the official copies. She handed the packet back to Calli and said, "Have a wonderful day."

Calli tried to smile. She was doing a lot of trying today, but that's about all she could muster.

Her lawyer shook her hand. "Congratulations, Miss Lindley." With a quick hug, she left Calli standing alone in the courthouse hall in a lingering cloud of Fucking Fabulous.

With her rates, of course, she could bathe in the wildly expensive perfume.

Looking down, the name on the papers certified Calli's new—as well as her premarriage—identity: Callista Linnea Lindley. She inhaled, exhaled, then pulled out her phone, snapped a photo, and texted the image to the group chat.

After receiving a series of happy and celebration emojis, she flipped over to the app RydeShare and ordered a ride home. The app said five minutes and Wally would be there to pick her up at the front door in a black sedan. Walking toward the door, she chewed her lip and scrolled through her contacts. Selecting Mom from the list, she hesitatingly attached the photo of her name change and tapped the paper airplane. She waited for a reply, hoping her decision to change her last name back would gain her mother's approval. No response came immediately, so she dropped the phone to her side and pushed through the door to catch her Ryde. The phone buzzed as the wind bit her cheeks and lifted her hair. Her heart skipped a beat as she looked.

Mom: I'm so very sorry, honey. This is such a sad day. I will pray for you.

That definitely didn't warrant a reply, so she waved to Wally, her driver. He acknowledged her, and Calli slid into the backseat. After confirming her address, she dialed her sister.

"Hiya, Cal," Cat answered. "Big day, huh?" The words were muffled, indicating she was eating something, but at the sound of her twin's sympathetic voice, Calli relaxed into the backseat.

Watching the buildings pass outside, Calli said, "It's done, Cat."

"And . . . do you feel like a new woman?"

"It really just seems surreal."

"Did you call Mom?"

"I couldn't force myself to call. All I get from her is how much of a tragedy it is to have a divorced daughter." She ran a hand through her hair, sweeping it out of her eyes.

Wally pulled onto the highway toward suburbia and her upper-middle-class neighborhood.

"Cal, she means well."

"I know. I just hoped that changing my name back to the family name would go a little further than it did. She just told me she'd pray for me. I'm kinda dreading going home next time. I'm sure we'll see her church friends, and they'll give me such a sympathetic look. I just don't know if I can handle that."

"I'll be there with you. If nothing else, we can get them to pray over Liam's cast. I told you he broke his leg in soccer, right?"

Calli giggled. "Yeah, how's your little man doing?" Her sister Cat did know just how to lighten the mood. Though they saw each other so rarely, they were always close at heart.

After a few minutes of catching up, Calli said, "Hey, sis. I'm almost home. Can we chat later?"

"Yeah, I'll give you a call tomorrow. Take care of yourself, Cal!"

"Love you!"

"Me too. Kisses."

Inside her bag, Calli traded her phone for keys just as

Wally pulled into her drive. She thanked him, hopped out, and punched in the garage code. If she left now, she should be just in time to pick up her boys, Kent and Jackson, her only remaining joy resulting from the twenty-one years she'd given to Bennett.

ᗪOMINIC MORETTI WRAPPED A TOWEL around his waist as he stepped from the shower. Workout complete, he ran through his day's agenda. He had an appointment with Kyle at Moffitt & Hall down in Cloud 9 to discuss his latest restaurant investment. Afterward, he'd meet with his personal assistant to review his books, and then, for the evening, he'd transform into Nic Moore, restaurant manager, and his evening would be spent with the love of his life, his flagship restaurant, Moretti's. Supervising the 1920s-style atmosphere was the proverbial cherry on top of his day.

He strolled casually to locker 719, opened the door and dressed, sliding into his Brioni slacks and blazer in preparation for the day of business. Grabbing the brush, he slicked back his hair while making sure the image in the mirror appeared perfectly professional.

Joe Cates, probably his only friend and also his lawyer, appeared at his side after his own shower and opened his locker. Dom had always been a natural introvert, and with his job at the restaurant and busy travel schedule, he had little time for friends. Joe, however, had gotten close over the course of countless business trips. The constant togetherness had given Dom adequate time to warm up, and he wouldn't trade their friendship for the world.

"That was a kick-ass workout. You were a beast out there. I'll be sore tomorrow," Joe said.

Dom cocked a half smile and fastened his shirt and tie. "You're behind. We're going to be late for the call.

"What are you talking about? We have half an hour."

Dom fastened his watch, catching a glimpse of the diamond-inlaid face just to be certain Joe wasn't exaggerating. He wasn't, but that was still cutting it too close for Dom's taste. "Joe," he said, "the call starts in thirty minutes. We have to get out of here, drive downtown, and get to the nineteenth floor within that time."

Joe was a last-minute kind of guy; just in time, he liked to remind Dom. In fact, if he could predict—

"We'll be just in time," said Joe, hurrying to gather his business clothes.

Yep, there it was, Joe's mantra. The man had always been there for Dom, so there was no arguing his loyalty. Dom gave his friend an accusatory look.

Joe held up his hands. "All right. All right! I'm moving." He threw on his clothes, making quick work of belt and buttons. "Let's go, I'll finish up in the car."

"You know, for a lawyer, you really could stand to sharpen up." Dom hesitated, then with a look at his pants, added, "Your attire, that is," giving the respect due to Joe's talent with contract negotiations.

Joe looked down. "They're not that bad. Plus, they're wrinkle-free, so they'll straighten out as I wear them."

Passing the trainer's desk, Dom raised his chin to the young brunette manning the computer. He considered giving her his card, thinking she'd probably make for a fun roll in the sack. That was about the only kind of relationship he had time for, but then he reconsidered: the young ones always got attached. He ran a hand through his hair and took the stairs, as usual two at a time. Stairs were designed for short people, and he didn't fit that bill.

Outside, Dom popped the trunk as they approached his car. Both men slung in their gym bags, then he slid into the leather driver's seat of his M3, and kicking down the clutch, he pressed start and slid the stick into reverse. With a full-on grin, he revved the engine just a bit before backing out and punching the gas.

"This is one beautiful machine," Joe said as he finished buttoning up his shirt. Then he hauled out a stack of documents and rustled through the papers. "The owner's name is Jean Claude, and it's valued at just under a mil."

The owner's name didn't ring a bell, but that was nothing unusual. Names frequently escaped him; it was the food and the atmosphere he gravitated toward. "The restaurant is Chez Phillippe, right?"

"Yes, that's it."

That connected the dots. "Thanks, I'd forgotten his name, but his little French seafood bistro had the most delightful lobster bisque. I'd like to add that to Moretti's menu once we seal the deal. What is our offer?"

"Two-twenty at a twenty-eight percent share."

"And what was Kyle's assessment on the investment?"

"Low risk. High profit. Highly in demand with customers. Top-notch ROI."

"And do you think Jean Claude will bite?"

"Really . . . who could resist being offered a partnership with the Dominic Moretti? And we're offering him a dedicated episode on The Dinner Shark on the Food Network." Joe slipped the papers back into his folio. "You bring an offer that no restaurant entrepreneur can resist, my man."

As Dom swung into the parking garage, he slid into a spot in the first row.

"I swear," said Joe. "You have a horseshoe stuck up your ass."

Dom widened his eyes and replied, "I have no clue what you mean."

"I usually drive around for fifteen minutes before finding a spot in this garage." Joe gathered his things and opened the door.

Dom cut the engine, put the M3 into neutral, and pulled the parking brake before stepping out of the car. He clicked the fob to lock the doors, and they strode onto 9th Avenue. Hanging a right, they headed for Moffitt & Hall.

*I*NSIDE THE SOUTH CONFERENCE ROOM on the second floor at Moffitt & Hall, Dom and Joe met with Kyle, Dom's financial advisor. With his prematurely thinning hair, pointed nose, and tapered chin, Kyle painted images in the mind somewhere between a bird and a human. He wore glasses on the end of his nose as he scanned over the latest reports and reported only a slight increase in portfolio value over the last month. It wasn't what Dom had hoped for, but any increase in this market climate was a good thing. The clock on the wall behind Kyle's head signaled it was half an hour past his schedule, so he stood. "Excuse me. I need to make a phone call to delay my next appointment. I'll be right back."

Outside, he pulled out his mobile. The battery indicator was flashing red and the screen had dimmed in an attempt to conserve battery life. He lowered it, thinking it was time to get a new phone. He went to the reception desk and asked the redhead if there was a phone he could use. Fortunately, there were small rooms for such a purpose. Dom closed the door, sat, and lifted the phone.

He pulled up his personal assistant, Pauline, and squinted to read the numbers on the screen. After dialing, he waited. At the third ring, he was certain she wouldn't answer, but then her voice came over the line with a sigh. "Monroe Professional Services. This is Pauline Monroe."

"Pauline?" said Dom with relief.

Her voice immediately perked as she said, "Oh, Dom. Good . . . "—she paused as if briefly distracted—" . . . afternoon. I didn't recognize the number."

"My battery's low. I'm calling from Moffitt & Hall."

"I wasn't expecting to hear from you before our meeting today. Is there anything at all I can do beforehand?

"I need to push our time back by half an hour. My appointment here is running over."

"Oh," her voice was a little quiet, then she added, "Okay, I'll be at your office above Moretti's at four thirty."

"Wonderful. Thanks for your flexibility." He ended the

call and returned to his meeting.

ON THE MORETTI BUILDING, A historic building originally constructed in 1923 and refurbished with additional floors in the late '90s, Dom sat in his office on the second floor reading an article about the latest trends in French cuisine. It seemed to be more of an opinion piece than to contain anything of substance, but he kept his eyes on those too. Sometimes they would offer something of value, either to his own restaurant or one of his many investments. At four twenty-five, Dom heard footsteps on the old wooden stairs outside his office. His personal assistant was five minutes early. When the steps stopped across from his office door, he walked over, opening it inward just as Pauline was about to knock.

Dom smiled, welcoming her, and invited her into his office. Her hair and makeup looking very fresh this late in the afternoon, it seemed she'd put a little too much effort into her appearance. He shrugged that thought off and said, "Hi, Pauline, thank you for accommodating my ever-changing schedule."

Her eyes shifted. She gave a shy smile and nervously tugged at her shirt as she entered. "Of course. Anytime." Her gait seemed unnaturally shortened by her too-tight skirt, and her high heels echoed on the wooden floor.

Dom looked out the door before pushing it closed to see her coat hanging on the hook right next to his. There were twenty or so hooks in that row. He lowered his brow, wondering why she'd gone all the way to the end to hang hers there. She wouldn't be here long enough to need to make room for his staff who would only show up around six.

He joined her on the guest side of the desk as she was extracting the computer from her bag. Pauline looked sideways to his chest before raising her head and blinking rapidly as their eyes met.

Also, too much mascara. Everything about her is overdone, Dom thought. A strong flowery scent accosted him, and he turned slightly. He stopped breathing through his nose. "Shall we?" he asked, checking his watch. "Moretti's opens soon, and I plan to be on the floor tonight." He sat down.

"Here is your mail and your financial reports." She handed him the mail and a folder with all the reports, then opened the laptop and sat primly in the other chair, dropping her eyes hesitantly. When the graphs appeared, she pointed to the screen, a fake nail pointing to one of the pie charts. "You'll see that you've exceeded your expectations for profitability here at Moretti's by a landslide." She swallowed and seemed out of breath as she continued, "Regarding your investments, I've worked with Kyle to create a visual that shows your top ten and bottom ten here. You can drill into the data to see how each investment is trending. You can access this information in real time through your personal portal. All that information is in the folder for your reference. Do you have questions on that?"

"I don't right now, but I might when I dive into the numbers." He stared intently at the screen. This was good. He was happy to have it all here and was happy that she'd gone above and beyond in putting that together. Satisfied with the results, he looked at Pauline. She placed a hand at her open collar and ran it up her neck while dreamily holding his stare.

His brows peaked, and he moved away as he asked, "Is something wrong?"

"No, no . . . uh . . . let's look at your balance sheet and cashflow. We have some new software." Pauline fumbled with the touch pad, her fake nails clicking as she worked. "Here, this graph shows your liquid assets, as well as your totals in accounts payable and receivable. Again, you can simply click here to get the details. This is all updated as I receive payments or pay your bills."

"Excellent!" Dom said. "Those numbers are better than I'd expected. I'm flying to San Francisco the day after tomorrow to meet with my latest investment opportunity." He stood and circled to the chair behind the desk, then breathed deeply through his nose, thankful for the unscented air. "These numbers make that investment even more feasible." He gave her a small smile and tilted his head.

Pauline closed the computer and leaned both elbows onto the desk. She pressed forward, accentuating her cleavage between her upper arms. Her voice dropped a note. "Is there anything else I can do for you, Dom?"

He'd gotten the uninvited non-business vibe, clearly, and looked at his watch again. Voice forcibly leveled, he said, "You've done a fabulous job keeping my accounts up-to-date. I pay you well for a reason."

"Very well." She put her computer back in the bag and made to leave.

"Pauline?" Dom cringed as he called after her, not wanting to extend the meeting, but he needed to double check the schedule.

She turned.

"We have a meeting next week, correct?" he asked.

"We do."

"I'll ask Kyle and Joe to join us to go through the acquisition numbers. The deal should close by then. Thanks for all you do." Dom picked up the pile of mail and began sorting.

She gave a small nod and strode through the door. If possible, her heels clacked louder as she went. He watched the door close behind her, worried once again that he'd have to find a new PA.

Three

AMAZON'S ALEXA PLAYED RAP MUSIC in the background, a nice thudding base for Calli to dance to as she curled her hair in her now private en suite master bath. She vaguely recognized the song from the '80s or '90s . . . she couldn't really remember the decade, but the old-school pop station was an attempt to get her in the spirit to go out with the girls. To party. To celebrate being single.

Her phone had been buzzing constantly since she'd texted the photo of her name change, so she left it on the bed while she dried and curled her hair.

A white button-down oversized men's shirt tickled her thighs as she encouraged her muscles to remember the moves she'd carelessly used when she was in college. A mid-forties, post-two-children body just didn't move the same way. She took a sip from the glass of wine that sat half empty on the counter. Yeah, she'd started early in hopes of loosening herself up a little.

The first song ended and the next song started as Calli slid her hair off the hot iron.

"Oh, my God, Becky, look at her butt."

She yelled, "Alexa," and waited for the sound to dim. When Alexa beeped, Calli added, "volume 8." Louder, the music resumed, and she held the end of the curling iron to her mouth and sang along. "I like big butts, and I cannot lie. You other brothers can't deny . . . when a girl walks in with an itty-bitty waist and a round thing in your face, you get sprung." She raised both hands on the sprung. Then the volume suddenly decreased. She turned to find Jackson standing there with his hand on the top of the tower.

"Mom, you're ridiculous," he said with his head tilted to one side, brows raised, and his multi-colored ombré hair loose from its usual ponytail. Jackson was her oldest son and an artist—much to Bennett's dismay. In fact, his preference for art-related extracurricular activities and comic conventions had become the cause of many household arguments. Bennett wanted his son to play the big three—football, basketball, and baseball—and he didn't accept it well when Jackson took a different path. Furthermore, when their then sixteen-year-old son told his dad he wanted to go by "Jax," Bennett had sulked around the house for a solid week. In Bennet's mind, the name Jackson had been intended to set him up to be a corporate executive or prestigious lawyer. Calli just wanted Jax to be happy; whether it meant he lived modestly following his passion, pursued fame and fortune, or climbed the corporate ladder after his father, it didn't matter to her. She'd always encouraged a college degree, but it could be in art or animation or whatever he wanted. She'd adopted his new persona with enthusiasm.

Calli smiled proudly and put on a false pretense of

shock. "Wha-at? It's a good song."

"I'm not arguing that, but you don't have to bring the house down. I'm trying to do homework next door."

"All right, I get it. I'm sorry. How's school going, anyway?"

"Meh," he said and shrugged, a typical response.

"At least it'll be over soon. You graduate in seven months."

"Saving grace. Where are you going tonight?"

"I'm meeting Tory, Jordan, and Trina."

Jax snorted. "Do you want me to drive you?"

"No, I'll just grab a Ryde." Calli turned back to the mirror and ran her fingers through the long curls.

"I know, but what about your friend Trina? Didn't she get a DUI last winter?" Jax walked to the bathroom door and leaned on the jam.

"You're a bit too mature for your own good sometimes," Calli said, raising a brow. "She did, but I think she learned her lesson. We've all figured out this new Ryde app. She's its number one fan." She smiled toward Jax's reflection in the mirror.

"Okay, Mom, just be careful. Please?" He hugged her from behind. As he was leaving, he said, "You know I worry about you and drinking."

"I don't understand why," said Calli. "Your dad and I were always very responsible."

A shadow passed over his eyes, too dark for the youthful face.

"Hey." Calli turned to him. "Look at me. Nothing's changed from what we were doing before. The only difference is some ink on paper. The real change happened months ago when Dad moved in with Grandma Stockton." She sensed her son was mourning the loss just a little, but also that he wanted to be strong. He'd become a young man far too soon for her liking, but at the same time, it made her chest swell with pride.

Jax shoved his hands in his pockets and looked down. "Yeah, anyway, be safe." He left her alone.

Calli watched after him for a moment with her mouth quirked in wonder, then shook her head and went to the closet to shuffle through her clothes. As she feared, she couldn't find anything worthy of the trendy, yet 1920s-throwback restaurant Moretti's. She pulled out a sweater with a nice V-neck and some black pants. She threw them on and looked in the full-length mirror. Rubbing her hands down her sides, there were slight bulges on either side. She yanked the sweater over her head and threw it in the box of clothes that no longer quite fit. Sighing, she put the oversized button-down—probably Bennett's at one time—back on and a pair of boyfriend jeans she'd purchased more recently. Then she ran to the bathroom door and called, "Jax? Changed my mind—will you take me to the mall? I'll catch a Ryde from there. I need a new outfit for tonight."

"Yeah, give me five minutes."

Calli checked her makeup and hair in the mirror. At least those looked good. She had always been able to pull off a fabulous cat eye.

By default, she slid on her Toms and turned to her reflection. Changing her mind, she fished out a pair of heels for the first time in over a year. They didn't feel great but made her legs look awesome and distracted from the extra weight she carried. She flipped the collar of the shirt, considering going casual chic, then decided against it. Not for Moretti's, she thought. She'd keep enough room in her bag to store the jeans, but she would toss the shirt. It was one more memory of Bennett she didn't need, even if he hadn't worn the shirt in probably fifteen years.

"Okay, Mom. I'm ready," said Jax.

Calli checked the curling iron was off and swiped off the lights, then followed her son downstairs.

*T*HE COMPUTER LIGHT WAS THE only interior light on in Dominic Moretti's office, which overlooked the street corner. He logged into his account on the Monroe Professional Services website and studied the Moretti, Inc. finances as the sun set over the city. He hadn't needed to extend the meeting with Pauline to go through the details and didn't want to encourage her ill-placed infatuation, so he'd followed her instructions. It would probably be best if he addressed the issue head-on and started the search for a new personal assistant and accountant, but she was meticulous with his finances, so he simply tried to maintain a professional distance.

There had been commotion outside of Dom's office for about an hour as his staff arrived for the evening. He checked the time in the corner of the screen. A quarter to six. Time to check in with the guests. He logged off and closed the laptop.

The day's fading light gave his spacious office a moonlit, shadowy feel as he crossed to his private restroom and closet area. This would normally be the moment when he slipped into a suit for the evening, but he'd already been in slacks and a dress shirt for his meetings earlier in the day, so he just washed up and ran a comb through his hair. Then, before donning the matching slate-gray blazer, he lathered up and took care of his five o'clock shadow. He kept himself clean-shaven when overseeing the restaurant for two reasons. He'd felt that the image was cleaner and more suitable for Moretti's upper-class atmosphere, and he wanted to keep his restaurant manager persona separate from his on-screen persona. Nic Moore looked very different from Dominic Moretti of the Food Network's The Dinner Shark—his network television series where he showcased his search for restaurant investment opportunities. Though he prided in his appearance, ties were suffocating, so he left the top button of the eggplant-colored dress shirt open.

All lights extinguished, he locked his office door, put on his best smile, and descended the stairs toward the growing din of conversation.

Four

CALLI WALKED INTO THE RESTAURANT and shelled her coat for the host who wore no less than a pristine black bow tie and tails.

He asked, "Is there anything else I may take, signora?"

Calli considered before pulling her wallet and mobile out of her purse and handing him the oversized bag. At the hostess stand, she asked for the Lindley party. Jordan thought it would be appropriate to use Calli's reclaimed maiden name for their celebration happy-hour reservation.

The girl peered at the screen. "Yes. Right this way," she said, turning and walking into the dining room.

Calli followed, noting how the hostess's waist-length blonde curls dusted her swaying hips and the black minidress hugged her petite figure. A jealous knife twisted in her gut, and Calli ran a hand down the A-line printed dress that hung a little looser over her own not-so-tight curves. She felt pretty in the new clothes, but certainly not sexy.

Sucking it up, she lifted her chin. The girl was half her age, so why should it matter?

Trina was the first to see her approaching, and her eyes sparkled as she stood and circled the table and wrapped Calli in long arms. Reaching up, Calli returned the hug with a single arm.

"It's been so long . . . how are you, guurl?" Trina said, always with the drag. It was as if she really didn't know there was an I in the word.

"I'm fabulous!" Calli said with a bit too much enthusiasm, then tucked her hair behind an ear. "Really just happy to have it all done."

Tory didn't stand but put a hand on Calli's arm as she sat. "I'm sure you are. It's been ten years, but it seems like it was this morning that I signed those papers. Just be thankful you didn't have to see a judge." She rolled her eyes and sipped the red wine. Tory had been divorced when Calli met her, but since then had found and fallen in love with a wonderful man, Steve Amos. Tory joked that she was Tory-with-a-Y, but she relished the fact that people did a double take when she gave her name. Small, with long strawberry-blonde hair, Tory had often dressed for Halloween as the singer Tori Amos—a cop-out on costume effort if Calli had ever seen one.

"Anyway," Tory said. "Tonight, we need to be on the lookout for you a man, even if only a temporary one."

"Damn straight!" said Trina.

"I'm, uh, not so sure about that. The ink's not even dry," said Calli.

Jordan gave her a downright wicked look. "Calli—" Her admonishment lingered. "You have been alone for . . . what? A year? The ink was a mere formality."

It'd been a bit more, but Calli didn't correct her.

"What gurl here says is right," said Trina. "When did that douche of a man move in with the ho-bag anyway?"

Calli raised both hands. "You know what? Why don't we not talk about Bennett tonight?" She lifted her glass and added, "Thanks for ordering the wine," then took a bigger than necessary drink.

Jordan grinned, "It's that Petite Petit you like."

Calli relished the bite on her tongue and raised her glass. "To being single."

Jordan was the first to clink. "To being available!"

"On. The. Market," added Tory.

"Screw that," said Trina. "On the prowl." She purred. "Sorry, Tory. No offense to the married."

"None taken. Remember, I was single two years ago." She raised her glass to the trio already toasting. "I, for one, have faith you girls will find your magic men just like I found Steve."

"Oh . . . " Jordan got dreamy eyes. "He's so good to you. We really are happy for you both." Then she wagged her brows. "But tonight's not about all that."

Jordan had also ordered Moretti's famous prosciutto balls. Calli popped one into her mouth, took a sip of wine, and closed her eyes in taste-bud heaven. The combination was delectable—creamy mozzarella, salt, and the wine's full body.

The women laughed and joked and drank for quite some time. Jordan expressed more frustration than ever over her daughter's latest shenanigans and general lack of commitment toward adulting. As a single mother from the beginning, she was always challenged by the absence of a father figure to her daughter to help her out. She'd never been married either. After a bout of college debauchery, the baby daddy had ended up in some drug rehab program and never really gotten clean. He'd been absent for all of their daughter's life.

As Tory commiserated, Calli hid behind her wine glass, thankful for her boys. When the conversation paused, she set down the glass and looked across the table at Trina. "What about you? What's your latest on the dating front?"

Trina's brown cheeks flushed darker. "There's a prospect. Will see how well he . . . shall we say . . . performs." Another round of laughter ensued.

The waitress delivered the second bottle of wine and poured a fresh glass for each of the women.

"Ladies." A proverbial tall-dark-and-handsome guy in a gray suit, smelling like the morning after a storm, stood beside Calli. He rested one hand on the back of her chair and the other on Jordan's.

Calli looked into piercing light-green eyes, stifled a snicker, snorted instead, then covered her mouth and curled toward the table.

"How are we finding everything this evening?" he asked.

Trina kicked her shin under the table, and Calli's eyes started watering from struggling not to release the fit of hilarity. She wondered which of her friends had set this up, and feeling a bit wine-numbed, the hot man's sudden appearance got her giggly.

"Everything is wonderful," said Jordan. "Calli here was in seventh heaven with the taste of the prosciutto balls."

Calli bit down in reaction to the word balls. What was she—a thirteen-year-old boy?

Gracefully, the man lifted the bottle of wine. "They are especially pleasing on the palette with the Petite Petit. Nice choice."

Calli tucked her chin in tighter, trying desperately to control her laugh.

"Is your friend all right?" his rich, husky voice inquired.

Calli pressed her lips tighter as a bellow threatened to explode from her chest and throat.

"She'll be fine . . . maybe after some water," said Jordan.

"I'll send over the server for refills. My name is Nic Moore. Let me know if you need anything at all." He strolled away.

Trina waved a hand in the air and said, "Guuurrl, what is wrong with you?"

Calli's restrained laughter erupted, and it felt like a good five minutes before she calmed down and wiped the tears from her eyes. "Okay, which one of you paid to have the hottie stop by the table?"

"He's the restaurant manager," Tory whispered, leaning a little closer and looking after Nic. "See, he's greeting all the tables."

"Oh." Calli felt a little light-headed, whether from the

laughter or wine, she wasn't quite certain.

Tory stood and dropped her napkin on the table. "I need to visit the little girl's room. Give me your cards, there's one of those thingies up front. Maybe we can win."

Calli, Trina, and Jordan fished out their business cards. As Tory walked toward the front, Calli said, "I think everyone wins those silly drawings," and finished her glass of wine.

$\mathcal{D}$OM SCANNED THE RESTAURANT, TAKING note of which tables were finishing up, then walked back to the front to check the reservation schedule. His standard of service at Moretti's was to ensure that seating flowed without having people loitering in the entry for an hour as they waited for a table. Over the years, the restaurant had become enough of an iconic establishment that only the occasional drop-in happened before the late happy hour at ten o'clock, at which time the bar became quite crowded. The regular clientele knew well enough that reservations were a requirement.

"Good evening, Mr. Moore." The hostess passed as she escorted a couple into the seating area—a young, radiant woman and a man whose eyes shifted nervously to Dom's and away as he patted the breast pocket of his suit.

Reading an impending proposal in the man's twitchiness and worried eyes, Dom turned and, for a long moment, he watched the patron dote over his date. He pulled her chair for her to take a seat, then touched his breast pocket again. After she sat, he moved his own chair a little closer, keeping just enough room to eventually sink to one knee. Dom grinned.

In the reception area, he stopped next to Anton, the maggiordomo, and whispered, "Have the bartender chill a bottle of champagne, on the house, and make sure the waiter delivers it just after the man asks the big question." It was quite the show to have engagement events at Moretti's. It occurred with some regularity, and Dom loved being a part of so many couples' special moments. It was part of the reason he'd gone into the restaurant business originally. Ironic that I've never felt that temptation.

Letting out a small amused laugh, he returned to business and perused the evening schedule. Seven parties were due to arrive within the half hour, matching the seven tables he'd counted as he'd scanned the floor. Everything was right on—

"Excuse me?" A high-pitched voice interrupted his calculation. He turned to the short woman who'd called for his attention, wrinkling his brow. She shuffled some cards nervously in her hand and shifted her eyes between him and the dining room.

She'd been at the table with the four women . . . the one where the lady couldn't stop laughing when he'd greeted the table. An evening didn't go by when he wasn't propositioned by at least one woman, but this one wasn't one he'd expected to approach him.

"Yes? May I help you?" he asked.

"Can we—" She pointed to the hallway leading to the restrooms and stairs, then shimmied over to the wall beside the hall entry.

Dom noted the rock on her left hand, which further added to his confusion. He joined her.

"Nic, right?" She asked as she looked around him,

apparently to ensure no one was watching.

He nodded, keeping up with his persona, and leaned against the wall with one hand casually in his pocket. She was more than a head shorter, so the slump brought him a little closer to her height.

"This is a bit awkward." She swallowed, clearly thinking where to begin. Then, suddenly, she widened her eyes at something she must have realized too late, and added, "Oh. And not about me at all."

Dom relaxed a little as she flipped through the three business cards in her hand.

"My friend, Calli. I think you should call her."

Dom accepted the card, a familiar style, and read: Callista Stockton, Moffitt & Hall. So she worked at the same firm as his own investment advisor, Kyle. "This is the one closest to the door? In the floral dress?" When the woman affirmed, he raised both brows. "What makes you think I should call her? She didn't look up while I was at the table." In fact, she seemed to have found his presence quite hilarious.

The woman snatched the card from his hand, darted over to the hostess table for a pen, and scribbled on the back. Returning, she handed back the card. "That's her mobile. I've known her forever. Just . . . trust me . . . you two would have a great time together." She skirted around him and back into the dining room.

Dom shook his head. But you don't know me, he thought. He slipped the card into his pocket and went to the dining room entrance to see this Callista Stockton again. The lady walked back and took her seat as the taller, more sultry woman beside her made an apparently funny remark.

Callista tipped her head back, laughing freely and allowing her dark curls to spill further down her back. Then she exposed the curve of her neck by gathering the curls and pulling the weight of her hair over one shoulder. The floral pattern she wore said she was strong, yet sensual. It wasn't one of the dime-a-dozen, tight, plunging-neckline skin suits that most women going after him flaunted. Then again, she wasn't really after him, was she?

Behind him, Anton greeted the next Moretti's guests, and Dom returned to work.

Five

THE PHONE BUZZED ON THE desk in Calli's home office, and she reluctantly lifted her heavy head from where it lay cradled on her arms, her keyboard pushed forward to allow the room. The space between her temples throbbed in protest as she squinted at the phone's screen. It read, Lanesboro High School.

She groaned and slid the little phone icon to answer. "This is Calli."

"Good afternoon, this is Beth Meyer, the secretary for the Special Education department."

Her pulse caught in her throat as she worried about what she may have forgotten. "Yes?" asked Calli, her mind spinning through possibilities and preparing for yet another school-related misstep with her son Kent. She retraced the morning routine up to the moment she'd sent him off to school. They'd packed his backpack last night before she'd gone out with the girls. He'd showed her his homework, and he'd taken his backpack this morning. She had also filled a glass of water for him to swallow his ADHD medication, so there shouldn't be an issue there either.

"Mrs. Stockton."

"Miss Lindley," Calli corrected.

"Excuse me?"

"Never mind." It'd take too much energy to explain the situation, and her splitting headache prevented her from thinking straight at the moment. "Is Kent okay?"

"Oh, yes. I was simply calling to remind you and Mr. Stockton about the yearly meeting to review Kent's individual education plan at 3:00 p.m. next Thursday."

"Yes. I have it on the calendar," said Calli. She heaved a sigh of relief, but at the same time, a knot formed in her stomach. She'd have to call Bennett to make sure he'd be in town then to make sure he would be at the meeting. Maybe she could just call the administrative assistant who managed his calendar. Later—when her head wasn't pounding.

"Thank you, and have a wonderful afternoon," Beth said and ended the call.

Calli didn't reply, didn't even press the button to hang up. She simply let her arm fall onto the desk and released the phone while blinking to bring the time in the corner of her computer screen into focus. Three forty-five. No one else should be calling and no appointments, she thought. She took a long drink of water, hoping that the dose of ibuprofen combined with the rehydration attempt would give some relief from the hangover. How many glasses of wine had she consumed? She couldn't remember.

Pressing her temple with one hand, she checked her e-mail one more time, then turned the computer volume up so she would hear any notifications, took her phone, and went to the couch. She grabbed the blanket, curled up in the corner, and considered going to sleep.

The boys both had activities after school, then would be staying at their dad's townhouse for the evening. She had no reason to prepare dinner; she'd just eat some of the leftover pizza she'd ordered for Jax and Kent the night before. She grabbed the remote from the sofa's arm and turned on the television.

The last story of the early news show had just wrapped up, and a slanderous political commercial started. Calli groaned and flipped through the channels. After a handful, she hit the Food Network, and a bearded man with piercing greenish-silver eyes popped a mouthful of some crab and pasta dish into his mouth, then hummed as he chewed and nodded. Something about him was . . . familiar.

"Oh, dang," she said and grabbed her phone, scrolling to the group chat.

ME:	HEY GUYS . . .
ME:	REMEMBER THAT RESTAURANT MANAGER?
JORDAN:	OH YEAH!
TRINA:	MAIN DISH LOL
TORY:	DID HE CALL?
TRINA:	*MAN DISH

ME:	WHY WOULD HE CALL?
ME:	ANYWAY . . .
TORY:	UH, NO REASON. 😊
ME:	WHAT WAS HIS NAME?

The name of the show and subtitle flashed across the screen before switching to commercial: The Dinner Shark with Dominic Moretti.

TRINA:	NIC
TORY:	YEAH, NIC MOORE, I THINK HE SAID.
JORDAN:	THAT'S IT. WHY?
ME:	HE LOOKS HELLA LIKE DOMINIC MORETTI
TRINA:	WHO'S THAT?
TORY:	MORETTI? AS IN MORETTI'S THE RESTAURANT? GTFO!
JORDAN:	DOMINIC MORETTI FROM THE TV SHOW?
ME:	YEAH THE DINNER SHARK
TORY:	I BET MOORE WAS SHORT. HE'S PROBS THE OWNER.

ME: NAH . . . PROBS
BROTHERS . . . THE GUY ON
TV'S TOO OLD TO BE HIM

JORDAN: HAHAHA

TORY: LOL

TRINA: GURL, WHO CARES? HE
COULDA BEEN MY
MAIN COURSE.

ME: ALL RIGHT L8RS LADIES

ME: I FEEL LIKE POO

TRINA: I FEEL YOU

TORY: ME 2

Calli silenced the phone and resumed channel surfing. Thirty or so clicks later and she stopped on the scene from The Time Traveler's Wife when Henry slipped a ring on a sleeping Clare's finger. Clare woke up, looked at her finger in confusion, then Henry said, "I never wanted to have anything in my life that I couldn't stand losing."

The two-dimensional Eric Bana paused in his proposal. A knot formed in Calli's throat, her sinuses burned, then he continued, "Well, it's too late for that."

Her eyes stung and prickled . . . tears welled up and overflowed. She threw the remote to the other end of the couch and grabbed the box of tissues from the end table. Crying wouldn't make the headache any better, but the movie seemed too perfect for her mood. She'd celebrated last night, maybe she just needed to wallow now.

Movie Henry continued, "I don't feel alone anymore." She fell apart, fully sobbing, an ugly and snotty cry. But when Clare said no, then yes, Calli found herself laughing aloud through the sniffles while wiping the salt water from her cheeks.

$\mathcal{T}$WO HECTIC NIGHTS IN A row, Dom had emptied his pockets on his office desk before taking the elevator to his eleventh-floor loft where he'd shed all but his shorts and dropped into bed with little preamble. This morning, he'd packed for his trip to San Francisco, dropped his suitcase in his office, and driven over to the gym for the 9:00 a.m. fitness class. Afterward, he'd shaved and dressed in business casual, then returned to his office to finalize a few details before the driver arrived to take him to the airport.

He stowed the papers and his laptop, dropping his shoulder bag beside the rolling suitcase for the five days of business he'd be spending in California. His office was in order except for the junk from his pockets the night before. He swept the change from the desk and dropped it in a jar on his bookshelf, crumpled and tossed a receipt, then held a business card to the light.

CALLISTA STOCKTON, SR. FINANCIAL ADVISOR

MOFFITT & HALL FINANCIAL SERVICES, INC.

Maybe he could give Kyle a call and get the inside scoop on this woman. Flipping the card, he scanned the numbers and glanced at the phone, contemplating. She had been a sight in the dim light across the restaurant. The warm glow on her neck as she'd laughed with abandon had moved something inside him. Dom pressed his brows together, unsure why his thoughts lingered on that moment, then decided it wasn't worth the time. He had far too much on his plate to consider calling her now. Besides, as he'd noted before, she wasn't his type. Surely he just needed a little fun and release. He'd have no problem taking care of that in San Fran.

The phone rang.

Dom waved the card a couple of times, then flipped it into the trash and answered, "Moretti's."

"Good morning, Dom," his personal assistant, Pauline, said.

He skipped being pleasant and asked, "Have you checked me in?"

"Yes. First class as usual, seat 2D. Your favorite."

"And the hotel?"

"Westin Grand downtown. There will be a driver waiting at the airport for you when you arrive." Pauline ran down the rest of the list and finished with, "You'll have the full itinerary in your e-mail when we're off this call."

Yet again, Pauline had performed better than any of his assistants in the past decade. "Thank you, Pauline."

"You're very welcome. The pleasure is all mine." She emphasized the word pleasure, then her voice pitched a bit higher. "Is there anything else I can help you with?"

Keeping her at arm's length was critical. He'd been down the dating-your-assistant road before—more than once, unfortunately. It never worked. He might even have to address the situation outright, but he hoped it wouldn't come to that. He reminded himself to keep it strictly business. "That'll be all. I'll be in touch once I'm on the ground if I have any questions." He hung up the phone just as the driver's knock sounded on his office door.

Six

CALLI STOOD BY THE FRONT door, staring into the gray morning over a cup of creamed coffee. Upstairs, a series of footsteps rushed between the bedrooms and the bathroom— the boys hastily readying themselves for school. The clatter was music to her ears. Last night had been their first night back from Bennett's, and she'd ordered gnocchi, Jax's and Kent's favorite, from the Italian place down the street. Having them back made her feel whole again. She was tempted to keep them home from school today but talked herself off that ledge. Powering through the separation from her two favorite young men was really the only way to get through their new arrangement, and she had to work.

The house smelled of warm cinnamon and sizzling pork. In the small hours of the morning, Calli had prepared cinnamon rolls, eggs, and sausage for their breakfast. Last night had been the first real snow of the season . . . the one that stuck and started the months of white that would blanket the city. Her boys typically ate cereal for breakfast, but she wanted Jax and Kent to have something warm before they stepped into the cold.

Thud . . . thud . . . thud. Kent ran down the stairs.

Calli looked away from the window to greet him. "How is Superman this morning?" She grinned. When she'd been pregnant with him, she and Bennett had argued relentlessly over names. It was to the point where she had believed that he'd be called Baby Boy Stockton, but a week before, she'd seen an author named Kent Rogers. When she mentioned Kent, Bennett had chewed his lip for a long time. Her mind had gone to Clark Kent and Superman, but apparently the name had sounded professional enough for Bennett and he'd agreed.

Kent rolled his eyes and made a disinterested groaning sound as he half-heartedly hugged his mother. Jax followed his brother down the stairs with a bit more grace and a lot less noise. The differences in two boys who came from the same genetics never ceased to amaze her.

"Hey, Mom," Jax said.

"Good morning," answered Calli, looking toward the kitchen where Kent had disappeared. "Let's get breakfast."

"Smells amazing." Jax followed his brother, binding his hair into a ponytail.

When they had finished eating, the boys grabbed their backpacks, and she kissed them each goodbye on the cheek. "Have a wonderful day at school."

Jax only smiled.

Kent let out his standard disinterested groan again.

Jax started the car, and each grabbed a brush to sweep snow from the car before they left.

Standing by the open door with the cold stinging her face, she waved and called, "I'll see you toni—this afternoon." Calli had made the decision mid-sentence to work from home. She had no desire to trek through the snow to the bus, and she certainly did not want to drive on the first snowy day of the year. Traffic would be a nightmare. She eased the door closed and flipped the lock into place before climbing the stairs to dress for the day. Nothing fancy, maybe some yoga pants and a frumpy sweater were in order.

Scooting up to her desk in her home office, Calli opened the computer and connected to her work network, then typed out an e-mail titled WFH. She made sure her boss and teammates were all included, then threw Jordan in the bcc line. They worked in the same office but on different teams.

GOOD MORNING,

> WITH THE SNOW TODAY, I'LL BE
> WORKING FROM HOME. AVAILABLE VIA
> NORMAL MEANS.

CALLI

A trail of similar WFH e-mails came in from her coworkers and one from Jordan where Calli was in the bcc line. She deleted them all without reading . . . they all said the same thing. Her Outlook calendar indicated she was free until after noon, so she responded to the other questions and inquiries, then made a list of clients to follow up with. She called probably a dozen that morning before she heard a car outside. Confused, she looked out her office window to the driveway.

The door to the black Jeep Wrangler opened, and Jordan slid out. She slung a laptop bag over her shoulder and grabbed a paper bag and a Chinese take-out box. Kicking the door closed, she shuffled up the steps to Calli's door.

Calli met her, relieving her of the takeout and led the way to the kitchen island. "What are you doing here?"

"Working from home." Jordan smiled and dropped her computer bag on the chair. She hung up her coat and went to Calli's cupboard to retrieve bowls. She handed one to Calli and kept one for herself, then fished out two large soup containers from the paper bag. "I never said whose home." She raised her brows, then added, "Anyway . . . I thought Taom Yum was appropriate for a cold day."

Calli's mouth watered as she grabbed two spoons from a drawer.

"You doing okay? This is your second time working from home in a week. I wanted to check on you," said Jordan.

"Everyone is working from home today." Calli rolled her eyes.

"Still."

"I'm fine . . . feeling wonderful, in fact, since Jax and Kent are back from their father's." Calli dumped some rice in a bowl and poured in the soup.

Jordan raised a brow. It may have been Calli's imagination, but it formed an almost perfect question mark.

Calli gave a short laugh. "I'm telling the truth. Last Friday, I was wallowing, but today, I'm tight."

"I don't know why you're upset over him." Jordan lifted

her bowl and took a spoonful.

Calli did the same, savoring the lemony broth and chewing an oyster mushroom. "I'm not upset over him. We fell out of love just after Kent was born. He had his first affair then, although he still won't directly admit it started that soon. The signs were there though . . . once I figured them out and looked back. Well, anyway, we all know how things worked out."

"Why'd you stay with him so long?"

She shrugged, not really wanting to go into all the reasons. "You know, marriage isn't only about the intimacy."

Jordan sucked in air to cool her mouth from the hot soup. "But it's a really big part."

"I know. We just got into a routine. I spent time at school functions and made friends with other moms. When he was around, he constantly was taking the kids to try new sports. Those nights, I had freedom to go out with you guys."

"I guess . . . " Jordan eyed her suspiciously. "You always were the first to instigate happy hour."

"For the most part, I just kept myself busy enough that I didn't have time to think about what was going on beneath the surface."

"Call me crazy, but I just don't get it."

"It was more of a business arrangement after I figured out his patterns." Calli shrugged. "I wanted the boys to have their father—still do. What blows is that while he slept around, I never once cheated." Not that she'd say it out loud, but somewhere deep inside, Calli wondered if she'd just turned frigid as a result of their less than romantic relationship. The thought of the work she'd have to put into either trying to bring Bennett around or have an affair herself had been just too much. While her friends seemed to think she'd been walked all over, she knew she played some part too—albeit less than his part—in their years of growing apart.

"My gawd . . . he's such a douche-bag!"

Calli chewed and swallowed, nodding. It was why Trina had nicknamed him DB.

"Well," said Jordan, putting both hands on the counter. "We're going to get you back to the you before DB."

Holding the bowl so that it would warm her hands, Calli eyed her friend suspiciously. "What do you mean?"

Jordan dug in her bag, then slammed a piece of paper onto the counter, pointing. "I signed us up for a class—Tuesdays, Thursdays, and Saturdays at 9:00 a.m."

Calli stared at the paper and the class name—Team Conditioning. She had a membership to the gym, but this class was one of those hard-core classes where people were in excellent shape. "What the hell, Jordan?" Calli rolled her eyes and walked into her office with soup in hand.

Jordan followed. "You've been saying you needed to get back into a workout schedule. So have I, for that matter."

"Yeah, but I meant starting out slow . . . maybe on the elliptical for half an hour." Calli sat behind her desk and glanced at her screen. Nothing new, and she had an hour and a half before her next meeting.

Her friend brought her bag into the office, then disappeared toward the kitchen and reappeared with her own soup. "I'm right there with you, Calli. But look at it this way, the class is paid for, it's a twelve-week commitment, I got permission from your boss for the time on Tuesday and Thursday. He said as long as you get your job done, all is good. Plus, there's no better way to develop the habit than by diving in headfirst." Jordan pulled her laptop from the bag and fired it up.

Calli drained what was left of her soup. She had been feeling self-conscious as of late and needed to stop buying clothes in larger sizes to accommodate the weight. "Argh. All right. Tomorrow at nine, I guess."

THE CELEBRATION LUNCH SAT IN front of Dom as his mind drifted. They'd closed the deal, so he should be here, in the moment with Joe. Instead, he idly swiped his thumb through the condensation up the side of his beer. This trip had been flat-out weird, and his mind hadn't been into the business, nor had it been into the pleasures he normally took when he came to San Francisco. When the waitress he normally toyed with had called, he'd made up an excuse, then stayed in his hotel alone all evening.

Callista Stockton. Why wouldn't her name or the vision of her leave him? Her dark curls reaching down her back lingered in his memory.

"Dom? Dom? Dominic!" Joe's fingers snapped in front of his face.

Dom blinked and sat straighter.

"Man, you've been distracted this whole trip. What's

up?"

"Nothing. I'm just ready to be home. You were saying?"

"I was toasting." Joe held up his Guinness Stout.

Dom lifted his IPA and forced a smile.

"To the latest in the Moretti investment chain," said Joe.

Taking a drink, Dom let the hoppy beer rest on his tongue before swallowing. He placed the mug on the coaster and asked his lawyer and friend, "How's Bets?" Joe's wife, Betsy was pregnant with their first child and due within the next month.

Joe's face lit up, and Dom felt an odd pang he couldn't explain as his friend gushed. "She and the baby are wonderful." Joe leaned in a little closer. "And Bets is sexier than she's ever been, if you know what I mean."

Dom furrowed his brow and stifled his shock. Bets looked like she had a basketball strapped around her midsection. How could he find that arousing? "Really?" he asked. Never having had the desire for children, or really even for a wife, he couldn't identify with finding a woman's stretching and rounding body arousing.

Joe rolled his eyes and breathed, "Oh my God, man. The fullness . . . she's tighter than ever. And the weight." He gave a quick moan. "It's hard to explain, but it's damn hot."

Dom laughed. "I'll have to take your word for that. No kids in my future." He took a large drink and swallowed, checking the time on his watch.

Joe finished his beer and raised a hand for the check. The waitress scooted over and glanced nervously at Dom as she fished through the stack in her folio. Dom eyed her back like she was the most beautiful thing he'd seen all day. That was, of course, untrue. But it'd make her feel better, and that was his only goal.

Joe handed over a card, and she scurried away. Joe smiled and said, "I have hopes for you, my man. One day."

Callista Stockton. Damn, there was that name again. Dom jerked his head to refocus and asked, "What's today?"

Joe, obviously ignoring him, said, "Not sex, Dom. Real love. It's out there for you."

"Mmhmm," Dom said. "The day?"

"December sixth."

"No, the day of the week."

"Oh, Wednesday."

"Excuse me for a minute. I need to make a phone call."

$\mathcal{H}$IS PERSONAL ASSISTANT ANSWERED THE phone, "Monroe Professional Services. Pauline speaking." She must not have looked at the caller ID because she usually greeted him by name.

"Hi, Pauline."

"Dom?" she squealed. "This is unexpected. You weren't on my agenda at all today." He heard papers rustling in the background. "I mean, I'm always happy to hear from you, but—"

Yep. Definitely off guard. "Yes, I know. Hey, I need you to do something for me."

"Of course, anything, just name it," she said eagerly.

"Before I left, I tossed a business card in the trash at my office. Can you run over and grab that before the cleaners empty the trash?"

"Not a problem at all. I have some errands to run downtown anyway. Will you be"—she paused and emphasized—"home tomorrow as you planned?"

"Joe got our flights bumped up. We arrive late tonight."

"Oh." Her voice sounded shocked and mildly pained, but she recovered quickly. "In that case, did you need me to have a car waiting for you?"

"Nope. Joe has us covered. Thanks, though. Please log your drive time, too, so I can make sure I pay you for all the time you spend on this. It's kind of a personal thing."

"Can I—"

"Look, Pauline, I have to run soon or we'll be late for our flight. There's a number on the back of the card. I'd also like you to call and arrange for a coffee date. She works at Moffitt & Hall, so somewhere near there would be great. Tomorrow afternoon if possible."

"Yeah, s—"

"I'm sorry. I have to run; we're leaving for the airport. Thanks again!" Click.

DOM HAD HUNG UP SO quickly he didn't catch Pauline sputtering as she deflated and sank into the chair.

Seven

$\mathcal{L}$ATER THAT AFTERNOON AT MOFFITT & Hall, the phone rang at the reception desk. "Good afternoon, Moffitt & Hall," Sara, the front desk receptionist, answered in her sweetest phone voice.

"Good afternoon," the woman's voice on the other end of the line said. "This is Pauline Monroe, Dominic Moretti's personal assistant. I'm calling to confirm our appointment with Kyle Newman for tomorrow at 1:00 p.m."

"One moment," said Sara. "Let me pull up Mr. Newman's calendar." The line was silent as Sara clicked into their shared scheduling software. "Yes, I show Mr. Moretti on his calendar in the North conference room. Is there a problem with the time?"

"No, no. Thank you for checking. One more thing. Is Callista Stockton available?"

"She's working remotely today, and it looks like she's currently on a call. I can either take a message or forward you to her voice mail."

"Wonderful. I can leave a message." Pauline paused. "Actually, can you check her calendar too? Mr. Moretti wishes to meet with her tomorrow—after his meeting with Mr. Newman?"

"Of course, but are you aware that her name has changed?"

"No, I wasn't," said Pauline with a lilting voice. "Did she just get married? How exciting."

"Oh." Sara's face fell as she belatedly realized she shouldn't have brought that up. "No, it's just a legal name change," she stammered. "Anyway, her last name is now Lindley. Can you communicate that to Mr. Moretti?"

"I can. Thank you. I'm sorry, what did you say your name was?"

"Sara Bishop."

"Well, Sara. You've been most helpful. Thank you." The phone went dead.

Eight

$\mathcal{D}$OM HAD ALWAYS BEEN A morning person, and the morning after returning, he sprang from his bed and went to his sink to shave. After filming a new episode of The Dinner Shark, he'd caught a flight back from San Francisco. Today, it was time to return to his restaurant manager's persona, clean-shaven Nic Moore. The trip had gone off without a hitch, and after his workout this morning, he and Joe would review the investment with Kyle at one, then he'd have coffee alone with Callista Stockton after. According to his calendar, Pauline had been able to arrange that. It still niggled at him that he hadn't even talked to this woman, but he couldn't get his mind off of her.

He put those thoughts aside, dressed, and went to his kitchen to prepare his protein shake with a healthy infusion of berries—a perfectly balanced breakfast that was easy to make and provided the energy necessary for the Team Conditioning class. He sipped and scrolled through the news on his phone. After some time, a calendar reminder for his workout flashed across the top of the screen. Dom grabbed his bag and called the elevator.

When Dom arrived at the gym, Joe and his very pregnant wife met him at the front desk. Dom went over and kissed her on the cheek. "Bets, you look lovely," he said.

She laughed. "I look like a blimp."

Joe grinned knowingly and nodded at Dom.

Dom ignored him, trying to not think of his friend's strange desires, and said to Betsy, "Are you here for the aqua class?"

"Nah," she said. "Thought I'd join you and Joe." Her face was deadpan.

He and Joe were scheduled for a class with the fitness coach, Trish, who had been nicknamed Beast Lady for her grueling classes. Dom peaked his brows, but her face split into a large smile.

Joe kissed her temple.

"I'm joking," she said and walked past reception toward the pool, then stopped and called back, "Though it might convince Little Joe here"—she rubbed her belly—"to come quicker. You boys have a good workout."

Joe issued a low groan and turned toward the locker room. Dom rolled his eyes. They dropped their bags in the normal lockers, each grabbed a towel, and returned to the gym where class was scheduled. As they crossed to the far side, Dom took inventory of the attendees and jolted at the sight of two new students. He halted mid-step, flashing back to a week ago at Moretti's. One was the boisterous blonde who'd done all the talking and the other one, stretching her calves, was Callista Stockton.

$\mathcal{C}$ALLI SHIFTED HER WEIGHT FROM one foot to the other and hugged herself, rubbing her bare arms. It was cold in the gym for now, though she knew it'd heat up as soon as she started to move. She couldn't recall the last time she'd been to the gym. Apparently, her running shoes had also gone into hibernation. So she'd gone last night and purchased new Brooks in hopes that she would save her arches and shins, or at least ease their stress as she jumped directly into this crazy workout regimen. She still couldn't fathom why she'd let Jordan commit her to six weeks of torture.

"Jordan," she said, "couldn't you have signed us up for one of the easier classes?"

"You'll be fine," she said, as bubbly as ever as she tied her blonde curls into a messy topknot and slipped on a headband.

"I'll be in pain is what I'll be." Calli took a drink of water and stretched her calves. She remembered the routine; warm-up would likely be a mile-long run. She took deep breaths trying to pre-oxygenate her muscles, doubtful though that it would help.

As she came out of the stretch, she saw Jordan's jaw hung open, her eyes wide. She tugged on Calli's arm. "The restaurant manager from Moretti's is here."

Calli started to turn, but Jordan held her and snapped in a whisper, "Don't look. He's staring this way."

"That's ridiculous, Jordan." Calli turned and locked stares with his green-gray eyes. She didn't giggle this time but felt heat rise in her cheeks under the pressure of his stare.

He gave a lopsided smile and followed the other man toward the class. His friend stopped to talk with another student, but he wrapped the towel around the back of his neck and came right toward Calli. "Hi, again," he said.

"Good morning. Nic, right?" Calli said.

"I'm surprised you remember." He stood a little too close, and it was suddenly not so cold in the gym even though the workout hadn't started. "You were in a state of hilarity at the restaurant," he said.

Calli's face burned. Words had left her brain.

"Yes, I'm Nic." He held out a hand. "I didn't catch your name though."

"Calli." She wiped her hand on her towel and slid it into his warm hand. The temperature difference made her small hand feel like ice inside his strong grip. Calli pulled back, shifting her eyes shyly from his, down, and back to Jordan who smiled broadly with her arms folded across her chest.

Music started—loud and blaring—and the fitness coach called everyone over. Calli breathed a sigh of relief for the reprieve from the awkward situation. Time to focus, she thought. One step at a time. You can do this, Calli.

Her prediction came true, a mile run on the upper track. The class was off, and she and Jordan fell in step behind those who'd clearly been attending for a while. Nic and his friend led the pack, and Calli felt incredibly inadequate. The text on the door into the upstairs track read, 12 laps = 1 mile. The class was only an hour, so Calli had little hope of finishing the full mile. Nic and the other guy passed the door in long strides on their second lap as she entered and started her first. When she was about two-thirds of the way around, he lapped her again, but she kept running. Each time he passed, she picked up her step slightly but then eased back into a pace that she felt was doable. Jordan outpaced Calli as well, but at least she didn't lap her.

Calli lost track of the number of laps, but when the students started exiting the track, she decided that she'd only finish one more, then head back down. Apparently, Jordan did the same because she waited at the door. Calli pressed on the stitch at her side, and they both were gasping for breath so much that a half smile was all the communication either could manage. The circuit had already started when they made it back to the group. Trish came over and explained the move at their first station.

Dead lifts with a kettlebell. Calli could handle this, and it gave her time to catch her breath. But by the time the two-minute bell sounded above the music, her hamstrings were on fire. Rest. She looked at the tablet countdown. A full minute. Thank the heavens.

Across the way, Nic shook out his arms from the overhead presses he'd performed at his station. When their eyes met, he smiled and looked away. The buzzer sounded for round two. Calli started again.

The class completed eight stations, then took a break for water. Nic ambled over and said, "You've got really nice form."

Calli took a drink, wiped her mouth and face with the towel, and simply said, "Thanks."

A whistle blew. "Make it quick," Trish yelled. "On the

line for kettlebell killers!"

"What's that?" Calli asked.

"Grab a pair of fifteens"—Nic pointed to the red kettlebells—"and stand on the line. When she whistles, run to the free-throw and drop one. Run back to the line, then back to the free-throw and drop the second." Nic pointed up and down the court. "Home. Free throw. Pick them up. Home. Half-court drop one. Home. You get the picture?"

Calli looked around at the others who'd already started the drill. Yeah, she got the picture all right—hell. Nic picked up thirty-pound bells and started his drill. Calli and Jordan exchanged tortured glances and started. Trish came over yelling something that was intended to be encouragement, but Calli wasn't sure it worked.

When the circuits stopped and the equipment had been stowed, Trish led the class through a few yoga poses to cool down and stretch the muscles. Calli's arms trembled as she struggled to hold a proper downward dog, and she sighed in relief when they rolled onto their backs and stretched the glutes. Hers were gelatin, so much so that she feared she'd have trouble walking the next day. She breathed in through her nose and out through her mouth as her heart rate settled back to normal.

"All right, team, amazing work," Trish said as she sat and folded her hands at heart center. "I'll see you all on Saturday. I have a really fun workout planned."

Calli looked at Jordan and rolled her eyes. Fun meant painful, and they all knew it.

"Oh, come on," Jordan whispered. "Don't you love the sore muscles after a good workout?"

"Not especially," said Calli.

"Ladies." Nic appeared with a hop at Calli's side. Other than the sweat on his shirt and damp hair, she'd never know he had just gone through that ringer of a class. "This will sound odd, I'm sure."

"If you're planning to tell me anything about your mother's cat, I agree, it will sound odd," Calli said, nervously reaching to make a joke. After it was out, she wanted to palm her face at her lack of eloquence.

He laughed, a smooth and rich sound, and Calli smiled back. Jordan and Joe introduced themselves and walked ahead, leaving her with Nic.

"I'm dreadfully allergic to cats," he said.

"Really?" asked Calli, brows raised. "We are going to discuss cats . . . awesome."

"No." There was that velvety laugh again. "I wanted to ask you if my assistant called you?"

"I'm sorry. Why would your assistant call me?" Calli's stomach dropped. It sounded like something Bennett would ask, so she was immediately on guard.

"Oh, I suppose I should clarify. Your friend at the restaurant, not Jordan and not the louder one."

"That would be Tory. What did she do?"

"She gave me your card. I've been traveling since that night you were at Moretti's. I wasn't going to call, but . . . "

Calli stopped and blinked at him repeatedly. "Why would she give you my card?"

Nic shrugged. "She seemed to think we'd hit it off."

"Oh, my God," she said, smacking her forehead. "Those were supposed to go into the fishbowl. Wait 'til I get my hands on her."

"So, did Pauline call you?"

"Uh, no." Calli started toward the door, then stopped. "And I think that's probably okay. Listen, I just went through an ordeal. I'm not certain this is a good idea. Especially if you're having your assistant call me for dates." Calli threw a hand in the air and walked away at a brisk pace. The last thing she needed in her life was another Bennett. If she was going to date, she'd do so with someone who wanted to talk to her directly, not someone who scheduled her into his busy life.

Nine

$\mathscr{W}$HEN CALLI ARRIVED AT THE office, she immediately popped three Advil and guzzled a liter of water followed by a protein recovery shake. Given any luck, the sore muscles would be minor, but that was unlikely. She logged into the computer and double-clicked the graph icon she had pinned to her taskbar. As her investment management application loaded on the screen, she remembered Nic's approach, how he had watched her intently as he'd entered the class, how their eyes kept finding each other during the workout, and how he'd fidgeted as he asked her . . .

No, Calli. Stop dreaming about him. Having an assistant schedule your dates is all Bennett, she reminded herself.

The app was taking forever to load, so Calli straightened her desk and noticed the blinking light on her phone. She lifted the receiver and pressed the button, and the receptionist's voice replayed. "Hi, Calli. A Pauline Monroe called on behalf of a Dominic Moretti. He has an appointment with Kyle at one, but she requested a meeting with you following that appointment. I have booked the South conference room for you at two-thirty."

The name familiar, Calli rubbed her brow as she slowly placed the phone in the cradle. At the gym, Nic had asked if Pauline had called. That was too coincidental. On her computer, the software had loaded, but she flipped to the browser and typed in Dominic Moretti. As soon as she hit enter, the first result read:

DOMINIC MORETTI – WIKIPEDIA

HTTPS://EN.WIKIPEDIA.ORG/WIKI/
    DOMINICMORETTI

And off to the right were a half-dozen images of a man who, despite the dark-brown beard, looked suspiciously like the man who'd fumbled to ask her on a date an hour earlier. Under the images it read:

DOMINIC MORETTI

RESTAURANT MOGUL

For some reason, she couldn't stop herself from reading through his vitals, learning that he was only a couple of years older than her and his net worth was $7.8 billion. Geez, if this was indeed the same man, why the hell would he be managing the floor at Moretti's himself? She smiled slightly when she read, "Spouse: None." Below the demographics, there was a section titled Movies and TV shows, in which six seasons of The Dinner Shark were pictured. More similarities . . . this had to be the same person.

At the whoosh of someone entering her cubicle, Calli

turned just as Jordan flopped into the guest chair. "So, do you have a date?" she asked.

"Ha," said Calli. "No."

"What? I was sure Nic was going to ask you out."

"Check this out." Calli leaned back and indicated for Jordan to look at her computer monitors. "His name is not really Nic."

Jordan reached for the touch screen and enlarged the images with two fingers. "Interesting," she mused. "Yeah, I think you're right."

"And, get this. He didn't ask me out. He asked me if his assistant had called."

Jordan eyed Calli blankly, shaking her head.

Calli sighed and mumbled, "Reminded me too much of DB."

Jordan rolled her eyes, sighed, and crossed her arms over her chest. "You can't let DB-Bennett keep interfering with your life." Then she held out a hand, palm up. "So . . . did the assistant call?"

"No. She didn't call me, but I think she called the receptionist here and scheduled a meeting between me and this . . . "— Calli circled her finger in the general direction of the images on her screen—"Dominic Moretti."

Jordan tiny-clapped and gave a wide grin, raising her shoulders. "Give it a minute, Calli." She looked back at the screen. "He is a quite beautiful man."

"Okay, but why a meeting? Is he looking for an investment? And for goodness sake, why is he insisting his name is Nic?"

"Duh," said Jordan. "Famous." She checked the time. "I have to run to a meeting. Don't discount it." And she was gone.

$\mathcal{D}$OM SLID INTO HIS M3 and gripped the wheel as his friend, Joe, settled into the passenger seat.

"So, did you get the date?" Joe asked.

"Why do you think I was asking her out?" Dom snapped.

Joe barked a laugh and held up his hands as if in surrender. "How long have we known each other? How many times have I seen you stalk a woman? You, my man, always get the girl. I just can't figure out why you don't hold onto any."

"Not this time," said Dom. While he tried to make the words sound casual, there was a bite to them and they tasted sour. Callista, no, Calli had brushed off his attempt rather easily. He changed the subject. "Why are you riding with me anyway? Where's Betsy?"

"Oh, she had a massage planned after her aqua class. She has the car."

"Should I drop you at your office?"

"Nah, I don't have any clients today, so I can work from your place until it's time for our meeting at Moffitt & Hall."

The car fell into silence, so Dom reached for the controls and turned up the music only for Shinedown to tell him that goodbye was sometimes a second chance. Dom pressed the skip key to silence Brent Smith's vocals. A new song started, and after a moment, The Calling sang the chorus of "Wherever You Will Go."

Dom shook his head, reached for the screen, and switched the playlist—Workout seemed safe. AC/DC's electric guitars screeched to life inside the car.

Joe looked at him sideways with peaked brows.

Dom shrugged, downshifted, and punched the gas.

$\mathcal{D}$OM AND JOE ENTERED MOFFITT & Hall and approached the reception desk. The fake redhead brushed her hair over a shoulder and looked past Joe to greet Dom. "Good afternoon, Mr. Moretti." She slid a paper across the counter as she stood. "Your meetings today will be in the South conference room on the second floor. The elevators are through these doors. May I take your coats?" She led them to the double glass doors to her right. Opening one, she placed a hand on her slightly jutting hip and looked pointedly at Dom with a suggestive smile.

She wasn't hard to look at, but the display was too typical, too forward. As he didn't want her to feel wounded, Dom returned the smile and said "Thank you" as he walked through.

In the conference room, Kyle and Pauline were already waiting. Kyle had prepared his latest statements, and after a formal greeting, he got straight to the numbers. Pauline listened intently, asking questions from page to page. Dom struggled to pay attention. He glanced down at the agenda that the redhead had given him.

Stradiotto

1:00–2:15	KYLE NEWMAN
2:15–2:30	BREAK
2:30–3:30	CALLISTA LINDLEY

His brow grew heavy. Apparently, Pauline had scheduled time, but he couldn't figure out why she'd called the office. He'd instructed her to arrange for coffee. He slid the paper over to Joe and pointed. Joe nodded and leaned in, whispering, "Second chance? Maybe that song on your playlist was kismet."

Ten

CALLI'S PHONE BUZZED, AND SHE fought the urge to look at it during the meeting with the hedge fund manager. "Thank you for your time today, Mr. Donaldson," she said.

"Of course," came the disembodied voice on the other end of the line.

Calli had worked with Mr. Donaldson for ten years but had never met the man. He seemed older and wiser, and he was always ready to crack a terrible joke. That was her life in this industry . . . dealing with some old geezers who worked magic with numbers and dollars. She sighed and lifted her phone to read the text.

Her shoulders fell when she saw Bennett across the screen. Reluctantly, she tapped the message.

BENNETT: HI CALLI

BENNETT: I HAVE A FAVOR

Of course, he does, Calli thought.

ME:	HI BEN WHAT'S UP
BENNETT:	ZOE AND I WOULD LIKE TO WTAKE JACKSON AND KENT TO SANTORINI FOR CHRISTMAS

"No!" Calli screamed at her phone though he couldn't hear. Maybe she should be thankful that he couldn't hear. She looked around the office to see if anybody else had noticed her outburst. She sighed her relief after taking inventorWy of the empty desks surrounding her cubicle.

"No. Fucking. Way!" she said aloud again. Then she took a deep breath, leaned back in her chair, and stared up at the foam-tiled ceiling. Why does the ass always put me in shitty situations like this?

Gathering herself, she typed back.

ME:	THAT IS NOT PART OF OUR AGREEMENT
ME:	I HAVE CHRISTMAS THIS YEAR
ME:	YOU HAVE THANKSGIVING
BENNETT:	THE AGREEMENT SAYS THAT YOU'RE SUPPOSED TO BE REASONABLE IN ACCOMMODATING REQUESTS THAT ARE AN EXCEPTION TO

<pre>
                THE RULES.

ME: THAT'S NOT REASONABLE
                BENNETT

ME: AN EXTRA WEEKEND IS
                REASONABLE

BENNETT: ZOE'S PARENTS ARE GOING
                TO SANTORINI
                WITH US, AND I WOULD
                LIKE THE BOYS TO SPEND
                TIME WITH THEM
</pre>

"Why the hell would they want to spend time with her parents?!" Good thing no one was around to hear her one-sided fight. Instead of replying with that, she tried to keep things civil.

<pre>
ME: I HAVE ALREADY PLANNED
                FOR US TO DRIVE
                TO MOM & DAD'S
</pre>

She hit send and then said, "You know, their grandparents, fucker!"

<pre>
BENNETT: TYPING . . .
</pre>

She waited. After an excruciatingly long pause, the text came across.

<pre>
BENNETT: YOU COULD DO THAT FOR
                THANKSGIVING.
                IT'LL BE AN EQUAL TRADE.
                YOU CAN HAVE THEM FOR
                2 WEEKS AT
</pre>

THANKSGIVING.

ME: 2 WEEKS?

ME: OUT OF THE COUNTRY FOR
2 WHOLE WEEKS?

ME: AT CHRISTMAS?!!!

BENNETT: GREECE IS NOT A QUICK
TRIP. YOU'VE BEEN
THERE.

Calli shouted to the phone, "I know I've been there, you asshole! It was our goddamn honeymoon." Back when she thought everything had been perfect. Back when she thought he was the most amazing and wonderful man on the planet. Back when she believed they'd be together until death did them part. Back when . . .

The request just wasn't fair. It, once again, showed how little he cared for the mother of his children. How did one just walk away from all of that?

ME: THIS IS MY 1ST CHRISTMAS
AND HOLIDAYS SEASON
ALONE

ME: AND YOU'RE GOING TO
JUST LEAVE ME ALONE

ME: YOU KNOW THIS IS MY
FAVORITE HOLIDAY

BENNETT: YOU HAVE YOUR SISTER
AND PARENTS. YOU

CAN STILL GO DOWN THERE.

ME: THAT'S NOT THE SAME

Calli's throat closed. Her eyes stung. The screen blurred, and she blinked to see the nonsense he sent next.

BENNETT: PLEASE CALLI. LET ME DO
THIS. I ALREADY TALKED TO
KENT, AND HE
IS SUPEREXCITED TO GO.

ME: HOW DARE YOU

BENNETT: WHAT? I HAVE A RIGHT TO
TALK TO MY KIDS.

ME: BUT YOU DON'T HAVE
A RIGHT TO MAKE PLANS LIKE
THIS WITHOUT
CONSULTING ME 1ST

BENNETT: I'VE ALREADY PURCHASED
TICKETS

ME: I NEED SOME TIME

ME: I'LL TRY TO GET BACK TO YOU
TOMORROW

BENNETT: TYPING . . .

Calli really didn't care what else he had to say. She needed to reach out to Kristi to see if she had a legal leg she could stand on. His request was just ridiculous, and the asshole didn't get it. Like always, he just wanted to run over her to get his way. Her head immediately started pounding, and she rubbed her temples. She started looking for an escape, even though she knew she wasn't trapped. Her chest tightened as her airways constructed.

Stop it! Calli schooled herself. Count through it. One . . . inhale. Two . . . exhale. Three . . . inhale. Four . . . By the time she had calmed herself, there were tears rolling down her face. She wiped them furiously, looked around, grabbed a tissue, and headed for the nearest conference room where she could have some privacy. She kept her head down and blew her nose. As she walked into the room at the south end of the second floor, the one nearest her desk, she closed the door behind her. Leaning back and dropping her head, Calli let the tears fall.

"Are you all right?" came a dark and spicy voice.

Calli jumped. "Holy shit! What are you doing here?"

Nic . . . Dominic . . . looked concerned as he moved slowly toward Calli. "It's 2:33. I believe we have an appointment."

DOMINIC CROSSED THE ROOM TOWARD the crying woman. Callista Stockton—no, Callista Lindley—stood before him, falling to pieces . . . yet moving him, drawing out some protective instinct he hadn't known existed. As she wiped the tissue beneath one eye, he took a step around the table. She looked at the damp black smudge and tended to the other eye. Dom took another step toward her, flexing and releasing his hands. Inside, he steamed, but not at her. He wanted to rip apart the person who had put her in this state, but more than that, he wanted to pull her into his arms and hold her so tightly she'd forget her worries.

"Wha—" He swallowed. "Can I do anything?"

She shook her head, turned her back, and blew her nose. After throwing the paper in the garbage, her back straightened, and she turned to face him. "I suppose your assistant made arrangements after all. What can I help you with, Mr. Moretti?" She'd nearly spat the word assistant and his last name. Her anger with him stung.

"So, you know who I am?" he asked, more to fill the space, make conversation, and stall.

Immediately after his words, she crossed her arms and raised both brows as she stared at him. He wiped his hands together; his palms were damp, so he dropped them to discreetly dry them on his pants. The suggestion in her stare was correct. He'd stated the obvious and appeared to be quite the inarticulate fool. He pulled out a chair and gestured for her to sit. "Please?"

She complied, and he looked to the ceiling, grateful but fighting the urge to celebrate just yet. Taking the seat next to her, he pulled the chair far enough back that he could lean forward in her direction and rest his elbows on his knees. "It appears I haven't made a great first impression. It's not often that I'm forced to correct that." His eyes drifted toward the floor. Usually, he didn't have to work so hard. Women normally pursued him. The receptionist's body language before was a case in point. This was new and delicate territory, and he knew he needed to move forward gently.

"Mr. Moretti, this is my place of work. Is there some professional matter, maybe an investment, that I can help you with today?"

"Ah, no." He hesitated. Still unclear why Pauline had arranged a meeting rather than scheduling coffee, he made a mental note to say something to her about her irksome solution to his request.

"Very well, then I really must return to work." Calli stood and made a move toward the door.

Dom placed a hand on her wrist to stop her. "Wait." He didn't look up immediately but felt her turn her eyes in his direction. "It was a mistake to have Pauline call. I'm sorry," he said. He raised his head slowly, hopeful that she'd listen. As he met her deep-brown eyes, rimmed in red from the tears, he buzzed all over.

"And what about your name?" Her tone was clipped. Obviously, she'd imagined him telling her falsehoods for some ill purpose. She added, "Why did you say your name was Nic?"

"I always go by Nic at the restaurant, and my TV persona is Dominic." He rose from his seat, not breaking eye contact but positioning them face-to-face with the top of her head at his chin. She followed his eyes until she was gazing upward. When her breath hitched, he smiled. "Call that a hazard of being a public figure. If you know who I am, you'll also notice that I'm clean-shaven here while I wear a beard on my show." He rubbed his hand down his cheek. "I go by Dom in my personal life, and I am very pleased to meet you, Callista Lindley."

She didn't pull away. He watched the tension drain from her pinkening face and her shoulders release as she took a deep breath. His eyes drifted to her lips and back, and she answered with the same drifting, suggestive look. Then she smiled, too, and gave a quick and nervous giggle.

"I didn't want a business meeting," said Dom. "I wanted coffee. Can we step out of here"—he motioned to the conference room—"and go with my original plan?"

"I . . . uh . . . " She scratched behind her ear, under the weight of her dark curls. "Well, let me check my calendar to make sure I don't have any meetings scheduled after you."

Dom followed her to her cubicle where she wiggled the mouse to wake up her computer and typed in a password. Glancing over her shoulder as nonchalantly as possible, he noted that her calendar was clear for the remainder of the day. As Calli gathered her jacket and scarf from a built-in coat cabinet in her cube, Dom leaned against the cubicle wall, waiting. The other woman, the talkative blonde who was with Calli at the restaurant, appeared at the end of the aisle. Apparently headed for Calli's cube, she stopped in her tracks, lifted her pen, and grinned at Dom before turning on a heel and retracing her steps.

"What is your friend's name?"

Calli looked over the cubicle wall, and said, "Oh, that's Jordan. You ready?"

Dom held out a hand for her to lead the way.

An uncertain look crossed her face, but she went.

He followed.

Eleven

THE MENTION OF COFFEE MADE Calli's mouth water, and this was at least a momentary distraction from the drama she had to manage with Bennett. Further, Dom had apologized easily for having asked his assistant to call her. Maybe she was being too hard on the man. She couldn't make everyone out to be like her ex. After all, she'd never heard the words I'm sorry slip through Bennett's lips. Maybe this was a small chance to separate herself from the compliant woman she'd been in her marriage and exercise a little risk. Coffee, at least, seemed platonic. And . . . she'd see this man at the gym three times a week for the next six. It'd be good to be cordial at least. So, she'd gone out on a limb and accepted the invitation.

Calli stepped up to the counter and greeted the barista at Bienvenue, the bistro around the corner from Moffit and Hall, and ordered a latte with an extra shot of espresso. Dom joined her and ordered the dark brew with two sugars. Dark brew, indeed, Calli thought as his clean scent overwhelmed her senses. He glanced down and they exchanged shy smiles, and Calli's gut twisted.

With their coffees in hand, Dom led the way to the armchairs in the back corner, and Calli observed how the crease in his gray dress pants moved and caressed him as he walked. Underneath, she envisioned his slightly bowed athlete's calves she'd seen in the morning's fitness class and hid a small smirk. He'd infuriated her with the assistant-arranged date thing, but now, watching him walk, she had to admit that he was one amazing package—at least to view. Maybe, just maybe, her friends were right, and he could be her rebound guy. Technically, it'd only been a week since the ink had dried, but she'd been separated for over a year, and her marriage had been in the toilet long before that. Calli couldn't recall the last time she'd actually been intimate with anyone other than her ex.

Calli placed her drink on the table and removed her coat, handing it to Dom who hung it beside his on the nearby coatrack. She sat and sipped her latte.

As Dom returned and took the empty chair, he said, "This atmosphere is much better."

"So," Calli started, looking around at the sparsely populated tables in the bistro. Most people grabbed a to-go from the Starbucks on the corner or the Caribou another block up. Coffee was the fuel for the financial professionals who worked in Cloud 9, and as a result, each block had one or sometimes two coffee shops. Bienvenue was the more upscale, sit-down version. In fact, the owner refused to provide to-go cups and instead created meeting spaces to invite people to use his space to conduct business.

"Yes, so," answered Dom, then offered a crooked yet charming smile.

Calli shifted and chewed the inside of her lip. The pause was uncomfortable at best.

At last, he broke the silence. "Tell me about yourself."

She laughed, again discomfited. "An interview?" She looked questioningly into his piercing eyes. "Is that what we're doing?"

"No. I just . . . " Dom rested the cup in the palm of one hand, pressing his lips together in a tight line. "I didn't really have much of an agenda. I just wanted to see if we had anything in common."

"Well, I can't say I'm overly experienced in the dating area," said Calli, "but maybe we should start with some casual talk?"

"Yeah, good idea." He looked toward the high ceilings, inlaid with copper-detailed cornices. "How did you end up in Trish's class this morning?"

Calli twitched a bit. The question reminded her of the ache settling into her muscles. "That's all Jordan," she said. "She signed us both up yesterday on a whim."

"But you're going. That's great!" said Dom.

"I'd planned to begin slow, but, well, I guess that didn't happen." Calli shrugged. "I'm going to hurt like crazy tomorrow, I think."

"Trish loves that. I think she's a bit sadistic in that way." Dom stirred in the sugar cubes and sipped. "You made it through okay, though."

"Barely. We'll see how well I'm moving by the next one

on Saturday."

"What do you like to do for fun?" he asked.

A waitress came around with a stack of saucers and empty mugs and interrupted. Staring at Dom with doe eyes, she asked, "How is everything here? Can I get you anything?" She glanced at Calli briefly, then refocused her attention on Dom.

It said something that Dom didn't flinch, his gaze never pulling away. Calli answered the girl, knowing full well that she was looking for Dom's attention. "Thank you, but we're good." She walked away, defeated.

Calli answered his question from before the interruption. "I don't have a"— she made air quotes—"quote, unquote, raging social life."

"But there must be something you enjoy," said Dom.

"I like wine, in case you didn't notice the other night."

"Ah, yes. The Petite Petit, if I recall."

Calli's eyes widened; that had been over a week prior. "Interesting that you remember that from all the tables you had to have visited that night."

Dom lifted one shoulder. "What can I say? It's one of my favorites too. Have you ever been to the Michael David vineyard in Lodi?"

"Can't say that I have." She hid her face in the latte, fighting away the sour memories. Back when she'd thought there might be hope for her and Bennett, she'd booked a trip to Lodi. Bennett's personal assistant had called to cancel the trip because Bennett had had a business trip to attend. Calli later learned that he'd used his ticket and rebooked hers under the name of his latest mistress, now fiancée she supposed. Swallowing, she changed the subject. "I like movies." She smiled. "And the theater. And concerts. What about you?"

"I have a thing for small breweries. I travel at least once a month for work, and I'm away for a week most times, so it gives me the opportunity to visit many of them across the country."

Calli swallowed hard. She didn't want to be involved with someone who traveled so often. She should have known—how else would he shoot his series? "That's right," she said. "You travel for The Dinner Shark, right?"

"Yes. My first love is Moretti's, but I invest in others to share the joy of owning a restaurant and seeing it successful."

She nodded and held the mug in her hands, allowing the warmth to seep into her palms. Breathing in through her nose, Calli counted mentally, then exhaled—her routine an attempt to eschew a bout of constricting anxiety. Despite her effort, the band around her chest was tightening, and she needed to get out. Travel. Investing. Déjà vu. She shook her head, breathing again and trying to maintain a semblance of socially acceptable behavior. "Listen, Dom." She looked up, into his light eyes—such a contrast with his dark hair and hint of a five o'clock shadow. Her chest loosened. The breathing seemed to be working.

With eyes locked, the space between them disappeared ever so slowly. "Yes?" he whispered, looking to her lips.

She let her gaze fall to his mouth as well, a strange force drawing her closer. Silence stretched out between them; the espresso machine gurgled at the bar and some dull conversation hummed in the air from other tables, but Calli forgot what she'd been thinking.

After a moment, the intensity of the connection passed, and he said, "Would you join me for dinner on Saturday?"

"Yes."

There wasn't thought. The word had escaped without permission. What was she going to do now? But she forgot about that, too, as the gap closed, and their lips met in a soft, chaste kiss that hid some underlying, electric, and base need.

<h1 style="text-align:center">Twelve</h1>

"GIVE ME HUGS," CALLI REACHED her arms wide to both Jax and Kent. Tonight was the first time they'd be leaving to spend the official four days with Bennett, and though they'd spent a night here and there with their father, this seemed more permanent. They were so close to leaving the nest for good, to going off to college or whatever path they chose, that it grated on her to know she'd be deprived of a third of what little time she had remaining. This was part of the hardship she thought she had been avoiding by staying in a dead marriage for so long. Reluctantly, though, she had to admit that her life away from the DB had been much better, even with the divorce negotiations and these times forced apart hanging over her. Heck, Jax was working now anyway, and Kent would likely be soon if he could keep his grades in a spot where he could spare the time.

Kent was the first to come into her arms. He was silent but tense.

Calli held his face to hers and said, "Hey, Superman." When he looked at her with eyes softening, she continued, "You have your mobile. Text if you need anything. Call anytime. I know you don't like to take them on the weekend, but don't forget to take your meds tomorrow and Friday before school."

"Okay, Mom," was all he said as he hefted his backpack and went out the front door.

She turned to Jax. He didn't look worried, exactly, but annoyed that he'd be away from his room and his setup for a few days. Being her young man and already setting his own ways, he liked his space. She pressed her lips into a line, then said, "I know it's not your responsibility to look after your brother, but . . . well . . . you know how he is, and you know how your father is with watching him."

Jax stepped closer. "Don't worry, Mom. We'll be okay. Just wish Dad didn't insist on picking us up. I'd like to have my car there."

"I know. He's being a little weird about it. Give it a few times, and I'm sure he'll be happy to not have to transport you." A honk came from the drive. She squeezed her son and tucked her head as she nudged him toward the door. "I'll see you on Sunday."

In the kitchen, she tossed a frozen dinner in the microwave and grabbed her phone.

CAT:	HEY SIS.
CAT:	I'LL BE OVER AFTER 7 AFTER HOCKEY PRACTICE.
CAT:	OH, AND I TALKED TO MOM

TODAY. DAD'S GOT SOMETHING IN THE
CITIES SOON. HE WANTS YOU TO CALL.

Calli's sister had a much better relationship with their mother due to her ability to just let things roll off her back. It didn't matter what good old Mom said, Cat just rolled her eyes and let it go. Calli wished sometimes she could be as tough, but most of what her mother said seemed judgmental or self-absorbed and stabbed her somewhere personal. When Calli decided to leave the family business, that had been the first divide that really stung. She wanted her mother to support her no matter what she did, and it wasn't like she had been off making nothing of herself or partying away her life. She had still gone to college and held a bachelor's degree with honors.

The microwave beeped, calling Calli from her musings. She pulled back the plastic, stirred, and put it back in for two more minutes. In that time, she picked up the phone and dialed her dad's mobile.

"Hi, Callista," Richard Lindley's rich voice came over the phone. He had been her rock growing up, and she always felt reassured by hearing him call her name.

"Hi, Dad. Cat said you wanted me to call?" She turned on the speakerphone and left it sitting on the counter.

"Oh, yeah. Hang on a sec." There was some rustling in the background, and she heard the distinct whine of the door to one of the greenhouses.

As she waited, her measly dinner finished cooking, and she plopped the plastic container on the counter to let it cool.

"All right. I have to come to the Cities to give a lecture at the U next week. I was wondering if I could stay at your house?"

"Of course, Dad. You don't ever have to ask that. You're always welcome here. When are you coming?"

"Oh, the lecture is Monday morning. I'll be up on Sunday night."

"I'll have the guest room ready. Is Mom coming too?"

"No, she has a benefit that she's hosting at the church that weekend. Will Kent be around?"

Calli grinned at him asking after her little superman. "Yeah, they come home on Sunday."

"Do you think he'd like to go to the lecture with me? We can go to the botanical gardens afterward."

"I'm certain he'll love that, Dad, but he has school on Monday." Calli's dad remained silent, and after a minute, she added, "But I think I can get him excused. It's educational after all."

"Thanks, Callista. I'll see you then. Love you."

"I love you too, Dad. Drive safely on your way up."

A FEW HOURS LATER, THE ALARM beeped on Calli's back door. "Hey, Cal, where are you?"

"In here, Cat," she called from the den.

From the hall, Calli heard some thumping and fumbling around as Cat took off her shoes and coat. When she was done, the fridge opened and glass clinked, then her sister finally found her way into the den where Calli was already curled onto the couch. She held two open beers and wore sweats almost identical to the black ones Calli had slipped into after dinner and a nice bath. Cat was her mirror image, a sensation she'd known all her life but one she knew was rare in the world. She had often wondered over the years how others would feel coming face-to-face with someone whose every curve, color, and structure was identical to their own. They'd had fun with it as girls from time to time, but had never quite pulled off a full swap. Their mother always seemed to know who was who. After becoming a mother herself, she understood how a mom learns the very essence and feel of each child as if they were a part of her. Confusing them would be like confusing your right hand for your left leg.

Cat plopped down beside Calli so that their shoulders touched and said, "How are you?"

"Happy you're here." Calli tried to smile but her lips just wouldn't turn up.

"Been a rough week?" Cat took a swig of the beer and came away with a loud sigh as she read the label. "That's hoppy."

Calli reached hers over and clicked the necks of the bottles together. "Just the way I like my beer."

"So . . . what are we watching tonight?"

"Something mindless."

Cat grabbed the remote and turned on The Princess Bride.

Calli giggled. How could anyone go wrong with that? She shifted a pillow behind her, getting a bit more comfortable, took a drink of her own beer, and said to her sister, "Cat, I really appreciate you spending the evening with me. It just makes it a little easier to not be alone."

Thirteen

After the class with Beast Lady on Saturday, Calli and Jordan met Trina for lunch. Aside from being difficult, the workout had been awkward—a combination of attempting new moves, her muscles protesting, and trading curious looks with Dom. When the hour had passed, he'd strolled over and given her a few instructions for the evening. Formal had been the most troubling part.

"Can one of you ladies explain to me why the hell I agreed to go on a date with Dominic Moretti tonight?" Calli asked at the girls' lunch after the conditioning class. She looked at Trina and Jordan suspiciously. "Where is Tory, anyway?" she added.

"Apparently, she and Steve flew to Italy, and they're taking a motorcycle around the boot," said Jordan, then sinking her teeth into her French dip.

Calli rolled her eyes and popped a grape in her mouth.

After a few chews, she said to Trina, "She always used to get down on you for riding with that one guy . . . what was his name?"

Trina answered, "Bill."

"That's right, Bill. He really wasn't your type," Jordan said.

Calli eyed Jordan and their boisterous and somewhat pretentious friend who sat across the table now scrolling through her phone. Trina, the friend who dated like there was no tomorrow . . . Trina, the partier who lived at the clubs . . . Trina, the one who always had her hair perfect, her makeup pristine, and her designer clothes matched to a T.

Sinking back into the chair, Calli left her sandwich barely touched on the table. Despite the grueling workout before lunch, her gut was in knots and food just didn't seem like the solution. A date. It'd been twenty-two years since she'd been on a first date. This was insane!

Jordan, still stuck on Tory and Steve, added, "Now look at her. They're off riding motorcycles every chance they get. I need to find someone to take me to Italy." She pouted, then smiled.

"Anyway," said Calli, "really, can somebody tell me why I chose to go on this date? I'm just sick over it."

"Guurl, relax!" said Trina. "It's about time you stepped out."

"Trina's right," said Jordan, holding a glass of ice water toward Calli.

"The man's hella hot. Wonder what he'll be like in bed," Trina mused, a little too loudly. Jordan nodded her agreement.

"Trina!" Calli admonished. "Jordan, really?"

Jordan said, "Don't tell me you haven't thought about it."

Calli's face heated and she reached for her own water.

"Oh, yeah, gurl, she's thought about it." Trina reached out and nudged Jordan's shoulder. "You can see it in her face. See that? She's imagined those strong arms wrapping around her and lifting her off the floor as she wraps her legs around his waist, clothes flying in all directions."

"Trina . . . shh!" Calli ducked as if she could hide from the stares turning in their direction from the other tables.

"I'm just sayin', gurl."

"You don't have to say it so the whole restaurant can hear," Calli pleaded and glared.

"If they got a load of that package, they'd all think the same damn thing." Trina crossed her arms and smiled slyly.

Jordan laughed. "Where's he taking you?"

"I have no effing clue. It all happened so fast and then the kiss just sent me into all kinds of confused. All I know is he told me to dress up, and he'd pick me up about eight fifteen."

"Wait?!" Trina slapped the table with both hands and looked between the two other women. "He kissed you?"

Calli took a sip of her water, trying for her best innocent look.

"Is he a good kisser?" Trina asked.

"Hard to tell. It wasn't like all hands-on. It was—" She didn't want to sound trite, but it was the only way to describe it. A grin crept across her lips, and she tilted her head slightly as she added, "—sweet."

"That man has sin dripping from every inch of his six-foot-something, muscle-ridden body, and his kiss was . . . sweet?" Jordan stared disbelievingly.

"Well, the conversation was awkward, but there was a strange undercurrent. I don't know how to explain it. Anyway, does it really matter? I can't see this going much of anywhere. I'm just not ready for something serious, so . . . I said I will go, and I will. Then it'll be done. Although . . . " Calli slumped. "I don't have anything to wear."

Jordan perked at that and raised her hands up as if she'd just won the lottery. "Shopping!" she sang.

"I'm in. Waiter!" Trina waved. "Check, please."

Jordan snatched the bill when it arrived. "My treat." She shoved her card in the sleeve and passed it back to the waiter. After his return, she signed, and her eyes sparkled as she said, "Let's go!"

Calli stood and bundled up as Trina on one side, Jordan on the other slipped their arms through hers and all but carried her away, likely destined for the most ritzy store they could find.

Trina pulled out her phone, selected a contact, and called. After a minute, she said, "Karla, I have an emergency." She paused as Karla obviously replied, then said, "Two hours is perfect. See you then."

"What was that?" Calli asked.

Trina lifted the ends of Calli's six-month-old cut and color and said simply, "Hair."

$\mathcal{D}$OM WALKED PAULINE TO THE door, then returned to his desk. Sitting back in his chair, he tossed a wadded-up piece of paper into the trash across the room. Score, he thought as it sailed right into the center. Likewise, he'd landed the date, but the interactions with Pauline today had been weird at best. She'd played innocent, stating that she had believed he'd only been looking for a professional arrangement since it was a Moffitt & Hall business card. He'd tried to give her the benefit of the doubt, but when she hesitated about going to pick up his suit for the evening, he started to suspect it wasn't as innocent as she wanted him to believe. He simply didn't understand why women were so needy, petty, and almost possessive even without a relationship.

He stared at the gray Canali micro-checked suit. It was one step away from a tux yet more expensive than what most wore on their wedding days. Dom didn't stock too many suits, and none in black, because they were a stuffy maggiordomo uniform in his restaurateur's eyes. Gray, on the other hand . . . The deep-eggplant threads and matching tie against a lighter-gray slim-fit shirt and the vest, coat, and pants were just what he needed to feel ready for the first date he was actually looking forward to since . . . when? He couldn't recall.

Grabbing the suit, he locked up his office and headed for the elevator and toward his loft above to shower and get ready for the evening.

Time moved more slowly than ever. After showering and dawdling as best he could for an hour or more, he glanced up; the clock read 7:28 p.m. . . . . close enough. He had plenty of time still to dress, do his hair, shave, get to his car, and drive to pick up this woman who'd infiltrated every single thought during his day. The workout this morning had been a series of him tripping over his own feet as he tried to get a glimpse of what she was doing or how she was doing in class. She'd said she would be sore, but she seemed to plow through the pain and did great. He was somehow proud of that—unreasonable though that feeling may have been.

At eight, he headed to the underground garage and slid behind the wheel of his M3. He'd already programmed in Calli's address—yeah, he didn't want anything to go amiss. He'd already biffed things with Calli once by having his personal assistant call to arrange a meeting, and he'd said a few things that obviously put her off. Tonight, he needed to learn how not to make those kinds of mistakes in the future.

As he drove through Calli's sleepy neighborhood, the houses grew into what he considered monstrosities. Far too large for someone single, he thought. He favored the size of his loft—an open living space, a single master suite, a smaller room tucked behind the kitchen that he rarely used, and absolutely no outdoor maintenance. Then again, she did work in Cloud 9. If the percentages his investment advisor, Kyle, took in fees were any indication, she could afford this lifestyle as well as any married couple. It was just a bit more . . . domestic . . . than he'd expected, and it was so dark. With the houses spread out, the mature trees, and only a streetlight at about every fifth house, it was hard to see anything. He felt like he was driving into the country.

The GPS said in her computerized voice, "Your destination is on the left."

He slowed to read the house numbers and easily confirmed the number he was looking for in the light from the front porch. Dom drove past her place into a cul-desac, backtracked to Calli's house, and pulled into the long driveway. He left his M3 running to keep it warm for his date and stepped outside. As he strode toward the walk, a dog started barking—a deep, growly bark, rapid and trying to warn someone of the stranger's presence. Fortunately, Cujo seemed to be a house or two away, so Dom buttoned the top button on his Canali suit jacket and pressed forward. Under the previously helpful spotlights, Dom felt like he was center stage, heart racing and his neck itching like he was about to break out in hives. Since that time in the fifth-grade talent show, when he was the fat kid that everyone laughed at when they weren't supposed to, he'd avoided that. How ironic that he had his own television show now. Somehow, though, it didn't feel the same, and through hard work, he was no longer fat.

He rang the bell and pushed his hands into his pockets, the light reflecting from his warm breath as it fogged the night air. Thankfully, no barking came from inside the house. He loved dogs, but dressed as he was, he didn't want to deal with fur clinging to the expensive suit.

The lock thunked, the knob snicked, and the door swung open into the house, revealing Calli with one shoulder leaning onto the open door's edge. She smiled, smoothing the simple, yet elegant gray dress. Dom lost his breath as he took in the beadwork that decorated her neck and chest. Her shoulders remained bare, but her rich brown curls rested over one shoulder, drawing his eyes down the length of her slender arm. The skirt brushed the floor. A soft pink color bloomed in her cheeks and his open-mouthed stare turned into a grin.

"Come in." She motioned with one hand. "I just need to grab my coat." She turned toward the closet, revealing an open back and the curved line of her spine.

Dom stepped inside, his mouth turning to cotton at the sight of her. He wanted to lean in and place his lips on that curve. Instead, he closed the door and reached for the coat she'd pulled from the closet. "Your choice in gown is delectable."

"Thank you. You don't think it's too much?"

"Absolutely not. You're radiant." Dom held up the coat for her to slide her arms into. As she did, a floral scent drifted up to him. He breathed deeply, savoring her soft smell. "Did you get your hair done too?"

Calli lifted a hand self-consciously and rolled her eyes. "Do you remember the ladies I was with at Moretti's?"

"Mmhmm."

"They had way too much fun with dressing me up today." Calli giggled, shaking her head. Then with a shrug she added, "You did say to dress. Though, even with that, I'm not usually so fancy."

"Well, you can tell them that they hit the mark."

As she grabbed a small bag and turned back to him, he shuffled from foot to foot. Why did he so want to pull her into his arms, forget the dinner, and have his way with her right here and now?

"Are you ready?" she asked.

He swallowed and said, "Yes," as he opened the door for her.

Fourteen

$\mathcal{C}$ALLI LIFTED THE LAYERS OF her gossamer skirt and walked down the sidewalk steps to Dom's still running car. Strike that thought—sports car. Typical. Just get through the night, Calli.

During the process of getting her hair foiled in a caramel color with deep-brown accents for depth, then coifed for the evening, she had grown increasingly nervous and, if she'd admit it, excited about the date. While she'd brushed off Dom's compliments, she was pleased that he'd noticed and appreciated her efforts. The dress and hair had cost a fortune that wasn't really in her budget, but she considered it her gift to herself for having come through the divorce to a good place. After all, a few hundred were a cheap price to make her feel like a million bucks and boost her confidence for the night. She wasn't the bumbling mess she'd thought she would be.

Dom opened the passenger door with one hand and

extended the other to her. His hand was warm and a bit rough; presumably, he needed to wash them frequently in the restaurant business. Even as strangers still, electricity shot up her arm when they touched, and the tension between them became palpable again. She cast her eyes downward, then back to his, holding his piercing gaze as she lowered herself into the car and gathered her gown.

He smiled, closed the door, and strode around the car. The light gray of his suit reflected the headlights' glow when his long legs passed through the beams. Calli looked down at the Jovani dress she wore. Good thing she had chosen the gray instead of the teal dress she'd considered as a close second. They looked like a properly matched couple.

Inside the car, Dom buckled his seatbelt and checked his watch—an intriguing double-faced gadget.

"Our reservations are for 8:15; we should be right on time." He shifted the car into reverse, the rear camera showing the entry to Calli's driveway. Once backed out, he pushed the clutch, put the car in first, revved the engine slightly, and they were off.

Not yet comfortable enough to sit with this man in silence, Calli said, "Nobody really drives a stick these days."

"I learned on one, and I've only had one automatic in my life. After that, I vowed that any vehicle I owned would have a manual transmission. I enjoy the feel of the engine and the connection to the machine as I drive"—he downshifted as they rounded a curve and shot her a crooked smile—"plus, it's a built-in car security system." He raised a brow. "And . . . it's just downright sexy. You can drive one, right?"

I'm sure I could drive yours, she thought, then wondered where that lewd comment had come from. Maybe Trina had invaded her brain. Instead, she said, "It's probably been fifteen years. I'm rusty at best." Unfortunately, that applied to both scenarios, and she was thankful for the low light to hide her heating cheeks.

He drove on, moving in time with the roaring engine, taking curves at precise acceleration and responding to the car's every need. Calli stared at him as he enjoyed the simplicity of working the machine beneath him. She had lost track of the lefts and rights through the city streets, but they were somewhere downtown and had parked underground by the time the engine whispered off. Dom helped her from the car into the heated garage. He removed his coat, then took hers and laid them both across the front seats. Then he slipped his hand into hers and led the way. Her heart flipped and flopped as they walked. She hadn't held hands with anyone in so long, it was a mixture of feeling like a foolish teenage girl and somehow arousing.

The door they approached read, Babette's. It wasn't the street entrance to the classy steakhouse but a private door.

Calli hesitated, drawing Dom's attention. He turned toward her, and before she knew it, he had his arms around her waist and they stood body to body. She raised her gaze, questioning his intentions, and they came nose to nose. Breaths mingled. Calli tasted mint in the air, and both of their breathing patterns became irregular. Hers hitched. Time stopped.

Was this . . . ?

Yes, it was.

Wordlessly, his hot lips met hers, and she felt the mint tingle on her lips. He coaxed her lips open, and she tasted the mint on his tongue. Her hands wandered up his arms to his neck as their lips moved together, each gasping for breath between kisses. He pulled her tighter, then slowed the kiss, and finally pulled back, smiling wickedly. Calli felt flushed from head to toe, throbbing lips begging for more.

"I'm sorry," Dom breathed. "I couldn't help myself."

"Yeah," was all Calli could say. Her eyes flicked toward the door.

"I know the owner."

Of course, he did . . . he was in the business.

"Anyway," he said but didn't move.

"Yeah, we should . . . um," Calli said, not wanting to let go either.

They both chuckled nervously. Dom reached up, running his hand from her elbow up her forearm to where her fingers still caressed the short hairs at his hairline. He pulled and held her hand, and she reluctantly released the other. He opened the door, allowed her to walk before him, and followed inside. Self-consciously, she ran a finger under her bottom lip, thankful she'd opted for lip gloss rather than a color.

A gentleman in a tuxedo with tails greeted them. "Good evening, Mr. Moretti and Miss."

"Lindley," said Dom. "How are you this evening, Bruce?" Dom held out a hand, and they shook.

"Doing well, sir. Your table is prepared. Right through there." He motioned to the open double doors.

Dom led, Calli trailed, and Bruce pulled up the rear. A private room waited, dark-wood paneled with a fire in a hearth and glowing candles dappling the mantle. Opposite where they'd entered was a second door, presumably to the kitchen. A round table, dressed in white and set for two, sat in the center of the room with two lit candles. As Calli scanned the scene with open jaw, the host silently moved around them to the table and pulled a chair for her to sit.

"It's the chef's table." Dom took the other chair.

Bruce draped black napkins across each of their laps and left them with a bon appétit.

The candles were positioned off-center on the table, perfect for a romantic dinner so as to not obstruct the couples' view of one another.

"This is amazing." Calli had never been in such a scene. At one time, Bennett had regularly taken her to the best restaurants, but he either hadn't known that such rooms existed or never thought her special enough to treat like this. Probably the latter. Then it dawned on her. "Does Moretti's have a room like this? Or a table?"

"Kind of. Moretti's has a private kitchen with eat-in dining as the chef's table."

"A bit more casual," Calli mused.

"That's not the intent." Dom pulled a bottle from the wine bucket near the table and poured a bubbling white. Replacing the bottle, he raised his glass.

Calli reciprocated the toast and asked, "Then what is the intent?"

"Intimacy with the chef." He raised a perfect brow, his green-gray eyes catching the candlelight.

"You being the chef, I suppose." She sipped, the sparkling rosé cool and crisp on her tongue.

"Only on very, very special occasions. I don't cook for many people anymore," he said.

"Oh," said Calli, looking down at the table. For some reason, that stung.

"One day," he said as the door opened.

The chef entered wearing the classic white hat with a pristine white double-breasted jacket with black collar, cuffs, and buttons. He placed a small, tented menu on the edge of the table. "Good evening," he said. "My name is Marco, and I'll be your chef for the evening. Your amuse-bouche will be a Maine lobster–stuffed petite portobello in a beurre blanc sauce; the soup an herbed French shallot; and the main course will showcase a quail breast presented on julienned baby carrots."

Calli's eyes grew progressively wider while the chef continued. "The salad course will consist of a bright pear, arugula, and pancetta mix. Your main course is a six-ounce bone-in ribeye with baked young russets."

She was thankful that she hadn't had much for lunch but still worried over where she'd put all that food. She glanced between her date and the chef.

Marco continued uninterrupted, "For dessert, a flourless chocolate soufflé with raspberry reduction. Naturally, my sommelier has chosen the perfect pairings for each course, with the exception of the main course. I believe you requested the Petite Petit, Mr. Moretti?" When Dom confirmed, Marco added, "Do you have any questions?"

"Marco, your menu sounds delightful. Thank you for the work."

The chef puffed out his chest and nodded toward Dom,

then to Calli, and retreated.

Calli reached for the sparkling wine—aperitif she guessed was the more appropriate terminology—and sipped. Setting down the fluted glass, she leaned toward her date. "Does everyone in the restaurant business try so hard to impress you?"

"Mmm, yes. Being famous in the industry comes with certain privileges, as well as a lack of privacy." He turned to look at the door just as an onlooker ducked away. "And you wondered why I introduce myself as Nic in public." He laughed, a deep and lush velvety sound.

$\mathcal{D}$OM GLANCED AT THE SUCCULENT medium-rare steak, cut the final bite of ribeye from the bone, and raised his eyes back to Calli across the table. He placed the perfectly prepared steak onto his tongue, following it with the last of his red wine, still watching his date. She glowed more and more as the evening moved into night, and he felt privileged to be sitting across from such a lovely and sophisticated woman.

They'd chatted endlessly through the first four courses, but when the steak arrived, they'd both fallen silent. It'd been a comfortable silence as both enjoyed how the fatty red meat cut the bite of the tannic red wine. Dom placed his fork and knife across his plate, pleased with the meal, the wine, and that she'd eaten almost everything placed before her. He hated when a woman only took a bite here and there and didn't enjoy her food.

As if timed, the door behind him swished open, and the waitress entered carrying dessert, a single plate with the chocolate soufflé dusted with powdered sugar and drizzled with the raspberry reduction, and two forks. The sommelier entered with the final wine of the evening and two glasses. After having Dom sample it, he poured a glass for each of them and disappeared.

Piano music reached a crescendo over the previously silent hidden speakers in the chef's dining room. They both looked up, then at the soufflé, and back to each other with mirrored smiles. "A little mood music?" asked Dom.

Calli lifted one of the forks. "Beethoven's Moonlight Sonata is one of my favorites."

"Then I guessed right." Dom cut into the soufflé, and they chuckled as it released a puff of steam and deflated. He scooped up a bite and offered it to Calli. Dom's pulse leapt as she leaned in, opening her delicate mouth for the prize. He couldn't let his mind go there just yet. "Now, follow it up with the wine," he said.

Her eyes danced.

"That sensation . . . chefs refer to it as joie de vivre."

"It's nearly orgasmic!" she blurted. Calli's eyes went wide and she raised her napkin to her lips, but he caught the O her lips made before she covered her mouth and shook her head.

Dom reached for her hand and pulled the napkin away to reveal her pointed little chin, the lower half of her heart-shaped face. After she slowly dropped the napkin into her lap, he said, "Don't be embarrassed. Food can be highly—" He paused, holding her eyes, wanting to ensure his suggestion was understood. He couldn't believe how much he wanted this woman. From that first night in his restaurant, to the gym and the coffee shop, to their real first kiss this evening, he desired her more than he could imagine. "—pleasurable."

"Yeah, um, well, I didn't have to be quite so crude," she said.

"Really? I'm mildly enchanted."

"Now you're just being nice." It bit that she brushed off his advance, that she obviously missed his meaning.

"I'm not. Truly, I'm being anything but nice."

Calli fanned herself and said, "Is it hot in here? Maybe I've had too much wine."

Still frustrated with her dismissal, he stood and stepped to her side of the table, grasping her hand. She allowed him to pull her to standing, and he wrapped one hand around her waist. With the other, he reached for the soufflé and dipped one finger into the hot and moist center. They swayed slightly to the backdrop of classical piano as he swiped the warm chocolate across her lower lip. Calli gasped but he shushed her. "My turn to taste," he said and licked her bottom lip. Without taking his eyes from her intense chocolate stare and with a wicked grin, he reached for a glass and drank.

Dom held the wine in his mouth as he set the glass back onto the table, then moaned, rolling his eyes in pleasure as he swallowed. "Oui, joie de vivre."

When their eyes met again, Calli laid a hand on his chest and breathily asked, "What does that mean?"

"Literally, it means joy of life. As does the more common joie de vie. But joie de vivre has an ongoing quality . . . kind of like living the joy."

"Oh."

"Oh?"

"Yes, oh," she said, but gave a hint of a smile that encouraged him on.

Dom inhaled her floral-vanilla scent, almost as intoxicating as the wine, and said, "Maybe the wine is going to my head too."

They swayed with the music, and as the song drew to a close, they stopped. Dom couldn't banish the kiss before dinner from his mind, and he wanted more . . . so much more . . . now. "I'm going to kiss you," he warned.

Calli's tongue darted out, wetting her lips.

He crushed his mouth to hers, tasting the chocolate and wine, and another dance began.

$\mathcal{C}$ALLI HADN'T FELT SO CAREFREE in years. After that searing kiss, her body had been loose and hungry for more. They'd both been a bit tipsy as they'd wandered through the skywalks to The Jazz. They'd cuddled up on a sofa in the back of the club and enjoyed the crooning saxophone soloist as they shared another bottle of wine. The evening grew late, and she doubted either were in shape to drive. Sadly, she'd probably have to end up ordering a Ryde, but for now, she was comfortable here in Dom's arms, and going home to an empty house wasn't something she was ready to face.

The club had cleared, and they were left almost alone in

the back. Dom took her empty glass and placed it next to his on the table before them, then turned back to her. Twining his fingers with hers, he looked down, appearing a little rueful himself. "Calli, tonight has been truly remarkable."

"Thank you," she said. "For everything. I haven't been on a date since, well, I don't remember my last date."

He shook his head. "No, thank you for joining me."

"Anytime," she said and found herself meaning it. She actually hoped he'd ask for a second date.

Instead, he leaned in and brushed his lips over hers. "Calli?"

"Mmm?" she answered.

Dom inhaled sharply, then said, "This may be forward, but would you like to come to my loft?"

Her heart stopped. She held her breath. She shouldn't.

He rushed to add, "It's okay if you don't want to, but I'm not ready to leave you. I don't think either of us is in a condition to drive. If you want to go home instead, I'll order a car and see you to your house first." He looked around, then smiled back at her. "Whatever you want." He dropped his head to her neck.

Chills ran up her spine as he peppered soft kisses from her shoulder to her ear. Her body betrayed her, heat gathering low in her stomach. Her throat was tight, but she considered his suggestion. What did she really have to lose? Her boys wouldn't know; they were at their father's. She wasn't married. There wasn't really a good reason for her to deny what her body begged her to accept. She placed a hand on his bicep and shrugged back to search his piercing, hungry, green-gray eyes. At length, she said, "I should probably go home."

He sank further into the couch.

But feeling a bit devious, she cuddled into him. "But I don't want to just yet."

A grin spread across his face and lit his eyes.

Calli swallowed. "I don't want to give the wrong impression, though."

Questions were written all over Dom's face as he regarded her.

"I've told you that I'm not ready for anything serious."

Dom lifted her hand and kissed her thumb. "There is"—he kissed her index finger—"no pressure"—her middle finger—"no expectation"—her ring finger—"no implied promise,"—her pinkie finger—"only pleasure between us tonight." He pressed his lips to her wrist and whispered, "I want you tonight," and kissed the inside of her elbow. "I think you want me too." His lips skimmed across her shoulder. "That's enough for tonight." His hot breath trailed up her neck, and she melted, a throbbing ache growing between her legs.

Was she really going to do this? Yes, she was. "All right," she whispered.

Their lips met lightly.

Calli smiled. "Your place."

Their lips met again, this time eager, lusting, and anxious.

Fifteen

$\mathcal{T}$HROUGH THE SKYWAYS, DOM LED the way back to the Moretti building. They only passed a few others en route as most anyone else would be making their way to the garages when the club closed. Inside his building, he called the elevator and they rode upstairs, sneaking nervous glances at one another, then snickering when one was caught. Strange that he was nervous. He'd had his fair share of trysts over the years, enough to not feel nervous but somehow he trembled inside.

After thinking on it during the walk and elevator ride, he realized that he'd only ever invited one person back to his place. All the others had been at hotels or at their place. Was he nervous of what she'd think or because he sensed potential? Regardless, he was elated that she'd accepted not only the date but the invitation to his place.

The elevator opened, admitting them to his semi-private eleventh floor; he crossed the hall and punched in the code.

The lock clicked, and he opened the door. He reached for Calli, securing her around the waist, and pulled her into him. Moving them both inside his loft, he kicked the door closed.

With a light touch, he flicked her purse from her shoulder and let it fall to the floor. Then, looking into the depths of her brown eyes, he backed her against the wall. He wanted her to feel his arousal, and by the way her eyes stretched wide, she did. He smirked and seized her mouth, driving a hand into the heavy brown curls at the base of her neck. Damn, he'd waited all night to do that. She responded with both arms around his neck as they moved together in the embrace.

Calli pulled at his jacket, but he didn't want to move away from her. He kept his lips sealed to hers as he slipped one arm, then the other, from the coat and let it fall next to her purse. Breaking the kiss, he moved one hand to her breast and teased her nipple to a peak as he trailed his tongue down the perfect curve of her neck, tasting her salty-sweet skin again.

"Oh wow." She sighed and let her head fall back against the wall with a slight bump.

Dom kissed his way back to her chin and said, "You're magnificent." He nodded toward the bedroom with a questioning eye.

Calli nodded, licking her lips.

OH. MY. GAWD, CALLI THOUGHT. Her body had taken

over, and every nerve was on end. She needed this . . . needed him inside her . . . soon! Her panties were uncomfortably wet as she followed the beautiful man through his minimalist loft into a bedroom with a clean white duvet covering a king-sized bed.

With his free hand, he removed the tie and dropped it without looking, then started to unbutton his shirt. "You're sure?" he asked.

"Yes," she said, well beyond the ability to say otherwise. Her body was certain that this was going to happen, regardless of any of her mind's reservations.

Dom removed the shirt, standing gloriously naked from the waist up before her, defined muscles twitching from time to time. He hadn't turned on any lights, but the city provided an ambient and romantic glow. Calli reached up to release the buttons behind her neck, but he stopped her with a soft touch and turned her so that she was facing away from him and out toward the city. The view was breathtaking but nothing compared to the sensations running through her body. Dom lifted her hair and draped it over one of her shoulders. He kissed her neck again and said, "I've been imagining this moment all night."

Calli was speechless.

He unbuttoned the small pearl buttons at her neck and let the dress fall, leaving her breasts exposed. Her nipples tightened, whether at the cool air or anticipation she couldn't be sure. The shadowy reflection of them both in the window was as erotic as anything Calli had ever seen. Dom unzipped the dress and the layers of gossamer fell.

Standing in the puddle, wearing only lacy panties, Calli turned and reached for Dom's belt. He allowed her to remove the belt but stopped her at his pants.

"Your turn first," he said with a smile, lifted her easily at the waist, and carried her to the bed. Starting at her neck, he trailed kisses down her chest, stopping at a nipple and running his tongue around one before moving to give the other the same attention.

Calli fought to hold still. It wasn't really squirmworthy . . . yet. She sucked in her stomach muscles as Dom moved lower and placed slow kisses at the waist of the lacy underthing. Of their own accord, her hips started to tilt from side to side, urgency building.

Dom lifted up and slipped the panties down, smelling them before he tossed them onto the floor. Running his hands up her legs, he settled back down and gave her body the attention she'd been yearning after for hours now.

Licking gently at first, his pace increased with each of her tiny jerks under his mouth until at last he found the right spot and sucked her into his mouth. One—two—three—and on the fourth time, Calli called out, gripping the duvet and riding the waves of her release.

$\mathcal{D}$OM KEPT HIS EYES ON Calli's face as she reached that perfect state, then he stopped and wiped his mouth. He caressed her waist and watched as she came down from the high. His erection throbbed, begging to be released, but he denied it for a moment longer while Calli recovered.

When her eyes opened, he stood and shed his remaining

clothes, slid on a condom, and turned back to Calli. He basked in her widening eyes as she took in his body, then leaned over where she still stretched languidly across his bed and said with a sigh, "Damn, you're beautiful."

"You're not so bad yourself."

Dom smiled and kissed her gently, then said, "I'm not sure I can go slow right now. Are you okay with that?"

"After that, I could stand it a little bit rough." She smiled wickedly.

Dom kissed her long and hard, a preamble to what was to come, then he slid to the end of the bed—the perfect height for what he intended. He grasped her around the waist and pulled her to the edge, too; easing her legs to wrap around his waist, he positioned himself at her entry. Slowly, agonizingly, he entered. She was tight and held her breath. When he was fully seated, he said, "Breathe, beautiful." She did with a grin, and he felt her loosen in waves around him. He tensed, trying to make this last longer. When it seemed she'd fully adjusted, he asked, "Ready?"

"Oh . . . yes!" Her voice was almost a whimper.

He slid out almost all the way, then pushed quickly back in, testing. He tried again, at that pace, one more time. She gasped. He groaned. Then he set a punishing pace, her breasts bounced as he moved, and when he felt her walls contracting, milking his cock, he let himself go, gave his body permission, and released a loud shout echoed by her outcry. Pulsing and spurting paralyzed him, and Dom closed his eyes until the white-hot pleasure faded, leaving his body weak. He fell onto his elbows atop Calli. Both sweaty, he found her lips and felt her smile against his own as she wrapped her arms around his back. As all sensations passed, they melted into the bed.

Dom pulled away and turned down the duvet. They crawled in and cuddled together. She fits so nicely, he thought. Placing a gentle kiss goodnight on her forehead, he whispered, "Joie de vivre."

Sixteen

Calli awoke in a cloud of white, the room painfully bright, and squinted through the glass wall over the city. *Oh shit, I just had sex with someone on the first real date. And . . . I slept over. One for the record books, Calli.* She looked under the covers and gasped. *I'm still naked.* She took in the lay of the land, the door they'd fumbled through, kissing and unable to keep their hands off one another. Calli blushed. Her dress lay in a pool on the floor beside the window. *Damn, those are the only clothes I have to put on.* She rolled her eyes and searched for a dresser or closet—none—only another open door leading to a bathroom. *Speaking of . . .* Calli flipped the covers and scurried to take care of morning necessities.

She breathed a sigh of relief when she found a thick terry cloth robe hanging behind the door. It smelled of Dom, clean as a fresh spring morning; she smiled as she slipped into it and tied the belt. Washing her hands, she caught a glimpse of her disheveled hair in the mirror and makeup smudges beneath her eyes. He's up, and he's already seen me like this . . . geez, what a wonderful impression. She ran her fingers through the tangled curls and braided her hair over one shoulder. The ends remained loose, but it held well enough to control the flyaways.

She scrubbed under her eyes with wet fingers and wiped away the black smudges with a tissue—at least he kept those handy. Calli ran her tongue over her teeth and cringed at the taste in her mouth. Rummaging through the drawers, she found a tube of toothpaste and a toothbrush. They'd shared a lot more than a toothbrush at this point. She considered. No, I couldn't, she decided at last and brushed her teeth with some of the paste on her finger. It wasn't perfect but much better.

When she emerged from the bath, the bedroom was still empty. At least he wasn't waiting with the oh-so-cliché breakfast-in-bed scenario. Calli straightened the bed, reimagining their shared need the night—or early morning—before with a smile. She admonished herself mildly; but considering that she was a mature woman, they were safe, and it was the best night she'd had in probably fifteen years, she easily came to terms with it. And it had been like puzzle pieces fitting together. They'd each been a match for the other's wants and desires, an improvised call and response.

Calli picked up her dress and his jacket, draping them both over the bed. She was beginning to wonder where he'd gone, or maybe it'd all been a dream. No, that was simply a silly thought. She'd woken here in his apartment, naked, and the soreness had been more proof. She went for the door.

Outside the bedroom, Dom's loft was enormous, made to look only larger by the full glass walls and the blue sky above the city skyline. Calli turned from the view. The apartment was minimalist with two white hard couches presenting a formal sitting area and a square table with four straight-backed chairs. Stuffy was the word that came to mind. The kitchen, though, was 100 percent gourmet with an island offering eat-in seating for six.

"Hi, beautiful." Dom, dressed only in gray jersey casual pants, stepped off the stool at the island bar and sauntered over. Without hesitation, he slipped his arms around Calli and landed a kiss on her temple. Calli placed a hand on his washboard stomach and looked into his smiling eyes and smiled back. "Enjoy the view?"

"Mmhmm," said Calli, inhaling the rich smells deeply through her nose. "Coffee?"

"I'll make you a cappuccino," he said but didn't move. Instead, he lowered his head to kiss her good morning. Thank the stars she'd found the toothpaste.

His lips made her feel all warm and fuzzy inside, and when he stepped away and behind the counter, it left her cool. Stop it, Calli. It's too soon, she reminded herself, but her eyes betrayed her by thoroughly enjoying the sight of him in the kitchen, bare-chested and preparing the espresso machine to make her a gourmet cup of coffee.

She circled the island to watch as he worked the machine. He glanced up and asked, "Sugar?"

"No," she said, shaking her head.

"Foam: a lot or little?"

"A lot."

"The way I like it too." He placed two shot glasses under

the drips, poured milk into the metal carafe, and turned the knob to start the steamer. As it swished, then gurgled, he slowly pulled the carafe away, allowing the foam to thickly form. After he'd poured the espresso into the cup, he topped it with foam. He stepped behind her, cradled her back into his chest, and brought the cup to her hands. A stack of brown hearts decorating the white foam looked back at her. Accepting the cup, Calli grinned and rested her head against his shoulder.

"Thank you," she said.

"My absolute pleasure." Dom kissed her neck, sending a thrill up her spine again.

Calli stifled her shiver in an effort to save the coffee and willed herself to enjoy the feel of his soft, warm mouth on her body again.

"Did you want breakfast?" he asked. "I'd love to cook for you."

Calli sipped the coffee, then swallowed and wiped the foam from her upper lip. "Can I take a rain check on that? I have a few chores to get done before work tomorrow." She didn't know why, but she didn't feel ready to tell him about the details of her life—the boys, that her father was coming, or least of all her ex.

"Of course," he said, but dropped his head and stepped away.

Again, she felt cold when he moved away. Sensing a small sadness, Calli rushed, "Hey." She paused for him to turn back and look at her. "I definitely want you to cook for me someday." She stepped into him. "But I get the feeling it could be something that could take a very long time and lead to other activities."

A spark flashed in his eyes. "There's no need to cook for the other activities." He tugged on the robe's ties.

Calli eyed him with raised brows.

"Okay, okay." He held up his hands, clearly understanding her unspoken words and thankfully taking it with good spirits. "Drink your coffee and I'll take you home."

Calli lifted the coffee and sipped again; the woodsy, dark flavor was delightful on her tongue. "I hate to ask this." She dipped a finger in the foam and licked it.

"If you keep making suggestive motions like that, all your attempts to resist are going to be quite ineffective." Dom raised a brow over one silvery green eye.

"What?" Calli said, faking innocence, then dipped her finger in the foam again.

Dom seized her hand and put her finger in his mouth. Closing his lips around it, he sucked gently, reminding her of similar actions the night before.

Calli groaned and, in the daylight, blushed. "All right. Point made. But, unfortunately, I really don't have the time today. I'm sorry."

"What do you hate to ask?" Dom said.

"Oh, do you happen to have any sweats I could wear home?"

$\mathcal{D}$OM PULLED HIS M3 INTO Calli's drive. In the light of day, the neighborhood reminded him of the home in the country where he'd grown up. The houses all had small seating areas and flowers or wreaths on the porches welcoming guests. The colors were all warm browns, obviously intended to be inviting. Unfortunately, it had the opposite effect on him. It was the quaint upper middle class he'd run from with everything he'd had. He'd watched his mother cater to his father for years and his father have affair after affair. His mother had known all along but stayed. She'd believed that her only son needed his father. What a fucking joke that had been!

Dom cleared away the memories and turned to the amazingly sexy woman in his passenger seat. He grabbed her hand, soft and delicate inside his, and said, "Calli—"The words stuck. He worked his throat and at last said, "I don't think I've ever met anyone who I was so comfortable just being with."

Calli rubbed his thumb but didn't reply. In fact, she looked nervously between him and her house.

"When is our second date?"

"I-I'm not sure," she said. A tension had overtaken her as he'd pulled up to her house, and she stared toward the front door with hollow, distracted eyes.

Dom didn't want to push or pressure her, so he just waited, staring at their intertwined hands sitting on his sweatpants she wore.

"I need to check my calendar. I'll text you . . . or let you know on Tuesday at class." She pulled toward the passenger door.

Dom tightened his grip, causing her to turn back to him. With his other hand, he cradled her face and searched the depths of her brown eyes. "I meant what I said last night that we can take things slow, but I do hope we can continue to take things."

Her eyes flitted down, then back to his. "Yeah, I think we can take things," she said breathily. He kissed her long and deep, willing his desire into her, and she responded, pulling away with a wistful sigh.

"Have a wonderful day doing chores, beautiful." He let her go.

As she stepped out of his car, she waved back, then ran up the steps to the front door. Dom flipped through his contact list on the car's infotainment system and pressed the phone button next to the entry for Joe. The phone rang as Dom shifted into reverse and backed out onto the sleepy street.

"Yeah?" answered his friend. "How'd the date go?"

"I need a workout. You up?"

"A little tense?"

"A bit frustrated . . . I'll tell you over a good run. Meet me at the gym?"

"Yeah, okay. See you there in ten."

"Make it twenty-five. I have a bit of a drive."

"Really? You devil . . . sleeping somewhere else last night?"

"I'll see you there."

Joe was laughing as Dom clicked the red phone button on his system. The music thumped to life and he pressed the gas, upshifting to gain speed on the highway. His options at this point . . . a hard workout or spend an hour in a cold shower. He opted for iron and a treadmill. Hopefully his brain would be focused, and he'd be fit enough to work in the restaurant that evening.

Seventeen

CALLI CHECKED HER WATCH AS she closed the door. Two hours before Bennett would be dropping off the boys, and she needed to hit the grocery store to have something to feed her father. She'd made it home in plenty of time to clean up and settle in before she had to face anyone else in her life. She didn't want to share her boys with Dom and didn't want to share Dom with them either—or Bennett for that matter. She sighed as the M3 sped away, then she climbed the stairs destined for a good scrubbing. This new dynamic complicated everything that was just becoming simple in her life.

Still clothed, she leaned into the shower and turned the dial to hot, then closed the door to let the water heater kick into full gear. She inhaled Dom's crisp spring-morning scent as she pulled his sweatshirt over her head and let it fall to the floor. Dropping the oversized sweatpants on top of the shirt, Calli closed her eyes and re-envisioned the scene she'd acted out with the gorgeous man in the wee hours of the morning. Her mouth went dry, and she ran her hands down her sides, imagining the touch was his rather than her own.

Stop it, Calli, your boys will be here soon. Your dad will be here this evening. Time to get back to reality.

She stepped into the steam, the hot water stinging as it pelted her skin. Sinking back under the rain, the water flowed over her head and face, and she re-imagined his mouth trailing down her stomach. She stepped forward and swiped the water from her eyes, looking up. Then she reached for the handheld, giving in to the lingering need.

DOM PRESSED THE UP ARROW until the digital readout flashed six point five. The mill sped to life, and he hopped onto the belt. The pounding of his feet soon matched the heartbeat that sounded in his ears, and sweat sprouted from his brow.

Joe took the treadmill next to him and set his speed to six. "So, what gives?"

"Dating. I really just need to stick to the restaurant business."

"So, what? Did she grow a third head?"

Dom laughed. "No."

"Psycho?"

That word typically covered it, but . . . "No. She's not showing any signs of psycho."

"Then . . . ?"

Dom didn't answer, struggled to admit how wonderful the date had been. He simply shook his head and pressed the up arrow and his body faster until he didn't have the breath necessary to hold a real conversation. Beside him, Joe kept a leisurely pace—the beauty of treadmilling with friends. You didn't leave them in the dust. Though Dom loved running, it was the sole reason he'd never become a runner. He enjoyed having a workout partner. Dom could see Joe's reflection watching him surreptitiously until, apparently, he couldn't bear the suspense anymore. Mirror Joe stepped off his belt and halted the mill, then reached across and pressed Dom's down arrow.

When both treadmills were silenced, Joe pressured him again. "This isn't like you. Usually, after a date, you're more certain than ever about yourself and your business. Why are you torturing yourself?"

Dom let his breathing return to almost normal, grabbed the towel, and wiped the sweat from his face and neck. "Everything last night was right." With a hesitant look away, he added, "Hell, everything this morning was right."

Joe's eyes grew to saucers. "You stayed at her place?"

Dom shook his head.

"Aahhh, a hotel?" Joe nodded as if that was par for the course.

Hell, it was. Dom shook his head.

Joe inhaled sharply. "You didn't?"

He remained silent, lips sealed.

"She slept at your place?"

Dom nodded.

"Oh. Shit. Well. That's something new."

"You're telling me!" Dom stepped off the treadmill, grabbed a couple of wipes, and returned. Handing one to Joe, he started wiping down the machine. "Come on, let's hit the weights," he said, and headed for the free-weight room.

"Leg day?" asked Joe.

"Yeah," Dom said, stepping to the leg press machine in the back corner and loading it up.

Joe grabbed a barbell, loaded the ends, and started a set of dead lifts while Dom pressed. After his first ten, he said, "So, this is more than a one-nighter?"

"I"—Dom grunted as he pushed out his final press—"freakin' hope so."

"But you didn't confirm the second date?"

Dom stood and walked off the set while Joe kicked up his legs, shaking out the hamstrings. They switched for set two. Dom wiped his hands on his shorts and reached for the barbell. In between lifts, he said, "She's supposed to text."

After the set, Joe stood and play-punched at Dom. "Well, man. I'm happy you've found one that makes you think twice about dying single. Should be fun to watch."

Dom raised a brow at his friend and sank back into the leg press machine. This set he decided to add a calf press at the top. *Man, he's right. I've got it pretty bad. When did I turn into the hopeless romantic? But she was . . . they were . . .* He pressed harder, tightening his quads and groaning at the burning muscles. *That's right, Dom. Tire out those muscles and get her off the brain.*

$\mathcal{C}$ALLI LET OUT A SATISFIED groan as she stood from the table and the late family dinner. Though her body was tired from the late night, her heart was full at having her father there for dinner and to spend a little time with Kent. Her dad motioned to help, but she held out a hand to forestall him, shaking her head. "You catch up with Jax and Kent. I'll clean these off and grab dessert."

"You're sure?" Her father sank back into his chair with a wary eye. Clearing the dishes at their family home, Lindleyi Manor, had been handled by her parents' live-in servants for as long as she could recall. His offer alone had been nice enough, but he really wasn't suited to working in the kitchen. And she wanted to give him the time with Jax and Kent before everyone went off to bed to prepare for the Monday morning routine.

As she brought the plates to the sink, rinsed them, and put them into the dishwasher, she also eavesdropped on the conversation. Kent, who'd been slumped in his chair and had picked at the rotisserie chicken salad with mild disgust, now leaned on the table with both elbows and turned with bright eyes to question his grandfather, Richard Lindley, the geneticist. Calli paused in mid-stroke as he asked a few particularly intelligent questions about how her father was conducting his latest research.

Her father's face lit up, too, when Kent asked the question, and he nearly preened when he replied, "I've been using fluorescence resonance energy transfer and reviewing the physical interactions of the proteins with a high-powered microscope. You're coming tomorrow to hear my lecture, right?"

"Yeah. Can't believe Mom let me out of school for it, though."

Calli jumped in. "It's still educational. Your case worker said you might need to do a presentation in your bio class to justify it."

Kent groaned.

"If it's something you like," she challenged her son, "shouldn't you be happy to share it?"

"I guess," he said with an eye roll.

"You'll be fine, Superman." Calli finished washing the plates and wiped down the counter.

The conversation at the table continued for a bit around her father's orchid research while she brewed some decaf coffee for herself and her father, and plated the banana pudding she'd ordered from the tavern down the street. She served and rejoined the family just as her dad turned the conversation to Jax.

"What's your latest art project?"

Jax had been trying to act engaged throughout the scientific discussion, but his mind had obviously wandered. He scooted upright in his chair. "I'm working on four pieces for the art expo at school this spring. I have one painting and one 3-D piece that's really hard. Dr. Brennan says it's coming along great, though."

Richard sipped the coffee. "And the other two?"

Jax glanced deviously at Calli and said, "Those are a surprise. No one gets to see them until the expo." He grinned

148

widely, obviously trying to build up her anticipation.

His efforts worked, and Calli gave a resigned smile. "I've been trying to get it out of him since the end of September." She lifted a spoon full of the creamy dessert. "If you get him to dish, you have to let me know," she said to her dad.

Richard put a bite of the pudding into his mouth and hummed. "This is delicious, Calli."

She demurred. "It's not the family recipe, but I thought it was pretty close."

They leisurely enjoyed the remainder of dessert, and when done, the boys cleaned up the dishes and went upstairs to get ready for bed, Jax giving Calli a quick hug and whispering, "Good to be home, Mom."

"Goodnight, Papa," called Kent.

"Hey, what about me?" Calli called with feigned insult.

"Nite, Mom," he droned.

"Nite, Superman." She smiled after them as they climbed the stairs.

When they were gone, her dad said, "You seem in good spirits. I'm sorry we didn't make it up before now."

"It's all right, Dad. Cat's been here, and I'm doing great." Yeah, after last night, she was on a high that she thought might be a bit dangerous for her current position as recent divorcée and single mother.

"Your mother gave me a list of things to check on while I'm here."

"Let me guess . . . " Calli sighed. "They're all things a husband would do, right?"

He made a small affirmative noise. "You know she's just worried about you."

"I do, but it feels a bit disapproving."

Her dad just nodded, and Calli let it go, aware he was positioned between two equally hard-headed women. She switched gears with a tight smile. "Well, might as well get through it. What's on the list?"

Eighteen

CALLI HATED DRIVING DOWNTOWN, SO she'd gotten in the habit of either taking the bus or calling for a Ryde to go to work. She stepped from the car in front of Moffitt & Hall, then opened the app and tipped the driver. When done, she noticed the little red dot on the Messenger app with the number twelve inside. The girls had been blowing up her phone since last night, but she didn't really want to share just yet. She ignored it again and went inside.

Through the revolving door, she offered a wave to the receptionist before entering the double glass doors to Moffitt & Hall. Instead of taking the elevator, Calli turned left, opened the door to the stairwell, and climbed to the second floor. She passed identical rows of cubicles until she reached hers and hung a right. She stepped into her foam- and metal-walled workspace and dropped her bag onto the guest chair. Monday morning, and back to the grind, she thought as she reached for the computer in her bag.

Stradiotto

While she waited for the computer to fire up, she checked the texts.

<table>
<tr><td>JORDAN:</td><td>SO . . . DISH.</td></tr>
<tr><td>TORY:</td><td>YEAH!</td></tr>
<tr><td>TORY:</td><td>HOW WAS THE HOT RESTAURANT MANAGER</td></tr>
</table>

7:46 P.M.

<table>
<tr><td>TRINA:</td><td>NO REPLY?</td></tr>
<tr><td>JORDAN:</td><td>NOPE. CALLI, WHERE ARE YOU?</td></tr>
<tr><td>TRINA:</td><td>MUSTA WORN HER OUT.</td></tr>
<tr><td>JORDAN:</td><td>YEAH, DYIN FOR THE DEETS</td></tr>
<tr><td>TORY:</td><td>ME TOO!</td></tr>
<tr><td>JORDAN:</td><td>UGH, MAYBE SHE STAYED UP ALL NIGHT AND IS ALREADY IN BED.</td></tr>
</table>

8:22 P.M.

<table>
<tr><td>TRINA:</td><td>CALLI! YOU CAN'T JUST DISAPPEAR, YOU WERE ON FIRE WHEN WE LEFT YOU LAST NIGHT! BET HE COULDN'T KEEP HIS HANDS OFF.</td></tr>
</table>

JORDAN: I'LL CHECK WITH HER FIRST
THING TOMORROW.

TORY: YEAH, LET US KNOW!!!

9:50 P.M.

Calli smiled; she'd let them squirm a while longer. She logged in and checked her calendar. She noted the Monday morning assignment meeting in twenty minutes and locked the computer. Pulling her wallet from her bag, she slid it into the coat she was still wearing, grabbed her mug, and headed downstairs. There was just enough time to run down to the corner, grab a triple latte, and get back for the meeting.

In the large conference room, all of Moffitt & Hall's investment advisors gathered for the weekly meeting. By the time Calli walked in, there was only standing room remaining. Jordan locked eyes with her across the table and mouthed, "Where have you been?"

Innocently, Calli held up her mug full of coffee from Bienvenue and smiled.

The principle partner walked heavily into the room, greeting people as he made his way to his seat at the head of the table. Ronnie Hall followed, and their administrative assistant, Mackenna trailed with a stack of folders. Ronnie scanned the room, obviously taking inventory of the faces present, then nodded to the end of the table.

Frederick Moffitt sat forward with his elbows on the table and fingers folded, then said, "We have some tough news to share this morning."

The silence in the room grew louder than if everyone had spoken at once. Everyone gave their undivided attention to Mr. Moffitt. He nodded to Mackenna to pass out the folders. As she began, Mr. Moffitt continued, "Kyle was in a car accident over the weekend." Several hands flew to mouths, and the other investment advisors looked around at each other with uncertainty. Moffitt held up his hands to ease the confusion in the room. "He will heal eventually but will be in the hospital for several weeks. Flowers on behalf of Moffitt & Hall have already been delivered. Mackenna will e-mail out information as to where you may send personal messages and the likes. Yes, Jake?" Moffitt asked the junior advisor who'd raised a hand.

Jake said, "Do we know any of the details?"

"Not at this time, but we'll share what we can when we know more," answered Moffitt. "In the meantime, the folders Mackenna is handing out are Kyle's accounts. Everyone will need to pick up a little extra while he's on medical leave."

A murmur went up around the room. From the administrative assistant, Calli accepted a stack of three folders—the same number given to each of them. With a small nod, she cradled them into one arm.

Mr. Moffitt continued, "Ronnie and I have chosen who we felt was the most capable for each account. Please see one of us with any questions. Now, I believe there are only two new accounts this week for assignment, true, Ronnie?"

"Yes."

As Ronnie Hall went into the stats and description of the first account, Calli pulled out a notebook and listened intently to see if she needed to take notes or if the account might fall to her. When he announced that the client was a sportscaster, she tuned out, confident that it'd go to the junior advisor, Jake. He was the newest and most athletic of the advisors at Moffitt & Hall, so he was a slam dunk. Calli hid a small laugh at the punny thought.

The second account was a pro golfer and likewise would go to an advisor who golfed, probably one of the four who already spent most of their time on the courses with clients.

When the meeting adjourned, Calli walked slowly toward her desk. Jordan caught up, and nudging her shoulder, she said, "Well?"

"Well what?" Calli asked, but her blush betrayed any feigned innocence.

Jordan inhaled sharply with a wide-open mouth. "You didn't?"

"So what if I did?" Calli ducked her head and pressed on toward her desk.

Her friend and colleague removed the computer bag and sat in her guest chair, rolling it closer. She leaned in and said, "Then I want all the dirty details."

"Jordan?!"

"Okay, fine. Maybe only half the details." She smiled slyly.

Calli shuffled the folders on her desk, her eyes flitting to Jordan and away. "It was nice."

"All right, let's start from the top. What does he drive?"

"A beamer. Silver."

"Did he come to your door?"

"Of course he did."

"Where did he take you?"

"Babette's"

"Ohhh . . . wow. That's upscale!"

Calli didn't share the bit about dining in private with a personalized five-course meal.

"And . . . " Jordan pressed. "After?"

"We went to The Jazz."

Jordan placed a hand on her chest and swooned. "Be still my heart."

"He did a wonderful job in planning the evening," said Calli.

"Sounds like. What about after?"

Calli chewed her bottom lip.

Jordan pounced, placing a hand on Calli's arm, her eyes glinting mischievously. Calli nodded slightly, and Jordan sat back. "I'm so happy for you. Do you think you'll see him again?"

"I'm considering."

"Well, even if you don't, you couldn't have done much worse for a first time after the DB."

"Yeah," said Calli. "It was an awesome night." Then she switched the course of the conversation. She couldn't pine over Mr. Amazing all day. She had a job to do. "Who'd you get?" she asked Jordan, nodding to her folders.

Jordan looked at the labels, "Cox, Hamilton, and Smith. You?"

Calli glanced down. "Jorgensen, Schultz, and . . . " Her eyes widened, and she looked up at Jordan's waiting stare.

"You have to take this one. I . . . um . . . can't."

"What are you talking about?" asked Jordan. She snatched the folder and read aloud, "Moretti." Laughing loudly and standing to leave, she said, "You heard the partners, they chose us to match the client. I'd say they did a good job on that one!" Her laughter trailed as she walked away.

Calli didn't read the file. She neither turned on her computer nor did she check voice mail. She stood and marched to the elevators bound for one of the partners' offices. She punched the button for the elevator twice and looked up to the floor indicator. Twenty-one, twenty, nineteen, . . . Good it was coming. Waiting and holding the manila folder shakily in one hand, she searched through her brain for an excuse—some plausible reason that she couldn't take the account.

On the nineteenth floor, the elevator slid open, and Calli stepped out into the prestige of Executive Row—all cherry wood with black leather accents, walled offices, and not a cubicle in sight. Moffitt & Hall was a small firm, and the space they rented consisted of space on the second and third floors, and the nineteenth floor for the directors and partners. Calli made her way to the administrative assistant's desk and waited for Mackenna to look up from her computer.

When the admin smiled at her, she said, "I need to see Mr. Moffitt or Mr. Hall about one of the files they assigned."

Mackenna looked at the calendar. "Mr. Hall is in a meeting, but Mr. Moffitt's calendar is open right now. Let me give him a call."

Meanwhile, Calli picked at a cuticle and tried to wait patiently.

"Okay, he said to come right in."

Calli walked past the desk and into the suite with a separate reception area that led to six office doors. She crossed to the largest, the corner, office and knocked.

"Come," the booming voice called.

Calli opened the door and stepped inside. Frederick Moffitt stood tall and lanky, and buttoned his blazer jacket. As she approached, he reached his hand toward the guest chair across from his desk. "Please, Calli, have a seat."

She obliged, sitting with a straight back and placing the folder on her lap. The principle partner before her slicked back his white hair, smiled, and unbuttoned his blazer as he returned to his seat. His suit-wearing habits are seriously ingrained, Calli thought.

"Mackenna said you have a concern with one of Kyle's accounts?"

"Yes, the Moretti account." Callie inhaled, counting to control her anxiety. "I'm afraid I've never worked with any investments in the food service industry. I think this might be a better fit for Becca or even Dale."

Moffitt reached a long arm across the desk, silently asking for the folder. Calli placed it in his hand, then folded her own hands in her lap. Keep them still, she reminded herself, hoping that the excuse was good enough. She hated the prospect of having to explain that she'd been intimate with this man only a couple of nights ago. He opened the folder, read for a moment, and sat back. Turning his chair and crossing one leg over the other, he said, "Calli, this account is a stretch for you, I'll agree."

"Yes. I'm not sure that I'm ready to venture into another

industry at this time."

"I disagree. You've been holding your accounts very well. In fact, across your accounts, the gains are better than those of every other advisor in the firm."

Calli's mouth opened. "Really?" she asked. She had known they performed well, but better returns than all the other advisors?

Moffitt made a small, affirming noise. "Looking at the numbers again, this would be your largest account. I think you could do wonders with it. It's been pretty flat with Kyle, and we were considering moving it to your portfolio anyway."

"With all due respect, Mr. Moffitt, I know absolutely nothing about the restaurant business. I don't really even know how to cook. My food groups consist of boxed, canned, frozen, takeout, and make it yourself."

That solicited a laugh, but Calli could see that she hadn't swayed his thought process.

"The commissions on this account alone will equate to a sixty percent increase in your annual income."

Calli swallowed but couldn't reply immediately. Those numbers would be perfect for her situation. She hadn't wanted to stay in her large house but had agreed not to disrupt the boys in their final years of high school as a concession to Bennett. This would make her less dependent on his alimony checks and more secure in her own ability to support herself and her boys. Really, she needed this income. "And there aren't any other accounts that would do the same?"

Frederick Moffitt leaned onto his desk. "Not a solo account. And with a little research and study around the market trends for this industry, I think you could grow Mr.

Moretti's portfolio better than Kyle. You're reserved, Calli, but you see the opportunities in a way that most of our advisors don't. Yes, this pushes you, but it is the right time." He closed the folder and handed it back to her.

She accepted the folder with an unsteady hand, her throat dry, and nodded to Moffitt. She did need it, and she couldn't admit the reality of the situation. She'd have to just suck it up. This probably meant that the dating thing was a thing of the past. At least she'd had one great night. Calli sighed as she left, mentally already saying her personal goodbyes to the amazing man she'd only just met.

At her desk, she checked her phone. The group chat was still open.

JORDAN:	C HAD A GREAT TIME
JORDAN:	♥
TORY:	WOOOHOOO!!!! CAN'T WAIT TO HEAR ABOUT IT!
TRINA:	UHM . . . DETAILS?
JORDAN:	I'LL LEAVE THOSE TO HER. 

Calli rolled her eyes and hit the back button. Two more unread messages—Jax and Bennett. Not wanting to face her ex, she clicked on the one from Jax.

JACKSON:	I HAVE TO WORK TONIGHT. CAN YOU GET KENT FROM SCHOOL?

Calli checked her calendar and typed back a quick reply.

ME: YEAH NP

ME: WHAT TIME WILL YOU BE
                       HOME?

JACKSON: ABOUT 8:30

ME: K-LOVE U

Dreading it, she flipped over to the unread message from Bennett.

BENNETT: YOU NEED TO CHECK YOUR
                       ACCOUNT TO MAKE SURE
                       THE PAYMENT WENT
                       IN OK. THEN LET ME
                       KNOW. IT'S A LOT OF MONEY.

She groaned. It was sooo him—so controlling, so full of himself, and so belittling—that he treated her like a child when it came to managing money. Hell, she fucking managed money for a living, and according to her senior partner, she was damn good at it too. And . . . she had managed herself before she met him. The only reason she let him manage all the money while they were together was his obsessive and controlling nature over the whole thing.

She kicked herself now for taking the easy way out of that one too. He'd given her a hefty spending account while squandering away a great deal of his executive-level salary. It was how he'd funded his indiscretions. And it both made her sick that he was still trying to control her, as well as gave her a tiny bit of smug satisfaction that he no longer had the control he so desperately desired. She texted back.

ME: I DON'T HAVE THE TIME

RIGHT NOW. I'LL CHECK THIS EVENING
AND LET YOU KNOW.

She grinned as she hit send, silenced the conversation, and fired up her computer and the client account management program. She had an hour still before lunch, and she wanted to check the details around the Moretti account before she called to arrange a meeting. As she read through his demographics, the numbers in each of his investment accounts, and the summary graphs, her shock and surprise at his significant wealth astounded her more and more. By the time she was done, she felt inadequate in some strange way—like she should be working for him.

Obviously, the date had been expensive, and obviously his loft would be worth a great deal given the location and the amenities, but she never imagined that he ranked among the top twenty in net worth in the country—and all that money made in the restaurant business. Not married. No children. No siblings. Only a charity, the Moretti Foundation, a private fund providing scholarships to children who wished to develop culinary careers with a preference for those less fortunate.

Calli sat back and crossed her arms over her chest. So, he's a philanthropist, billionaire, sexy as hell, body like a rock, and effing amazeballs in bed. Too perfect in every way. Except she had a choice to make, and securing her own future was at the top of her priority list. She picked up the phone and dialed the number in the file to setup a meeting about their new business relationship and to close the door on the other stuff. She wasn't really ready for that anyway.

After two rings, a female voice answered, "Monroe Professional Services. This is Pauline Monroe."

Calli lost her voice and all thought.

"Hello? Is anyone there?" again came the disembodied smoky voice.

Really, Calli. Stop it. Business. At last she found her words. "Yes, my name is Callista Lindley from Moffitt & Hall. I'm looking for a Dominic Moretti."

There was a pause on the other end of the line, then the voice came back. "Yes, I take care of almost everything for Dom." She uttered his name as if he were her lover. "How may I be of assistance?"

You can't be jealous, Calli, she thought as she closed her eyes and rubbed her brow. "I need to meet with him regarding his accounts with Moffitt & Hall. When would he be available to come down to the office?"

Smoky voice replied, "It looks like he has some time this afternoon, but let me touch base with him and get back to you. What is your number?"

You goddamn well know my number, Pauline, thought Calli, but she gave her office number and her mobile just in case she was away for lunch. After Bennett's philandering and how much his assistant had covered for him, the rich man's assistant was a proverbial thorn in Calli's paw. It was for the best that this was taking the form of a business relationship.

Calli pressed the button on the phone to end the call and dropped her headset onto the desk. She stared at the phone for what seemed like five solid minutes before dropping her head into her hands. Could her situation with this get any more complicated?

Buzz. Buzz. Buzz. Calli looked at the screen on her phone. She didn't recognize the number, but the snippet

Stradiotto

read, Bienvenue 3:00 p.m. Can't wait–Dom.

Nineteen

$\mathcal{D}$OM HAD SMILED AS HE'D typed out the text and hit send. He hadn't expected to see Calli today, but he was giddy at the prospect. Even if it was under the pretense of a business meeting, they'd be in the coffee shop where they had shared their first, albeit chaste, kiss.

He'd showered and dressed conservatively, yet nicely, in a tapered blue dress shirt and gray pants. He'd left the collar open and grabbed his wool overcoat and scarf as he stepped into the cold to walk the four blocks to Cloud 9 and to Bienvenue. He arrived early, ordered the double latte Calli had ordered the last time they'd been there, and took a seat in the same chairs in the back of the café. He flipped open his tablet, opened the Restaurant Business website, and under the financing section, he clicked on an article titled "The Inside Story of the Twisted Kilt Sale."

Apparently, his investment competitor, Rick Akam, CEO of two breastaurant chains was branching out into objectifying men, as well as women. Dom shook his head. It was a marketing shtick, and while he acknowledged that sex sold, he kept his investments on the upper-scale and tried to encourage a romantic atmosphere rather than a lustful one. Though the numbers for this type of restaurant were pretty astounding.

"Hi there."

Calli's sweet voice called him from his read, and he flipped the cover closed. Standing, he leaned in for a kiss, but she turned her head to accept his lips on her cheek. Fighting a falling sensation, he guided her to the chair to his side and handed her the latte.

"Thank you," she said and sipped. "You remembered my order."

He shrugged. "I pay attention to what I'm interested in."

Calli placed the mug on the table and shifted in her seat to face him. Her face twisted with whatever was on her mind. "Dominic," she said formally. Then she stopped and pulled out a file from her bag. "I don't know if you're aware, but your investment advisor, Kyle, was in a car accident over the weekend."

"Oh, that's awful. Is he okay?"

"He will be. We don't know all the details yet."

Dom nodded.

"Anyway, I have been assigned your account."

His chest flip-flopped, and he smiled. Grabbing her hand, he said, "That means we'll be seeing a lot more of each other." Between the gym, investment meetings, and dates, they'd be together more often than he'd thought to hope.

"Dom"—Calli's eyes shifted and her brows peaked— "What it means is that we can't have an intimate relationship. It would be a conflict of interest for me to manage your account and be dating you on the side."

"Oh." He rubbed her hand with his thumb. "Then you'll have to give the account to someone else."

As he held her eyes, he saw the ugly truth. She'd already made up her mind.

"I'm sorry," Calli said and pulled her hand away. "I already talked with the partners, and they are set on me having the account."

"Then I'll talk to Ronnie."

"No!" Calli looked down, then with sad brown eyes, searched his face. "Please, this account is good for me and my career. I told you that I wasn't quite ready for a serious relationship. I really can't pass up this opportunity. I'm sorry," she said again, now fidgeting with her hands on top of the folder.

Dom sat back in the chair and raised a hand to stroke his jawline; the stubble was getting thick already. He flew out in the morning for another shoot in three days and needed the beard—his trademark for the show. He wasn't ready to give up on this, but it seemed she'd already decided for them both. Anger warred with determination and hurt. Saturday night had been the best night of his life, and he was frustrated that she wouldn't have talked to him before making the decision on her own. He thought she'd enjoyed it equally as much, but apparently not.

She sat, picking at her cuticles beside him. "Would you say something?" she asked at length.

"If this is what you feel you want and need, I won't stand in the way of your career." He let his hand fall onto the arm of the chair. "Are you sure?"

Calli nodded, her throat working. She was obviously torn, but he didn't want to guilt her into a relationship. He'd give it some time as a business relationship and hopefully friendship. They'd see each other at the gym, and he'd see her at least weekly for meetings regarding his portfolio. Maybe over time, things would grow, and she'd give him another chance.

"Very well," said Dom. "Is there anything in my portfolio you'd like to review today?"

"Nothing specific. I've reviewed the numbers at a high level. I'll do some follow up analysis and we can discuss direction next week if that's okay."

Dom scooted to the end of his seat. "Sure. I leave tomorrow after Trish's class for another shoot for my show. You can arrange some time through Pauline. She manages my accounting, and she'll make sure my lawyer, Joe, is available too." Dom lifted her hand and kissed her knuckles gently, lingering for a moment. "I would have preferred pleasure over business with you." He smiled sadly.

Hesitantly, he stood and put on his coat, buttoning up. "I'll see you at class tomorrow."

CALLI SAT BACK, HER EYES glued to Dom's back as he walked toward the door. When he arrived at the door, he turned sideways, almost glancing back, but then running a hand through his hair as if giving up. It sucked that she had to walk away from the chemistry they'd shared on Saturday, but at least he'd accepted it gracefully. Now, she just had to get through seeing him three times a week for workouts over the next five weeks—the time remaining until the class was done and she could break that connection.

She looked down at her coffee with the slightly disturbed stack of hearts in the foam. Beside her cup, his black coffee . . . with two sugars, she recalled . . . sat nearly full next to hers. Calli swallowed the lump in her throat and blinked repeatedly against the sting in her eyes. Sniffing, she stood and cinched her coat tighter. Her eyes lingered on the cup-couple on the table—so near each other yet so far apart. She walked to the windows, pulling out her phone. Swiping to the next screen, she pressed the Ryde app and entered her destination. Home. She wanted to be there when Kent and her dad got home from the botanical gardens. As she waited, she texted.

ME: HOW WAS COLLEGE?

SUPERMAN: PRETTY COOL

SUPERMAN: WE'RE GOING HOME NOW.

ME: K-SEE YOU IN A HALF HR

ME: LOVE U

She dropped the phone to her side, holding it by the button on the back of the case, and watched for the black sedan with a driver named Jack. In the seven-minute window the app had given her, snow started to fall. Figured. And fitting for her mood. Jax would be leaving school about now too. Hopefully, they'd all be home and curled up in comfy clothes before the roads got bad, and thankfully, her dad had agreed to stay another night and wouldn't be driving back in the dark and snow.

Twenty

STANDING BEFORE HER OPEN PANTRY in yoga pants and an oversized sweatshirt, Calli rattled a box of mac and cheese, wondering if that was too informal to feed to her dad as a side dish for the pork roast she'd put in the crock pot that morning. She eyed the fridge skeptically. She had just enough milk and butter to make two boxes. Her dad probably wouldn't complain, but somehow, it just felt improper to serve to a guest.

"Ah, what the heck, I could use the comfort food today," she said to the empty kitchen.

As she opened the ingredients, the security system beeped with the announcement that someone was entering from the garage. A moment later, Jax threw his keys on the counter and asked, "Boxed for dinner?"

"Mmhmm." Calli licked butter from her finger. When she measured the milk, she had just a little too much, so she poured about an ounce in another glass and handed it to her son. "Sorry, have to use all the milk for dinner."

"It's all right." Jax took off his beanie and coat. "I can drink water too."

"I know. But you love milk . . . "

"Zoe figured that out too. Dad hates it, but they had three gallons in their fridge when we got there."

Calli froze mid-stir. Keeping her reaction steady, she disposed of the butter wrapper and milk carton. Normally, she tried to not hold it against Jax or Kent when they mentioned Zoe, but she hated that the other woman was such a big part of their lives now. Suddenly feeling inadequate, she said, "I'm sorry I didn't pick up more."

"Aw, man." Jax rolled his eyes and dropped his head forward, shoulders slouching. Then he walked over and wrapped his arms around his mom's shoulders. "I could have picked some up too. Sorry I mentioned Dad's. Where's Papa and Kent?"

"They're upstairs. It's not your fault, kiddo." Calli smiled, trying hard to make it genuine. "It shouldn't faze me anymore, either. And I really am happier that we're not together anymore." She wanted to add, *It's just that the time you spend there is supposed to be mine too. I'm not supposed to have to share you yet.* But she held her tongue.

Jax fished in his bag and sat down at the kitchen table with a sketch pad and pencil, turned on his tunes with the headphones only covering one ear, and started to draw. Calli watched him in her periphery as she drained the noodles and melted in the butter and powdered cheese. She plated the pork roast, transferred the pasta to a bowl, and asked, "Hey, can you set the table?"

As she placed the bowl of cheesy, comforty goodness among the plates and next to the roast, she grinned. "Bon appétit." At the bottom of the stairs, she called up for Kent and her dad.

Her superman bounded down with as much grace as a giraffe, about as lanky and awkward too. Just growing into knobby legs and arms, his voice cracked as he asked, "What's for dinner?" He hadn't even looked.

Calli, aware it drove Kent crazy, said, "Chicken and salad," and smiled wryly. When she was in training for the half-marathon, that had been pretty much a nightly thing, and they'd all gotten sick and tired of the lean protein and green, leafy vegetables. It had become a running joke in their house, and Kent had the least sense of humor about it.

"Mom. Seriously?"

"Thought it was your favorite."

He tucked his chin and glared. "Since when do you make salad in a saucepan?"

"Roast and mac and cheese." She touched her son's shoulder—about the closest she could get to a hug these days. Just as he sat, her father came down the stairs after his grandson and gave Calli a quick kiss on the cheek.

"Eat up, Superman. Hope you don't mind the informal dinner, Dad. It's been a rough day."

"It's just right. There's nothing better on a snowy evening than something warm and gooey."

She thanked her dad and offered him a tight smile, but her eyes dropped, betraying her mood. She quickly focused on something non-hurtful, not wanting to broach the topic of Dom with her dad or in front of the boys. "The snow this year has started so early. It's going to be a long winter. I'm glad you decided to stay overnight and give them a chance to get the roads cleared."

Observantly, he asked, "Is there something wrong, honey?"

She shook her head, and they all sat down to eat. In an unusual display, Kent babbled about the day, telling his brother all about the lecture hall and how Papa was going to send him the presentation on fluorescence resonance energy transfer and his research on orchid genetics from the lecture earlier so he could share it with his biology class. This reaction was a highlight in an otherwise not-so-bright day.

After dinner, the boys went off to do homework, or at least they pretended to. Calli and her dad went to the den where she curled up on one end of the couch with her favorite heavy quilt.

"You seemed so happy last night, Cal. What changed?"

Calli sighed. She wasn't bringing her dad into her real turmoil, but she could give him the background about the situation. "A coworker was in an accident over the weekend. He's in the hospital, so I have a boatload more work for the foreseeable future." Calli ran a finger around the rim of her mug and sipped, keeping her eyes on her dad.

He glared at her skeptically, placed his tea on the table, then moved closer and wrapped an arm around her. "You don't have to talk to me about it, but I hope you're talking to your sister or someone else close."

Calli snuggled into him, remote in one hand. His rich

and familiar scent infiltrated her nose, and she felt young sitting next to him, but it was nice—something that'd been off-limits to her as an adult for far too long. She missed this much like she missed working beside him in the greenhouse. Regardless, she had her life here in the Cities, and she needed to make the best of it.

In companionable silence, she clicked and clicked and clicked, then clicked faster when she came to the romance group—past Hallmark Channel, past Lifetime, and past Lifetime Movies. Certainly, her dad didn't want to watch any of that crap, either, and the last thing she wanted to be reminded of was how lonely she was—apparently the way she would remain as the muses, fates, stars, cards, and even her boss seemed to be aligned or stacked against her having a love life.

It was fine, she decided. Time to focus on herself, a chance to discover who she was without a man in her life. *My boys, my career, my friends, and my family.* She looked forward to being with her whole family now sooner than expected—at Thanksgiving—thanks to Bennett. Her well-meaning mother would express how sad she was over the divorce, and that sadness would be even more amplified because Bennett would be taking her boys out of the country on her first Christmas after the divorce.

Calli stopped on HGTV; a couple was trying to decide between staying in their newly renovated home or selling it and buying a bigger one. Good enough, not really romantic. She placed the remote on the arm of the couch and half-watched. She would have to work to show her mom how happily independent she could be, but it would be good. Cat and her brother Jon would be there with their significant others, and Alder would be there too. She wondered if he'd bring home a different girlfriend this year from Seattle. Turkey Day would give her a good chance to get out of the city and remember where she came from, maybe try to mend a few fences. With so much to look forward to, she didn't need anything else, right?

Twenty-One

$\mathcal{O}$N THE GYM, DOM GRABBED a towel, then stopped to fill his water bottle while Joe caught up. As his friend pulled up next to him and threw his towel over a shoulder, Dom said, "I have to cut out of class ten minutes early so I can catch the plane."

"Yeah, no worries. I'll just catch the bus over to my office." Joe didn't drive much at all. He and Betsy lived right on a bus route and only had one car. He left it for her most of the time. "Hey, what are you doing for Thanksgiving?"

"No plans. Probably spend the day in the kitchen at the restaurant . . . take advantage of it while it's quiet and the staff is gone. Sometimes, I really miss having a commercial kitchen to myself."

"What about your new girl? Calli? She was all you could think about on Sunday."

"Yeah, that's history."

"History? The story hadn't even started."

"Yeah, so Kyle . . . " Dom waited for Joe to register the name of his investment advisor. When Joe nodded, Dom explained the situation, finishing by saying, "She chose a business relationship. End of story."

"That blows, man! I'm sorry." After a few more steps, he said, "Betsy is so close to the due date that we can't really go anywhere. She suggested I invite you over for some stuffed bird."

Dom eyed his friend. "She shouldn't have to cook a full meal when she's almost ready to give birth."

"I think she's hoping it'll send her into labor." Joe laughed. "And I can't boil water."

"Doesn't she still have a few weeks?"

"Yeah. The baby's due the week before Christmas."

Dom pushed the door to the gym open. "Maybe the two of you should come to Moretti's. It's closed for the holiday, and there's nothing like a gourmet kitchen to make the food prep go faster."

"I'll talk to her and let you know."

Inside, they walked over to the group. Trish was setting up the speakers, so class would begin in the next couple of minutes. Calli's friend Jordan looked over, but Calli didn't turn. Dom sighed and did a couple of jacks to loosen his calves and shoulders, then sank into a runner's stretch.

Trish called the class over and handed out a sheet of paper, explaining the day's drills. Dom knew this one by heart—The Hundred, Trish called it. One hundred of each strength exercise and three sets of stairs in between, it was one of his trainer's favorites and always promised to leave the muscles fatigued, then sore, for the two days that followed.

Dom finished in forty-five minutes—record time. Calli hadn't looked over once from what he could tell. He said goodbye to Joe and Trish, then jogged off to the showers, telling himself, You need to move on, dude. She certainly has. Somehow, the thought of her moving on was less than helpful. At the gym entrance, he stopped one last time and looked back. When their eyes met, she immediately flinched away. He smiled and pushed the door open, stepping out into the weight room. Maybe there was a crumb of hope. Maybe she was fighting the attraction too. Maybe their connection would become even more obvious as they tried to work together on his investments. Maybe, just maybe, all he needed was to be patient.

$\mathcal{W}$ORKOUT DONE, CALLI WAS READY to be at work and lose herself in the numbers and meetings that'd pepper her day at Moffitt & Hall. Mentally, she'd been preparing for her first client since she stepped into the shower. She continued practicing her words as she dressed, and after, as she walked to the parking lot with her best friend.

"Seriously, Cal, you wouldn't even look at him during class." Jordan interrupted, slinging her bag into the back seat, and ducked into the driver's seat of her car.

Calli sat in the passenger seat with her gym bag in her lap. "There are so many reasons this is not an option, Jordan. Just get us to work already." She dropped her head back onto the headrest and stared out the window into the gray morning.

"But when you talked about him, everything about you lit up."

"Not anymore."

"Yeah, you're right. Now you're moping!"

Calli turned to her friend and ranted, "Listen, Jordan. It's just too much to deal with a new relationship already. I need to focus on me, on getting the boys graduated, and on my career to make sure I'm secure for my own retirement. Yeah, I got part of Bennett's 401(k) in the settlement, but I'm not sure we'd saved enough before. He always managed that, and I'm trying to get my arms around what I need. The Moretti account is a huge step toward my financial security. I know Kyle will be back one day, but Moffitt said he had been considering moving the account to my portfolio anyway. I just can't do anything to jeopardize that income right now." She sighed and turned back to the passing buildings. Quieter, she added, "It was a huge mistake. I think I'll save the whole dating thing until after Jax and Kent are on their own."

Oh, thank the heavens, Calli thought. Her rant seemed to have done the trick and shut Jordan up, at least temporarily.

"Would you mind terribly if I bowed out of the movie this Saturday?" Jordan switched topics.

"No," said Calli, turning back to her friend, slightly confused. Jordan was a movie-aholic; totally unlike her to skip out on the latest chick flick they'd planned to see. "What's up?"

"Well, I have a date." She gave a shit-eating grin, then rushed to add, "I was kind of hoping you'd have another one yourself." Jordan held up her hand. "I'm not pushing. I'm just not superexcited about bailing on you."

"It's not a problem, really."

"You're sure?"

"Of course. Why don't we just go on Monday?"

"Yeah, then we can head over to Fireside. They have half-priced bottles of wine on Mondays."

"That's awesome. The boys go back to Bennett's on Sunday afternoon, so I won't feel like I'm losing any time with them. It works out better for me." Calli smiled and shifted her gym bag to the back seat.

"What are you doing for Turkey Day?" asked Jordan.

"Going down to Lindleyi with the boys to see my parents. Why?"

"Oh. Never mind," Jordan said.

"No, what? You were going to ask something."

"Well, you know my parents retired last year."

"Yeah?" said Calli.

"I don't have anyone to hang with. Guess I'll binge Outlander or something that day." Jordan shrugged. "Just another Thursday, right?"

"Nonsense. If you don't mind my crazy family, you should come with us!"

"Really?" Jordan's blue eyes brightened even more than normal.

"Yeah." A satisfied smile grew on Calli's face. Not only did it make Jordan's holiday better, it'd give her a buffer with her mom. "Did I tell you how much fun Kent had with my dad when he was in town?"

Jordan turned to check her blind spot. "No. What did they do?"

"Dad had a lecture at the U, and Kent went with. He was talkative when he got home. It did my heart good to see him excited over anything except video games."

Twenty-Two

THANKSGIVING DAY ROLLED AROUND, AND Calli woke the boys early for the trip to Lindleyi Manor, the Lindley family estate South of Wabasha on the Wisconsin side of the Mississippi. It was only a two-hour drive, but they planned to stay through the weekend. They'd loaded the SUV for a stay through the weekend plus an empty suitcase. They picked up Jordan on their way out of town and stowed her suitcase in the only remaining space.

Calli had included the empty bag because Isabelle Lindley, mother, grandmother, and homemaker extraordinaire, would be loading them up with Christmas gifts. The conversation with her mom where she had to tell her that Bennett would be taking the boys out of the country for Christmas had been something akin to torture. With apparent disappointment that her famous family Christmas at the manor would be disrupted, Isabelle had also taken the opportunity to remind Calli that marriage was a lifetime commitment, making her disapproval of the divorce abundantly clear—again.

The drive she'd taken a million and one times went by in a blur of conversation and improvised karaoke in the car on the parts of Jordan and Calli. Jax joined in occasionally, but Kent put on his Beats and ignored the fun, rolling his eyes as soon as the singing had begun. They passed through Alma, then turned to the right along the river and climbed the cliffs to Lindleyi Manor.

Calli pulled the car into the circular drive, around a fountain, and alongside what could only be her youngest brother's latest automotive adventure—a small red sports car that didn't seem to have any door handles. Calli said, "Oh my lord, Alder has a new toy."

Jordan's mouth gaped as she took in the sprawling Tuscan-style façade, then her eyes landed on the car. "That's a Tesla, Calli! What did you say your brother does?"

"Something in computers out in Seattle. I'm not really sure what his exact job is." Her thirty-five-year-old brother had always been one to flaunt his latest thing. Everything he'd ever talked about was more techy than she could understand.

"Is he single?"

"Maybe. He's not married, but I haven't talked to him in a few months, so I'm not sure if he's dating anyone." Calli gripped the wheel as the car idled, steeling herself to face the family and her mom in particular. She cut the engine and sighed loudly. "All right, let's do this." She turned to the back seat. "Ready?"

Kent's eyes popped open, and he was out of the car without a word, circling the ostentatious machine. He reached forward, then pulled back as if he wanted to but couldn't bring himself to touch something so perfect.

"Go ahead," said Alder as he stepped from the front veranda, sliding a smartphone into his pocket.

Calli looked between her ogling son and her brother. Kent's eyes were Frisbee-sized as the door opened of its own accord. Alder strutted over to his nephew and his car with a smirk and threw his arm around Kent.

"Wanna drive?" asked Alder.

Kent's expression fell. "I don't have my license yet."

"Permit?"

"No." He met his mother's eyes.

Calli felt her heart crack for her youngest son. Their deal was that he had to pass all his classes before she'd put him in driver's ed. She couldn't give him the responsibility that came with driving if he couldn't be responsible with his schoolwork habits. He loved technology, and this machine was an embodiment of everything he wanted. Unfortunately, it seemed like his ADHD would be a blocker to the things he wanted to do in life—at least for the foreseeable future. Maybe someday, something would click for him. She hoped. "You know the requirements," was all she said to Kent's pleading look.

Her younger brother glared at Calli, then said, "Hop in. I'll take you for a spin." As Kent hop-stepped around the back of the car, Alder added, "How are ya, sis?"

"You know . . . livin' the dream." Calli smiled.

Alder walked over, looking between Calli and Jordan. Calli made quick introductions and cleared her throat when Alder lingered over an extra-long handshake with her friend.

When she cleared her throat, Alder looked over and said, "Mom's been on pins and needles."

"Why?"

"Think she's excited to have us all home but she's nervous about dealing with you." Alder raised a manscaped brow. "Go easy on her."

Calli was appalled. "On her?" She folded her arms across her chest and decided not to discuss this with her ladies' man, perpetually single, drop-dead gorgeous younger brother. "Yeah. Okay."

Alder wrapped her in a hug, then went to the driver's seat of his toy. Chatting with a glowing Kent, he started the car, then whipped the car around the fountain and out onto River Road.

Jordan elbowed Calli. "Single?"

"You're drooling." They both laughed, and Calli added, "He's not the relationship type. Jax, help unload the luggage."

Jax almost huffed but obviously stifled it. Just as he'd unloaded all the suitcases, a butler emerged from the house.

In a very southern accent, the man said, "Good day, Miss Lindley, Miss Shuler, Mr. Stockton. My name is James. Please join the family in the salon. I will tend to the luggage." James held out his hand toward the open front door.

"Please, James," said Calli. "Do call us by our given names."

"Very well, Miss Callista." James nodded deeply.

Calli shook her head. Outdated though it may be, her mother was quite the Southern belle, and obviously she'd imported a servant who fit her expectations of southern

186

hospitality. "James"—she smiled up at the tall red-headed suited man—"I am pleased to make your acquaintance." Though she'd been raised in Minnesota, the traditions under which Isabelle had raised her, her twin, and their two brothers came back easily. At his nod, she led the way into Lindleyi Manor.

$\mathcal{C}$ALLI STRODE THROUGH THE STONE arch entry, stepped lightly over the marble-floored foyer with ornately carved custom table, and walked alongside her image in the large matching woodwork-framed mirror. She ignored Jordan's small sounds of astonishment and marvel. It had been this way all of Calli's life; the first time she brought a friend home, there had been tons of ooh's and aah's. Funny, she thought, with her parents' home dripping with this much wealth, she shouldn't have been so worried about landing Dom's account—strike that, the Moretti account.

But the truth remained—The money her parents gave her when she married Bennett Stockton had gone to pay for his Ivy League master's degree, while she held only a bachelor's degree in finance from the University of Wisconsin at Madison. True, it was a good school, but it didn't compare to the Yale MBA that Ben had "won" in their divorce settlement.

The worst thing she'd done in her life was trust that they'd be together forever and that she was making the best decisions for their family. She'd asked her lawyer, Kristi, if she could go after Bennett for that money, but since they were married at the time, the state of Minnesota considered that money joint resources. The sum of money invested didn't matter, only what they had at the time of the divorce. Live-and-learn was the bucket she guessed she'd have to classify that mistake in.

"Mom?" she said quietly, tentatively, as she entered the opulent salon. High-backed chairs and scroll-armed couches formed a conversational area to one side while a six-foot curved cherry-wood bar, complete with backbar, stood out as the room's centerpiece to the other side. The family had gathered on the leather stools, Dad playing bartender even though James had likely prepared the drinks beforehand. A combination of wine glasses, beers, and highballs sat in front of the adults. None of her nieces and nephews were present.

"Calli!" squealed her sister, flying from one of the stools and grabbing her fluted glass before she rushed over and slung an arm around her mirror image. Twins, Calli felt an immediate rush of energy as she squeezed her sister in return—the other half of her fitting right back into place.

Calli's mom made similar movements but went straight past her hugging daughters to Jax. Over Isabelle's shoulder, Jax looked at his mom with questioning eyes and hugged his grandmother.

"How are you, Cat? How's Trey? And the kids?" Calli pulled back to get a good look at her sister. Outside of the icy-blonde highlights, looking at Cattleya was like sliding into her own skin. She thought about their shared middle name—Linnea, meaning twinflower. One thing of their mother's tastes that Calli absolutely adored. "You look fabulous."

Her sister lowered her voice, "Cal, I wish I could say the same. You look tired." Cat pouted as she touched Calli's cheek under her eye but the mood lightened as she added,

"Good thing we're scheduled for facials tomorrow." Cat hooked her arm around her sister's and pulled toward the bar. "Trey's great; kids too. Growing like crazy. They're all out back. You'll see them soon."

Calli stopped to give her other brother, Jon, a kiss on the cheek as she passed. Jon smiled and proudly pulled his wife into his arms. "We've already told everyone else, but Meg's expecting." He rubbed her stomach through a loose shirt. She didn't show yet that Calli could tell, but she held up a goblet full of ice water as if to emphasize Jon's point.

"Congratulations to you both!" Calli kissed her sister-in-law on the cheek too.

They had been trying for their first child for years, so the news was welcome, even before Calli had the chance to introduce Jordan. She smiled across the bar at her dad. Richard Lindley was the descendent of the Charles Lindley who'd discovered the Dendrobium lindleyi species of orchids for which the family was now famous. After marrying Isabelle, the resulting naming of everything in their lives had been quite predictable.

Calli introduced Jordan to her family who welcomed her with open arms—a little too open and falsely hospitable for Calli's taste but that was what it meant to be a Lindley. Her mother sashayed primly over and ensnared Jordan in a hug as well, asking immediately about the men in her life. Calli only shrugged as Jordan gracefully said that she had recently started dating someone who seemed promising.

Richard asked, "What can I pour for the ladies?"

"I'll take a red, Dad."

"The same, please," Jordan said.

He pulled the stemware from the carved overhead racks and poured two glasses. After handing Calli's over, he offered the second to Jordan. As she accepted, Richard Lindley told her to sit and started on his introductory speeches that Calli knew would lead well into the history of the Lindley family.

Isabelle preened. She, especially, loved the fact that she had married into such a prestigious family in the history of botany. She'd embraced the culture whole-heartedly with private greenhouses, a penchant for floral décor, and in the names of each of her four children. Callista and Cattleya were varieties of orchids. Their younger brothers sported names as masculine as their mother's creativity could come up with while keeping with the theme . . . Jon Quill and Alder Berry Lindley.

While Jordan humored her father, Calli leaned over to her mom. "How are you?"

"I'm good, Callista. How are you since the . . . you know." She couldn't even utter the word divorce.

"It's an adjustment."

"I don't know how you manage without a husband, dear."

"It'll be okay, Mom." She looked over at her dad as he glanced toward Isabelle with an admiring smile. Then she went on, "It had been a long time since we were a couple anyway."

"That is so sad, darling," said Isabelle, placing a hand over Calli's.

Calli turned her hand to take hold of her mother's. She fought the urge to ask for her acceptance. Instead, she just said, "It's hard but it'll be all right, eventually."

"I will keep praying for you and the boys."

"Thanks, Mom." She changed the subject. "How is dinner coming along? Are we having Mama's dressing?"

"Yes, we found a wonderful new chef. I gave Garvey the recipe, and he said he'd be happy to whip it up for our Thanksgiving dinner."

"Garvey?"

Isabelle shook her head. "I forget, it's been a long time since you visited. We have all new staff. The stress of hiring was horrible but we've lucked out with Garvey and James. You met him, right?" Isabelle pointed toward the foyer with a questioning look.

Calli nodded with lips pursed and brow crinkled.

Isabelle smiled widely, then added. "It's a little awkward though." She lowered her voice as if she were discussing something truly scandalous. "They're a couple, you know?"

"Really, Mom?" Calli chuckled. "That's common these days. But I absolutely cannot believe you gave your mother's recipe to someone outside the family."

"Oh dear." Isabelle flipped her hand nonchalantly in the air. "I'm beyond cooking and Cattleya wasn't here early enough to get started."

"I could have come down early to help if you had let me know."

"Nonsense. You're not really a chef either, darling. Garvey will do a fabulous job." The fingers of her crow's feet stretched as she smiled—small evidence for her sixty-eight years.

"Did they move into the servant's house?"

"Of course."

Jordan appeared at Calli's end of the bar. "Hey, lady"—she hesitated—"and Mrs. Lindley."

Calli's mom said, "How are you finding our home, dear?"

Jordan gave her decorating a few quick compliments and they were quickly on to a first name basis. Jordan said, "Isabelle, is there a . . . um . . . powder room I might use? The drive was long, and I had a good deal of coffee along the way."

Isabelle pointed down the hall and explained while Calli took a sip of her wine to stifle her amusement. She'd prewarned Jordan that her mother was proper to an extreme, but she'd never expected to hear the words powder room come from Jordan's lips.

"Darling," said Isabelle, placing a hand on Calli's forearm. "I'll be back shortly. I should check on Garvey and how dinner is coming." Her mom slid from the stool with her iced sweet tea and walked gracefully from the room.

Calli's father grabbed the remote from the backbar and flipped on the TV, finding the first football game of the day. Green Bay was at Detroit, something that was important for most of the locals, but the first game always just served as background noise at the Lindley home. The important game, and the one they'd go to the theater downstairs to watch was the Cowboys. Who were they playing today? Calli couldn't remember. At one time, Calli had been a number-one-Dallas fan and had religiously played fantasy football. She could recite the NFL rules with the best of football fans. But in recent years, work, the boys, and her strained relationship with Bennett had taken that from her. Maybe today would help her find that part herself all over again.

Calli looked around at her extended family. Jax stood at the end of the bar talking to Jon and Meg. Trey had slipped back in beside Cat. With their dad, they were engaged deep in a conversation too. Calli imagined she was a spectator watching a happy scene through someone else's window. Then, totally out of nowhere, her mind wandered into the taboo zone . . .

I wonder how Dom would fit in here at Lindleyi Manor with my crazy, wealthy, displaced Southern family?

$\mathscr{A}$LONE, DOM TURNED ON CHRISTMAS music in the kitchen at Moretti's. He wouldn't allow it before Thanksgiving as many other restaurants and retail stores did these days, but he secretly loved the holiday and waited with great anticipation for "Winter Wonderland," "Little Drummer Boy," and "Carol of the Bells." But as always, he started with his favorite: "I'll Be Home for Christmas." Maybe a strange favorite, definitely an old one as he demanded the Bing Crosby version, but one that he'd developed a hard attraction to in the holiday season after he lost his parents.

The turkey was half done on the rotisserie when Joe and Betsy wandered in, proffering a bottle of wine.

"That wasn't necessary. Have you seen the wine cellar?"

"I know, but what else were we supposed to bring to a dinner with a famous gourmet chef?"

Betsy came around the long stainless-steel island and leaned slowly toward Dom for a hug. "How is my favorite chef anyway?"

"I'm wonderful," lied Dom. All morning, and for most of the week, Calli had been on his mind. "Thanksgiving starts the most beautiful time of the year. Twelve days, my ass." With his knife in hand, he pointed toward the speaker playing the song.

"At least you don't start before Halloween like most other places," Joe said.

Betsy took off her jacket and hung it on the apron hook along the far wall. As she returned, she said, "Okay, what still needs to be done."

Dom smiled at his friend, Joe. Betsy's take-charge attitude was simply adorable—especially in her condition. She'd make a wonderful mother. He stepped to the block and grabbed another knife. "Do you know how to use this?"

Betsy glared at him.

"Yep, you'll do great as a mom. You've already nailed the look," said Dom. He reached under the counter and produced two russet potatoes and a sweet onion. "Paper-thin slices."

Betsy got to work.

Joe asked, "Can I grab a beer?"

"Yeah, I put some in the fridge." Dom nodded toward the wall of refrigerators.

Joe raised a brow.

"The third from the left. Second shelf."

Joe wandered over and retrieved a bottle. "So, anything new on the girl." He jutted his chin toward Dom's preparations.

Betsy focused on her work, glancing up surreptitiously

at Joe's question.

"What girl?" Dom acted ignorant, knowing good and well that he meant Calli, and continued to julienne the carrots for each of the four pre-plated salads.

"If there is nothing new with Calli, who is the fourth salad intended for?"

Dom remained silent for a few seconds, slicing and arranging the orange ribbons atop the bed of dark greens. It was probably a mistake, he knew, but he hated for her to be alone on Thanksgiving. No one deserved that. "Oh, I invited Pauline."

Betsy's knife clattered as it fell onto the stainless island top.

$\mathcal{D}$OM HAD GIVEN JOE THE non-culinary duties—fetch some bowls or pans, wash my knives, bring up a bottle of Chardonnay, set the table—really anything to keep him out of Dom's hair. Betsy on the other hand had been a wonderful little sous-chef. As they prepared a cranberry-pecan stuffing, some truffle mashed potatoes, and a pumpkin mousse pie, they'd sung along to the Christmas music at the tops of their lungs, using wooden spoons as microphones.

Pauline arrived in the middle of "Baby, It's Cold Outside" when Dom was serenading the very pregnant Betsy. Joe sat to the side and laughed at Dom and his wife replaying the scene from Neptune's Daughter. Pauline, holding a vegetable tray and obviously not thinking it funny, stepped into the kitchen with her jaw hanging open, but Dom didn't stop his silly imitation of Ricardo Montalbán until his performance was complete.

Betsy was a tiny little thing, even at eight-plus months pregnant. At the end, he dipped her easily, then made sure she was steady on her feet before greeting his new guest. Dom walked over to Pauline and accepted the store-bought veggie tray, then dropped it on the counter. "Come on in. Wine is on the table, beer or water in the third fridge."

Joe, who was nearly in tears from his mirth, said, "The two of you are insanely bad actors and singers."

"Happy Thanksgiving, Pauline." Betsy went over and shook her hand. She then walked over to her giggling husband, leaned in, and kissed his lips. "Ever the flatterer, my love."

Dom turned away, not really wanting to be reminded of the romance factor, washed the vegetables Pauline had brought, and re-plated them. He tossed the Hidden Valley Ranch plastic bowl into the garbage and went to the refrigerator for his signature Moretti's Garlic Ranch and a couple of bright pink-and-white orchid flowers to dress up Pauline's contribution.

Pauline trailed after him, asking, "How can I help?"

He handed her the dressed-up vegetables. "Put these on the table through the doors there, then have a drink. It's just about ready." Given that she had brought a ten-dollar veggie tray to his kitchen even after he told her not to bring anything but herself, he didn't want her stepping foot inside what he considered his ring of magic. He smiled at her, hoping to reassure but feeling that it fell quite flat. Her shoulders slumped as she pushed through the doors.

Meanwhile, Joe and Betsy watched in awkward silence.

Joe peaked his brows. "Why did you invite her again?"

"She didn't have anywhere to go. It sucks to be alone on a holiday." Dom shrugged.

Betsy rubbed her husband's shoulder. "Dom, she's your PA, right?"

Dom nodded.

She looked to her husband who dropped his eyes, then said, "That might've been a mistake, D. She's got it pretty bad"—the door swung open revealing an overly smiley Pauline—"uh . . . headache. Do you have any Tylenol?"

Nice recovery, thought Dom. Pointing with a pair of potholders, he said, "Upstairs in the bathroom in my office. It should be open."

Betsy excused herself.

Dom threw a second pair of gloves to Joe. "Come help me with the bird." They went to the open-fire stone rotisserie and pulled out the long spit. Normally used for roasting a line of chickens, it was seven feet long and unmanageable for one person. The fourteen-pound turkey looked miniscule in that setup.

They slid the bird off onto the cutting board, and Dom returned the spit to the fire. His kitchen staff would be in late this evening and would clean the spits and add birds to roast overnight for the next evening. He let the turkey rest for a good twenty minutes before pulling the wings and legs, slicing the breasts, and arranging the meat on a bed of gravy. He ran through his mental checklist for the meal, then sent everyone to the table and joined them with platter in hand. Between the two tapers, he placed the meat onto the crisp white tablecloth, then took his seat.

Pauline scooted her chair toward Dom's ever-so-subtly. "It looks delicious," she said, placing her hand on Dom's and leaning in. "Thank you so much for having me."

Dom looked at her hand, looked at Joe and Betsy who were both gulping water with wide eyes, then pulled away. "Of course, Pauline. I just figured it would be a wonderful Friendsgiving." He draped a napkin across his lap and spread his hands over the table as if making a formal presentation. "Let's eat."

CONVERSATION AND COMPLIMENTS FLOWED THROUGHOUT the meal. After Dom, Joe, and Betsy had gorged on the turkey, stuffing, and potatoes, the three of them sat back as if to give more room for the food. Pauline had sampled the food, but really only pushed it around on the plate. She didn't have much to add to the table's discussion, either, even though Betsy had prompted her for her thoughts on several occasions.

"Are we ready for the pumpkin mousse?" asked Dom.

Joe groaned.

Betsy rubbed the top of her baby bump. "Maybe give it just a bit." She smiled sweetly.

"Excuse me," said Pauline. She dropped her napkin on the table and left.

Dom propped his elbows on the table and let his head fall into his hands. "Yeah, inviting her was a mistake."

"Ya think?" said Betsy.

Joe added, "I think it's time that you found a new PA."

That was a prospect Dom hated. He'd desperately hoped not to have to let her go. He'd tried to not let anything develop between them, and he was still hopeful. He'd tell her before she left tonight that his intentions with her were merely professional. Hopefully, she'd accept it and they could continue with the working relationship.

Twenty-Three

THE AIR IN THE SPRAWLING greenhouse at Lindleyi Manor was floral thick, a familiar and comforting smell, as Calli strolled beside her sister on the Friday after Thanksgiving. When they reached the corner that hosted the fall of the yellow orchids with the ocher centers, Calli stopped and stroked a D. lindleyi's delicate blossom. Crushed velvet whispered against her finger. Since her ancestor, Charles Lindley, had discovered the species, orchids had been a sustaining force for the family. She'd once run from the business and science that her father had so desperately wanted her to embrace, but it was a proud history Calli missed now that she had arrived in her mid-forties.

When she was a young child, she'd spent every waking, non-school minute in the greenhouse with her father, a fourth-generation in the famed Lindley line. Richard Charles Lindley, he'd introduced himself . . . always using the famous Charles as a means of self-identity. Everyone between Red Wing and La Crosse knew the story of Charles Lindley thanks to her father. History tugged at Calli in the greenhouse by the river. At this moment, everywhere she turned, she'd see a ghost of the blonde-haired girl she'd once been, running barefoot under the glass ceilings, over the cobbled floor, down an aisle, or to her father's side as he'd tended the plants. In the lab, the little girl pulling over a stool and climbing up to watch her father work with one petri dish or another, hoping to invent a new variety that would make him as famous as his great-grandfather.

She reached up and swept her brown curls to one side. No longer the innocent little blonde, she thought. Her eyes prickled a bit as she considered how she and all her siblings had dispersed, leaving no one to inherit the family love for the flowers.

"Hello? Earth to Calli." Cat snapped her fingers in front of Calli's eyes.

Calli blinked and smiled ruefully. "I'm sorry, just a little lost in the memories."

Cat didn't say anything. Words weren't required. Sensing Calli's muddled emotional state, all she did was pull her sister into a hug and stand there in the humid-sweet atmosphere.

Thanksgiving dinner the day before had been a delightful meal with homely conversation and a little too much libation. Between the turkey and cocktails, their father had snored loudly in one of the reclining leather theater-seats as a backdrop to the game. Calli had watched the players on the big screen intently, trying to recapture her love for the sport, but something had just been missing. After the game, they had decorated a tree that Garvey and James had brought up from the fields and set up for them before joining the family for the fourth quarter of the game. Cat and Trey's young children, three-year-old Liam and six-year-old Olivia, had giggled and laughed as one adult after another or Jax or Kent took turns holding them high to put on a new ornament. Even Garvey and James had joined the family for the tree trimming. Each estranged from their own families, they merrily saw to every need of the family but also joined in the celebration. Through all the happy, in every little thing, there was just that little bit missing. The absence had tugged at her relentlessly.

Cat stepped back, holding her at arm's length. "Let's get Mom, Meg, and Jordan and head over to the spa for the facials. I think it'll do you some good."

"Yeah, that sounds wonderful."

$\mathcal{C}$ALLI FLIPPED THROUGH A COSMOPOLITAN in the waiting area at Lotus Rejuvenation Spa, the only spa for a hundred miles up and down the Mississippi River. Calli sat with Cat and Jordan, all three dressed in terry cloth robes and fuzzy slippers while a mandolin played over speakers hidden by the mechanical waterfalls in each corner of the room. The lights were dim, and it felt like sacrilege to utter sounds above a whisper.

An esthetician appeared in the arched door. "Cattleya," she said, and Cat stood to follow.

Jordan scooted closer to Calli. "All right, I feel like we've stepped into a movie set . . . some strange combination of Tuscany and a southern plantation. I mean, really, a limo, butler, and chef? Then a full spa day? I knew you grew up in money, but dang, girl."

Calli inhaled deeply and exhaled slowly. Though she'd let on with Jordan that her family had money, she typically evaded questions about the family history and stature. "Yeah." She gave her friend a small smile. "Just don't let it overwhelm you."

"Me?" Jordan covered her chest as if appalled. "Remember where we work, Cal? Rich is old hat in Cloud 9. It's more the feel of your parents' estate—maybe—and the fact that your mother is paying for all of us here today."

Calli just nodded as the next technician appeared in the arch and called for her. "I'll see you after. Enjoy!"

When Calli stepped into the hallway behind the technician in black scrubs, a well-known man's voice called her name. She turned toward her youngest brother, who also wore the traditional spa-goer attire. "Alder, what are you doing here? Girl's spa day, remember?" She looked him up and down, then burst out in laughter and covered her mouth. "Your knobby knees are showing."

Alder had always been superfit, but he was a long and lean kind of athlete. There wasn't one thing stocky about his six-foot-four frame, but being the tallest in the family and having been giraffe-like clumsy until he was seventeen left him with his own scars and insecurities.

"Very funny, flower girl." He snarked back.

"Are you here to get your toes done? A little waxing maybe?" She reached toward his brows.

"Massage." Alder jerked away from her touch, then shuffled his slippered feet. "Is your friend still in there?"

Calli nodded warily.

"You go have a relaxing facial. I'll keep her company until it's her turn."

She grabbed her brother's arm before he could enter the waiting area and pushed him back down the hall. "Oh, no, you don't! She's one of my oldest friends. The last thing I need right now is to have to pick up the pieces you leave behind. I've been in that boat far too many times."

Alder held his hands up as if surrendering. "All right. Purely platonic. But I can't just go in there and not talk to the only other person in the room."

Calli took a deep breath and closed her eyes for a moment, reopening them as she exhaled. "Promise me you won't try anything with her, please?"

When he smiled, Alder was about the hardest person on earth to resist . . . except for maybe Dominic Moretti. Calli shook away that thought and refocused on her brother.

"You gonna be all right there, sis?" he asked.

She had little choice but to trust that he wouldn't go against her wishes. Trust just wasn't something she was feeling a lot of these days. "Okay," she said reluctantly and joined the esthetician at the open door, waving to Jordan as she passed.

Twenty-Four

THE ALARM BUZZED IN THE dark and early hours on Monday morning. Calli rolled out of bed, silenced the buzzing, and was in the shower before really coming awake. She'd known today would be challenging, so had gone to bed early to make sure she was on her game. Her first meeting of the day was with Dominic Moretti, his PA, and his lawyer. She wanted to be more than prepared for the meeting. As the water poured over her, she coached herself.

Calli, you need to be strong. You're making the right decisions for your future. You've made too many wrong choices in the past which led to too much self-sacrifice. Now, it's time to focus on you. Do not let lust for this man ruin what you've worked for at Moffitt & Hall, and you sure as hell better not confuse that with anything more. In that room, today, you focus on the facts and the account. It's an hour today. You don't have to interact with him at the gym. Keep it professional.

She reached down and shut off the water, reaffirmed in her path. She dressed in the business suit she'd chosen the night before and woke the boys on her way downstairs. "Kent, I'll leave your meds on the counter. Don't forget. Jax, you working tonight?"

"Nah," came the groggy reply.

She still had the boys. Had it not been for the traded extended holidays, they would have been back at their father's this morning. This felt normal as she watched each of them begin their morning stirring. Reluctantly, she said, "I'll see you both later. Love you."

She decided to drive this morning; it was a bit more predictable, and that's what she needed today. Everything had to be just so. She was in complete control. Looking at the clock in the dash, exactly thirty-four minutes had passed since her alarm. Slightly ahead of schedule, she thought.

At the garage, she parked in the empty row of slots labeled Moffitt & Hall and checked to make sure she had her badge. Arriving before eight meant that the receptionist wasn't there yet and she'd have to let herself in. It also meant that she'd probably be the only one there for the next hour or so. Again, that was on plan. Before entering her work building, she visited Bienvenue for her customary latte. The barista started her order before she'd even placed it, and by the time she'd paid, the cup was waiting on the bar. She picked it up and poured it into her travel mug. Looking back to the cashier, Calli considered how to get a black coffee with two sugars to go—Dom's drink of choice from what she knew—but she readily gave up on that idea, kicking herself for it even crossing her mind.

This is business, Calli. Keep it that way, she told herself

as she walked to the other end of the block and into her building.

Inside Moffitt & Hall, she badged in and climbed the stairs to the second floor. The motion detectors tied to the lights turned on the overheads in each area she entered until she reached her desk at the far end.

She put on a pot of coffee for the meeting and ensured there were cups and sugar to accompany the drink in case he wanted a cup. Still alone in the office and waiting for her computer to fire up, Calli looked up as the white noise kicked in overhead. When her computer had fired up, she printed off four copies of the portfolio reports for the Moretti account, showing significant growth, and a copy of the agenda for the meeting. They'd review the current state, look at his cash position, and evaluate any legal risks that he might be facing. Finally, they'd discuss the go-forward strategy. With the packets ready for the meeting, Calli decided to filter through some of the guides to restaurant financing and some trends in the restaurant industry. She still had a lot to learn about this industry before she'd be able to guide him effectively in a strategy. Meanwhile, she jotted some notes of things to ask during the meeting.

With ten minutes to spare, Calli went to the conference room down the hall to wait for her guests. The lights were on. Puzzled, she slowed and peeked her head inside. Instead of an empty conference room, Dom sat at the far end of the table, alone. He stood as she entered and grinned widely. "I was hoping you'd be here a few minutes early," he said.

Calli placed a stack of folios on the table and stammered, "G-good morning. I wasn't expecting that you'd arrive before me." She idly flipped through a folder to keep from looking into his green-gray eyes.

Dom stood, walked to her, and placed a hand on top of the papers.

Damn. She raised her gaze to meet his and forgot to breathe.

He flashed his eyes to the door and back to her. "Before we start down this road of business relationship, I wanted to ask you one more time to give my account to someone else." He leaned close to her neck, his warm breath reminding her of that night.

She stepped away. "Please don't. This is what I want." Isn't it? C'mon, Calli, yes. It is.

Joe came into the room. "Good mo—" he started, then stopped in his tracks, looking between Dom and Calli.

Calli smiled.

"I guess maybe not as good as I thought," he said.

Dom walked back to his end of the table, Joe taking the seat to his left. A few unintelligible whispers were traded, and Calli schooled her breathing back to normal. Keep to what you'd practiced. One hour, and we're done. One step at a time. She passed out the folios placing one in front of each of the men and a third in front of an empty chair beside Joe. As she was returning to her end of the table, a woman appeared—red trench coat, brassy brown hair, too much red lipstick, and the smell of the perfume counter at Macy's.

"Good morning," said Calli.

The woman looked up. "Oh. Hi." She scanned the room, eyes glowing when she found Dom at the other end of the table.

Calli knew the feeling, but brushed that off, too, and

210

held out a hand. "I'm Callista Lindley."

"Oh." She shifted a too-big bag and placed a cold hand into Calli's. "Pauline Monroe, Mr. Moretti's personal assistant."

Pauline clomped in her high, very high, heels to Dom's end of the table. She grabbed the folder beside Joe and went to the other side of Dom, pulling a chair close to his right side. Slinging her jacket over the chair beside her, she threw the bag on top of the table and went digging. Dom's PA pulled out a wrapper and spit her chewed gum into it, folded it up, and stuffed it into the side pocket of her purse.

Calli wrinkled her nose and looked down. Where the hell had Dom found this one? Recalling the minimalist condition of his loft, she didn't seem to fit his idea of business or pleasure. Calli decided she must be one very talented personal assistant . . . or maybe it had to do with the mouth she highlighted in glossy red.

Calli blinked hard. Stop it. You don't have a right to be jealous, she told herself as she closed the door. Sitting at the far end of the six-person table, Calli kicked off the meeting. "In your folders, there is an agenda. Since I am new to the account, I'd like you to provide an overview of how you feel the management of your accounts have been handled so far. What you'd like to see continued and what you'd like to see changed." She waited.

Dom sighed, then straightened and started discussing the history of his investments. As he talked, Pauline leaned closer and closer. Calli tried to ignore her. She'd seen this relationship before with Bennett's string of personal assistants. It was amazing that her ex had never ended up with Human Resources on his case for his inappropriate behavior with his youngs and leggies, as Calli had come to know them.

When Dom finished, Calli said, "I've done some research on the latest trends in restaurant investments. It seems that there are some up-and-coming chains that might be worth considering."

Dom held up a hand. "Calli, you've eaten at Moretti's, true?"

"Yes." She swallowed.

"Have you watched The Dinner Shark at all?"

"Uh, no." Well, she'd scanned past it once. It was an excellent question though. She should have watched it before now to try to educate herself about his career and investments.

Pauline laughed, then said, "Oh . . . " dragging it out this time as if she felt sorry for Calli. "You should probably do that, sweets. It's as entertaining as it is educational." She stuck the end of the pen between her teeth.

Calli scanned both Dom and Joe for their reactions. Either they were accustomed to this strange woman or they were better able to hide their reactions than she felt capable of at the moment. Calli had met Dom's lawyer at the gym. Here, now, Joe sat silently, holding the pen at each end with one hand and observing the room as everyone talked . . . the exact portrait of a competent, professional, unflappable lawyer. Him, she liked. Pauline, not so much.

Dom rubbed his chin and nearly rolled his eyes as he said, "Anyway,"—he paused emphatically, glancing at his PA—"I'm not sure about the education value but it would be good information for you to have about my investment strategies. You might say that I enjoy quality over quantity. Though, I think you're aware of that."

Pauline stifled a little gasp at Dom's insinuation and Calli's cheeks grew hot. She quickly moved on to the next topic. "Joe, can you share the legal risks around Dom's investment strategies, his current investments, and any that are being presently evaluated?"

When Joe had completed his summary, Calli turned to Pauline. "Do you have Mr. Moretti's cash position available?"

"Oh, yes." Again, she went digging in the canyon that was her purse and brought out a stack of papers that had suffered some corner damage from the trip inside Pauline's bag.

Calli reached across the table and accepted the reports. "I'll need some time to review these. Are there any new investments on your immediate horizon?" she asked.

"Actually, yes," Dom said. "There's a rumor about a Mediterranean diner—tiny little place—that recently popped up in New York. Apparently, it's owned by a young man from Greece who has been experimenting with some interesting blends. I'm traveling there next week. Would you like to come along?"

"Ahh, I don't think that's necessary." Calli blushed again and checked the agenda. She quickly covered a few more items and adjourned the meeting twelve minutes early. She quickly shook hands with Joe and Pauline, then Dom. He held her hand longer than necessary, until she pulled away.

"We do have a meeting next Tuesday, correct?" he asked.

"I believe so."

"And I trust that you'll study up before then." Dom slid on his thigh-length navy-blue coat and secured it around his waist. "I'll also send you some more information about what I consider a great investment."

Pauline cut in. "I can handle that for you, Dom."

He didn't take his eyes off Calli as he said, "That's all right, Pauline. Ms. Lindley might have questions that only I'd be able to answer. Also, I think she likes dealing directly with her clients rather than with their assistants. True?"

"Yes," Calli breathed, then blinking, recovered. "Um. Yes. That is true. I'll look for the information. Joe, it was good to see you. Have a wonderful week." She turned on her heel and left the room unconcerned about protocol in her present state of confused frustration and, dare she say, jealousy. The man really, really listened. It was so unlike everything she'd experienced with Bennett, but she couldn't help envisioning the trollop in the meeting with those red lips wrapped around his . . .

"Argh!" she said aloud, then balled her fist and stomped down the hall. Fuck. Ing. Stop. It. Callista Linnea Lindley!

Twenty-Five

$\mathcal{B}$EAST LADY'S WHISTLE BLEW, AND Dom sprinted. It screeched again, and he walked. Joe wasn't in class this morning because Betsy had gone into labor the night before and delivered a healthy baby boy. Dom had stopped in first thing this morning to congratulate the happy, yet exhausted, new parents before coming to the gym alone. He hadn't worked out alone anytime in recent memory. Joe had always been at his side—even in classes. He couldn't say it was his favorite.

As for his professional life, it had been two weeks since the working relationship with Calli had begun, and they'd met in the offices of Moffitt & Hall twice, the second time more electrically charged if that was possible. They probably didn't need to meet a third time but he hoped the constant contact would sway her. She was indeed learning a great deal about his world. That brought a smile to his face. Then, he'd had the opportunity to see her at the gym on Tuesdays, Thursdays, and Saturdays, and they'd started bantering during and after Beast Lady's classes. At the thoughts of Calli, he looked around the track to see where she was. Nice, he thought, I'll catch her on the next sprint.

The thought wasn't out before Trish's whistle sounded again. He sprinted, this time with a finish line in mind. As he approached her, his fingers itched with desire to touch her bare shoulder. He only slowed when the next whistle blew but kept jogging until he reached Calli's side. "Hi," he said, only a little winded. "Where's your friend today?"

"Sick. At least that's what she said." Calli breathed deeply. "What about Joe?"

"His wife gave birth last night."

"Oh, that's awesome!" Calli's eyes lit up.

They walked in silence until the next whistle sounded. Dom matched her step to not leave her behind. At the next interval, he asked, "So, if the drills are partners today, guess we're paired up?"

"Yeah. Looks that way." She put a hand to her side. "Have you even worked up a sweat?"

Dom laughed. "I've been at this a little longer than you. You're doing great!"

"Thanks for the approval." Calli rolled her eyes.

"I didn't mean that . . . ugh. Never mind." Damnit, he'd screwed up again.

But then she smiled widely. "Joking."

Trish's double-whistle called them back to the door for the rest of the drills to begin. Dom said a little thank you to whatever gods might be listening when Trish told them to pair up. The workout was another of Trish's favorite—boxing—so he barely listened as she explained the sequences. As they started, he helped Calli with the jabs, hooks, and uppercuts. They teamed well, anticipating and responding to each other, and fell into easy conversation in between.

"Ouch," Dom said. "You have one hell of an uppercut."

She glared at him. "And you're being overdramatic."

"No, I'm serious. Have you had any self-defense classes?"

Calli laughed and punched the boxing pads harder. "My dad signed me up for one when I told him I was moving to the Cities for college. He said I was small and needed to know how to do more than—I quote—kick 'em in the balls. So, yeah. But that's been twenty years."

"I hear the instinct doesn't really go away."

"Well, you're about to knock me over with yours. We're not a great pairing, physically."

"I think you're wrong there." He looked at her suggestively.

"Dom. No."

"All right." He held up his hands in surrender.

WHEN THE WORKOUT AND COOLDOWN were done, they walked side by side to the locker rooms. Dom wanted desperately to pull her to him, but he resisted and watched her walk into the women's area. Then he decided and quickly rushed into the men's locker room, showered, dressed casually in jeans and a sweatshirt, and headed for the parking lot. He pulled around and parked, quite illegally, with the passenger door facing the door to the gym. Stepping out, he pulled on his gloves and tightened his scarf around his neck. He leaned on his car door and waited for Calli to come out.

$\mathcal{C}$ALLI SHOWERED AND DRESSED FOR work. The workout had been a killer but partnering with Dom had been good. They'd fallen into a nice platonic rhythm. She turned on the hair dryer and blew her hair in the wrong direction. After a minute, she turned it off and pushed the brown veil out of her face. Shit . . . Joe's out. There's a good chance my first meeting will be one-on-one with Dom . . . or worse . . . Dom and Pauline. She grabbed the round brush and started shaping her almost-dry hair. She couldn't call off the meeting, she'd just spent the morning working out with him. She'd learned a ton about the restaurant industry over the last two weeks, but the meetings had been growing more and more charged. This was a munitions warehouse, about to explode.

She dressed, absently thinking of possible excuses to get out of the day's meeting. She needed to stall until Joe could be there. He was safe—her buffer zone—and kept things level in the room. Without him there, Calli was afraid she'd do something foolish like calling Pauline out on her overt flirtation in the middle of the business meeting or asking her to leave due to nonprofessional behavior. Or, if she didn't attend the meeting, Calli hated to think what she might do if she were alone with Dom.

Still considering how to get out of the meeting, Calli

packed up her bag and headed out of the locker room, then passed reception and pushed open the doors into the cold. Her feet stopped, rooted in place, when she saw Dom straight ahead leaning against his car and smiling as if it were the best day of his life.

Shouldering her bag, Calli started walking . . . she had to pass him to get to her car. "What are you doing?" she asked as she neared.

"Isn't it obvious?"

"No."

"Waiting on you. The way I see it, your first meeting is with none other than . . . me." He pointed to himself with both thumbs and grinned. "I think I should give you a ride."

"I have my car here." Shit-shit-shit! Definitely not getting out of it.

"I'd be happy to pick you up and bring you back here after work."

Calli looked around the parking lot, the wind biting her cheeks. "Dom, it's cold—"

"My car is warm." His cheeks were red. How long had he waited?

She tilted her head. As many times as she'd told him it wasn't a possibility, he remained optimistic. "Why?"

"Because I'm still trying. I've thought it through, and here are my thoughts . . . I don't pay you directly. You make money off the money you make for me. We're both paid by your work. You don't technically work for me, so there's no nepotism." He held his arms wide. "Therefore, I think we should be able to give us a shot too. Outside the office."

Calli pursed her lips. He had a point. There weren't any explicit rules. But what if things didn't go well? She'd still have to face him on office time.

He leaned toward her. "I see the gears turning."

She slumped and jutted a hip. She was going to regret this, she just knew it. "Okay."

"Okay?"

She was sooo going to regret this, but she was struggling to deny it. Throwing her arms to either side, she harrumphed and nodded. "Okay."

"Yes!" He nearly jumped, but composed himself and opened the door, holding out a hand for her bag. He opened and closed the trunk, presumably putting her bag inside—next to his—and slid into the driver's seat. He shifted into first with a small crooked smile, and they were off.

He was right, his car was warm as he'd had the seat warmers fired up. Her backside nice and toasty, she wondered how long he would have waited while she prepped. She returned his smile, giving into the magnetism that she always felt when he was near.

"Do we have to meet at your office?" he asked, then rushed to add, "Pauline isn't joining us this morning, and . . . well . . . Joe's a little busy with Little Joe."

"Is that what they named the baby?"

"No, I think they named him Daniel. But since it's just us, it might be less stuffy somewhere else."

She thought for a minute. "I suppose we don't. I have my computer, and as long as I can access the internet, we can pull up the information. Where are you thinking?"

He hesitated, then said, "Moretti's? I can make espresso."

Calli's throat went dry and her stomach twisted as she remembered the morning after they'd been together. At least he hadn't asked her to come back to his place. She tucked her hair behind her ear and said, "O-okay, I guess that'll work." The words were no sooner out of her mouth than she remembered—his loft was right above the restaurant.

Twenty-Six

$\mathcal{M}$ORETTI'S DURING THE DAY WAS an entirely different environment—quiet, formal, and oddly stuffy. Calli scanned the dining room normally teeming with guests and wait staff while Dom made a path around empty, undressed tables and behind the bar where the espresso machine also sat silently. She followed, breaking through dust dancing in the streaks of daylight that filtered in from the reception area.

At the bar, Calli took off her jacket, hung it on a chair, and pulled out her computer as Dom pulled two mugs from a lower cabinet, milk from a refrigerator, and fired up the contraption. She'd checked in to work this morning before going to the gym and hadn't shut down the laptop. It had gone to sleep but flickered rapidly to life, asking for her password. Scanning the available networks, she found Moretti-Guest. "What's the Wi-Fi key?"

"In love at Moretti's," Dom said, glancing at her with a wry smile as he worked. "All one word, no caps."

The steamer squealed and gurgled as Dom frothed the milk, then he turned to her with two mugs full of coffee and placed them on the bar. Two little hearts decorated the foam of each half of the coffee-couple. Calli stared.

Dom pulled a stool closer and sat beside her—very close. "So, what have you learned?"

"Well, I binged a full season of The Dinner Shark."

"And? Your thoughts?"

"It is very entertaining. Enthralling, really. But more so, I learned that you invest in the chef rather than the restaurant."

Dom nodded his approval and sipped his coffee, motioning with one hand for her to go on.

Calli lifted the mug to her lips and tasted—better than Bienvenue's. She wiped a bit of foam from her upper lip and continued, "How am I supposed to help you with growing in that area? My business is watching finances, investing in the stock markets or real estate, watching the economics globally so that if one region is having a downturn economically, I can shift my clients' funds to another region to maximize their return on investments. I don't know anything about what makes a good chef."

"Precisely." His eyes glittered. "My investment strategy is not about what makes the most financial sense. If that were the case, I'd have been in the restaurant chain business ages ago. I'm all about the palate. I look for people who will be successful because of their passion. That is my space—sweet spot, if you will."

"Then what exactly does Moffitt & Hall do to help you with that?"

"Industry trends don't often sway my strategy, but I do pay attention to stay informed about the market and my competition. Secondly, I find that investment managers are pretty good researchers. When I have an investment in mind, I will likely ask that you do some homework. Finally, I ask that you watch my investments' performance trends. Typically, my structure involves a percentage of the revenues from the investment. I help grow each one individually, but I need to monitor how they are growing or not, to know when it's time to remove myself from the arrangement."

Calli was fascinated, hanging on every word and taking notes on her computer. Surprisingly, the meeting proceeded easily and concluded as their most productive one in the last two weeks. Without the distraction of Pauline, Calli was able to focus on what her client wanted from his investments and to begin to see where she would fit into his financial world. He provided a few potential investments for her to research, and she shared the performance of his current portfolio.

When the business concluded, Calli closed her computer. "This has been great information. Thank you for the coffee." She stood, stowed the laptop, then grabbed her coat, throwing it over her arm. It was a short four-block walk through the skyways to her office in Cloud 9. She should be there before lunch.

Dom stood, too, and when she turned for the door, she found herself staring directly at the Nike swoosh in the center of his sweatshirt. He took the coat from her arm and draped it back over the stool, took the bag from her shoulder and placed it on the bar, never moving from where he blocked her way. Her breathing hitched as she raised her eyes to his face. Green warred with gray in his eyes as he searched her face. His lips parted slightly and spearmint filled the air. Oh

God, what the hell was she doing just standing there, letting this begin?

"Calli," he said softly, then ran a hand up her arm and under her hair at her neck. "I'd like you to stay with me today."

She shook her head and swallowed. "I have work. Other clients I need to follow up on."

"It's one day."

She stuttered, searching for an excuse.

Apparently seeing that she wasn't just going to give in, he added, "Then until after lunch."

Damn. His breath was hot and sweet, and her mouth watered. "W-what for?" she asked.

His free hand caressed the other side of her neck, he closed the distance between them, and his lips brushed over hers ever so lightly. "To begin with . . . " He kissed her chin and fluttered kisses down her neck.

Calli tilted her head, reaching for his kisses. "Yes?"

She felt his lips smile against her neck. "I'd like to enjoy the way you smell." He inhaled deeply.

She herself was enjoying the crisp and clean scent of him as well. Her hands had found their way onto his defined biceps without her permission, feeling them flex and release. This. This was what she worried about. "Dom. It's the middle of the day."

"So?"

"I . . . uh . . . ," she started, but she forgot what she was about to say as he crushed her lips against his. Her body responded to the call of his. Hands roamed and tangled with urgency. He lifted her onto the stool and settled in between her legs, pushing her skirt up her thighs. Damn clothes, she thought and felt warm there . . . where his clothed body met her panties. Alarmed, she pushed him back, but just a little, searching his eyes. All she found was desire. It had been so long since someone had looked at her that way. She wanted this. She wanted him here. Now. But . . . She looked around nervously.

"No one will be here until after one, but if you want"— he licked his tongue up her neck and whispered in her ear— "we could go upstairs."

Chills ran down her spine. Calli dropped her head back, rolling her neck, then refocused on Dom's stare. "Ah . . . what the hell?" She pulled him back to her and they kissed, long and hard, turning their heads one way, then the other. Between her legs, she felt him grow increasingly harder and reached for his pants. He didn't stop kissing. She didn't stop kissing. It was as if blood would stop flowing if their lips parted for more than a mere second.

Opened, his pants fell from his slender waist over trim hips. No briefs, no boxer briefs, no boxers. He sprang free. She gasped. He grinned. Reaching down, Dom pulled on the drenched panties between her legs and pushed them to one side. She felt him at her threshold, throbbing.

"Wait." Calli put a hand on his chest. She could barely find air. Halting this was akin to breaking gravity's pull. She breathed, "Condom?"

He moaned. "Shit. Yeah. Good call." He pulled his jeans up and disappeared into the reception area. Footfalls echoed on stairs.

Calli breathed hard, trying to level herself. Then she

remembered the expensive Victoria Secret underwear, stood and slipped out of the lace, then tucked them into her bag. It felt scandalous to sit here in an empty restaurant, wearing nothing under her skirt and anticipating Dom sinking into her right here at the bar, where people would gather for drinks in a few short hours. Damn, that made her want it all the more.

He returned, holding up a silver package, and sauntered back over to the bar. Ripping it open, he laid it on the bar, and resumed his place. "Look at it this way . . . you get to undress me again." A sly smile danced across his lips before they took up the dance with hers once again.

Calli reached for his jeans, unbuttoning and unzipping them until they fell to the floor and he sprang free again. She took him into her hand and stroked the shaft, long and slow, causing him to groan. He rolled his neck, then reached for the open package and slid the condom into place.

Reaching under the front of her skirt and finding her bare, he slipped a finger between her very wet folds and grinned. "This is much better."

Now Calli groaned under the friction of his finger against her clit. But it wasn't there for long, soon replaced with the tip of his cock. Calli mewled and slid forward slightly on the stool to gain more access as he entered her slowly, his mouth forming an O and eyes rolling back in his head. Calli breathed deeply, exhaled as they both adjusted. He held there in place for what seemed like an eternity, then reached down and squared the stool legs, wrapped one arm around Calli's back under her arms, and braced his other against the bar.

He slid out and back in, painfully slowly, then repeated the motion, watching her intently.

Calli's breath hitched. "Oh, yesss . . . "

He stopped at full hilt and kissed her again, their tongues stroking one another, plunging and retreating . . . a precursor to their bodies taking over. But before he moved, he pulled away to look at her. "I'm so happy you gave me a second chance to do this properly."

Calli whined. He pulled out and pushed forward again, excruciatingly slowly, but even without urgent friction, her body started to bear down and she felt her orgasm building. "This is . . . " Out again. "So . . . " In again, long and leisurely. "A-a-amazing . . . "

Dom bit his lip, smiled, then said, "You're so ready. I can feel your body responding to mine. You feel so wonderful wrapped around me like this."

He retreated and returned, hard this time.

Calli squealed, then laughed.

"I love the feeling of you laughing with me inside."

"Oh God, I'm going to come," she said desperately.

"Faster?" he asked.

"Yes, oh yes."

As he took up a steady rhythm, Calli felt the chair tilt backward on two legs, felt him holding her weight, balancing the stool, holding her, and letting her take all of his strength. She needed this, and as his tempo picked up and his breathing deepened, she lost sight as to whether it was her body's need or her soul's. Calli's whole body seized, and she cried out over and over. In the throes of her own passion, she didn't hear his voice do the same. By the time she came back to herself, he had nearly collapsed onto her with the bar at her back, his head resting on her shoulder. He shuddered in her arms.

She laughed, he laughed, and she held him inside her as he softened.

$\mathcal{D}$OM RELUCTANTLY RELEASED HER AND moved behind the bar to find a bag for disposal. He'd make sure the trash was emptied after she left. That was the hottest, most gratifying experience he'd had in a very, very long time. They'd been doing the courtship thing during these so-called meetings, and he was overjoyed that today's had ended this way, though he was less certain how she felt. He moved back around and stepped back into his pants, socks, and shoes. As she straightened her clothes, she kept glancing up, and when their eyes met, they both smiled. Her body had responded but he still felt he needed to win over her mind.

"Well," said Calli. "That was a first."

"Yes, for me too. A good one." He leaned over and kissed her under her jawline in that one little crease.

She lifted her head in acceptance. "Not how I expected to end a client meeting."

Dom cleared his throat. "It was a better ending than I'd hoped."

"We can't do this every time." Her look was dead serious.

Dom only nodded.

She continued, "If we're going to try this, there must be ground rules."

He crossed his arms over his chest and pursed his lips. Rules were made to be broken but he'd hear her out. After all, he'd been trying to woo her since she'd put up the roadblocks that Monday after their first date. He wasn't going to object if she was actually accepting that they'd try. "Yeah, go ahead."

"We sh—"

"Wait. Let's eat while we talk. I'm starving after that!" Smiling lasciviously, he grabbed her hand. Calli hesitated toward her coat and purse. "Leave it. We'll get it after."

$\mathcal{D}$OM MADE TWO SANDWICHES FROM yesterday's roasted chicken and sourdough bread, garnished them with butterhead lettuce and heirloom tomatoes and spread on some garlic aioli, then handed one to Calli and sank his teeth into the other.

She played with the lettuce hanging out one end. "You know . . . I couldn't make a bologna sandwich if you paid me, much less something this delightful."

After he finished chewing, he said, "I don't know why on earth you'd want to make a bologna sandwich." Dom wrinkled his nose at the idea.

"Funny. I mean I can't cook . . . at all."

"Well, that's not a worry for me, now is it?" He quirked a brow.

She covered her mouth as she chewed, and when finished, she said, "Work hours have to be left out of this trying thing."

Dom swallowed. "Understood, but you'll see me after hours now, right?"

The smile she gave him stole any conscious thoughts he had remaining. "Yeah, I will. But." She held up a finger.

His heart sank, and he waited.

"But we need to start slow."

"I thought I took it pretty slow in there."

Calli backhanded him on the arm but they both giggled. "Again, I meant the trying thing."

Dom shrugged. "I knew what you meant, but funny, right?"

She gave a small laugh—music to his ears. And her brown eyes glowed when she laughed. He had to make her do that more.

She chewed the inside of her lip, twisting her mouth to one side, then said, "Maybe we should try one date a week to start."

"Formal, don't you think?"

She swallowed, her throat working, then turned to him with peaked brows. "Dom, I haven't dated in a very long time. This is new to me, and I'm kind of set in my ways."

"I see. And you believe it's old hat for me?" he asked, dropping his eyes and toying with the little of his sandwich remaining on the plate.

"I didn't say that, but I do have some issues with trust— thanks to a less than thoughtful ex." She smiled weakly.

"All right. I understand. We'll take it slow." He took their empty plates to the sinks and returned, clasping his

232

hands. "So, since this wasn't really a date, when can we have our first week's date?"

CHRISTMAS WAS THREE DAYS AWAY, and Calli stared at the sad little tree in the family's den with no presents underneath; they'd all been opened and already put away. She'd helped Jax and Kent pack for Greece, made sure that they each had their money belts and passports secured, driven them to the airport, and as she hugged them goodbye, told them to have a good time. That part was true enough . . . she wanted her boys to enjoy any experience they could. She'd fought a lump in her throat as Bennett strolled over with his young and yellow-haired Zoe in tow. He'd looked like a predator who'd just conquered his prey. Calli had begged him to please look after Jax and Kent—especially Kent as he was forgetful and aloof at times—and left without saying a word to Zoe.

Now, here, in front of the tree, she sighed and turned to the kitchen. She cleaned the counters and made a cup of tea, then returned to the sectional and sat, alone in the semi-silence of her house. As the heating kicked on, there was a small clicking before the whoosh through the vents. The sound of silence, she thought. Worst holiday ever.

At length, she decided to get up and put away the tree. All it did was remind her that she was alone. In the process, she examined each of the ornaments the children had made over the years, as well as the ones she and Bennett had bought for each of their first fifteen years. As she held the blue glass globe with a one engraved on the bottom, an idea blossomed. She walked to the kitchen, ornament in hand, and pulled out a cutting board. She dug through the tool drawer until she found her little utility hammer . . . a silver head with golden handle that unscrewed to reveal a set of hidden screwdrivers. This time, she didn't loosen the handle. She planned to use the hammer. She placed the ornament square in the center of the cutting board, raised the hammer in slow motion, and dropped it onto the delicate bauble. Glass flew in all directions, and her memories shattered along with the ornament—of her first Christmas with Bennett and the Stocktons during her junior year at Madison, Ben's young, hairless face and gray-free hair, them cuddling on his mother's couch . . . The feeling was amazing. Cathartic! Laughing hysterically, she went to the tree and retrieved ornament number two.

At year five, she shattered the memory of her pregnancy with Jax, when they'd both decided that he should go back for his masters and that they'd move out east. It'd seemed the right thing to do to spend her inheritance on securing their future with an Ivy League degree. Man, how she now regretted that decision and was even more ashamed to admit it to her family. When she arrived at number seven and was about to banish the memories of their first Christmas as a family of four, she stopped and opened a bottle of wine.

That had been one of their toughest years between her postpartum depression, her body's unwillingness to recover from the pregnancy, and the resulting hysterectomy. During all that, Bennett had graduated with his MBA and her hopes had been high as they moved back to Minnesota with two of the sweetest little boys. Unfortunately, the move and her improving health hadn't improved their marital relationship.

By the time she'd smashed every one of their family ornaments to pieces, she felt a little better. They'd abandoned the tradition at year fifteen. Calli guessed that was the year when they'd really stopped being a couple, but they'd stayed together, strangers in the same household, for the following six years—until that damnable letter had arrived and she'd kicked him out. Bennett moved in with Zoe and started his new life. It may have been partially due to the wine, but a weight was gone. She looked around her kitchen, now littered with glass and ceramic and glitter. The evidence of her broken marriage spread and fractured over the marble peninsula and hardwood floor. She refilled her glass and went to the den to finish dismantling the tree.

*A*FTER THE TREE WAS DOWN and stored away, Calli did clean up the kitchen mess, then curled up on the couch and draped a quilt over her legs. She flipped on the television and scanned through the channels. Finding nothing worth watching, she went to the office to pick out a book. She had a book addiction—so many she'd purchased over the years but hadn't read. She scanned the spines on the shelves, looking for something not depressing: no broken women, no romance, nothing about relationships. The choice was tough, since most authors' work that she tended to love centered around relationships and the human experience.

At length, she selected a hardcover and left the dust jacket in the empty space. Grabbing a glass of water from the kitchen, she went back to the den, curled up under her quilt, opened to the first page, and read Lord of the Flies, by William Golding.

ON CHRISTMAS MORNING, CALLI HADN'T gotten out of bed yet when her mobile rang. The caller ID said Bennett. She thought about rolling over and ignoring it, but her boys were with him.

"Hello," she answered.

"Merry Christmas, Mom!" Jax said. "We've been waiting all day to call you."

Calli popped upright in her bed; her heart soared. She was so happy to hear from them. After Lord of the Flies, she'd read two more books in the prior two days, trying to keep her mind off not having Jax and Kent with her. Her eyes prickled as she relished how they'd been considerate enough to call just as she had woken. "How's Santorini?"

"It's good. I guess you could say we're having a white Christmas, but it's really not the same as being at Papa and Mama Lindley's. What about you?"

"It's quiet around here. I've been catching up on my reading." She put away the second urban fantasy book in Cassandra Clare's Mortal Instruments series, City of Ashes, and pulled the third, City of Glass. Those were her plans for today too. "Tell me about your trip."

Jax talked about how long the flights were and how they had been so exhausted with the time difference but didn't go to sleep immediately to stave off the jet lag. He gushed over the Greek food, then asked what she'd like them to bring back for her.

"I don't need anything, Jax. Just you to come home to me safely."

"How about some olive oil. It's totally different here."

"I'm sure it is." She thought for a minute, not knowing what to do with it. Then she considered Dom. Maybe, just maybe, they'd last long enough for her to bring him home and introduce him. It wasn't something she'd considered yet . . . hell, she hadn't even told him she had kids. Returning to the conversation, she said, "That'd be great. Is your brother around?"

"Yeah. He's here. Love you, Mom, and see you after the New Year."

"Love you too. Can't wait."

Kent's deeper voice came over the line. "Hi, Mom."

Calli fought the urge to laugh at his clipped tone. He often brooded and used as few words as possible. "Merry Christmas, kiddo."

"Merry Christmas."

"Are you having a good time?"

"Yeah."

"How was the trip?"

"Long. Tiring."

"What have you done since you got there?"

Kent sighed.

Calli smiled—so typical.

"Akrotiri was cool. Lots of hiking."

"Oh, that's the Bronze Age city buried by the volcanic eruption, right?"

"Yeah. They say it may be the real Atlantis."

Calli chuckled at that. Of course, that's what Kent would equate it to—myth, legend, something fantastic like the superhero movies he loved so much. "How are the beaches?"

"They're not white and sandy. The sand is dark brown and rocky, but the water's super bright and clear."

"All right, well, have a wonderful time and take lots of pictures of you and your brother for me. I wish I could be there with you."

"Yeah, it doesn't feel much like Christmas."

"I'll see you soon."

"Later, Mom."

"Love you, Kent."

"Love you too."

She ended the call and cried.

MUCH LATER, AFTER CRYING HERSELF back to sleep, Calli was pulled once again from a half-sleeping state. She didn't check the caller this time, just swiped right. "Yeah?"

"Merry Christmas, darling," her mother said tentatively. "What are you doing today?"

"Hi, Mother. Merry Christmas to you too." Calli pinched her eyes shut, then opened them wide, searching for the clock. Twelve-thirty. Damn, she'd slept the day away. "You know, a little of this and a little of that. Just trying to keep busy with the boys away."

"I really wish you would have come down to Lindleyi Manor."

Calli rolled her eyes at the name dropping. It was rarely just home to her mom but always carried some prestige in her mind that compelled her need to refer to it formally. Calli could have gone home, but she simply wasn't up for watching Cat's happy family or Jon and Meg so happily doting over the pregnancy. "I know, but I have to work, and it's just not the same without Jax and Kent."

"I understand that. When you kids left, your father and I walked around the house, looking at each other and feeling simply lost. I'm sure that's how you feel now."

"Yeah, sure." No, Mom. Not really. You did your job and you had eighteen good uninterrupted years with each of us. But Calli didn't voice her thoughts. "What's Dad up to today?" she asked instead.

"He's down at the greenhouse. You know him . . . simply obsessed. Though I can't complain. He keeps my home decorated and smelling orchid-sweet."

"I knew Cat and Trey and Jon and Meg were coming, but did Alder make it home?" Calli rubbed her swollen eyes. Crying herself to sleep hadn't been a good idea. She hated the feeling the next day.

"Alder's here, and Jon was this morning. He and Meg had to get back to the Cities to do her family Christmas. I guess her family's superexcited that she's pregnant. It'll be their first grandbaby. I remember when Cat had little Liam; it was one of the best days of our lives. I thought becoming a parent was wonderful, but it just doesn't compare to being a grandparent."

Calli marveled over how her mother made everything about herself. She knew how selfish she was being by simply wanting to curl back up in her bed, but she should get up. She tossed back the covers as her mother went on about one thing or another. She looked at the screen and muted it to use the restroom. When she was done, she unmuted and interrupted. "Mom . . . M-Mom. I have a couple of things I need to get done this afternoon. Can I call you back?"

"Oh, that's not necessary. I just wanted to let you know that your dad and I are planning to come to the Cities the third weekend in January. He has another speaking engagement, so we're making a vacation out of it. I'd love to have dinner with you and the boys on Saturday night while we're there."

"Okay. That sounds great, Mom. I love you. Give Dad a kiss for me and tell him Merry Christmas."

"I love you, too, darling. Let us know if you or the boys need anything. We're only a couple of hours away, and I worry about you without Bennett."

Calli rolled her eyes and ran a hand through her hair. "I know, Mom. I appreciate it, but I'm adjusting okay. I'll talk to you soon." She pressed the red button before her mother could say more. Then she flipped to her calendar. Damn, she was supposed to go to the Orpheum that night with Dom.

Well, she'd have to deal with that later. Maybe they could do dinner on Friday instead of Saturday.

She dropped her phone on the counter in her bathroom and threw on some sweats and ran a brush through her hair before going downstairs. She glanced at the phone one more time and left it on the counter. In the kitchen, she popped in a K-Cup and waited for the coffee. Though it wasn't morning, it still was to her.

Coffee in hand, she went back to the cozy couch in her den. The third of the Mortal Instruments series waited on the table. She sat down and opened City of Glass.

"Let's see what Clary and Jace are up to today," she said to the empty room.

Twenty-Eight

$\mathcal{D}$OM CLIMBED THE STEPS AT Calli's house, excited for their day together. He'd spent Christmas yesterday with Joe, Betsy, and their tiny baby boy, Daniel. The baby was good, his cry didn't pierce, and his best friend told him that he'd only ever woken once per night. Dom held Daniel once, but only for what he felt was long enough to look sufficiently interested. He would never admit it to his best friend, but he'd kept thinking that Daniel both looked and sounded like a little old man. One thing Dom had known all his life, or at least since his parents had passed and he'd ended up in a group home with abandoned children of all ages squealing, screaming, and crying through every hour of the day, kids were not for him.

But that was yesterday, and while he enjoyed Joe's company, the warm home, and a nice after-dinner scotch and cigar—a treat Betsy only allowed once a year—today was what he'd been looking forward to. Today was his Christmas celebration. He tucked the small wrapped box into his inside coat pocket and raised his hand to knock, but the door swung inward before his knuckles connected.

Radiant, Calli stood in the open door wearing a white trench coat with a matching hat and mittens, and her dark-brown curls flowing over her shoulders. He slicked back a strand of hair that had fallen into his eyes, then welcomed her as she stepped into his arms. Over the last several weeks, he'd felt them growing more comfortable together, and the wordless hug was proof that she felt the same.

Not stepping out of his arms, she turned her head and looked up at him with her big, deep browns—eyes he could lose himself in for hours if it weren't for the pull of her lips. He leaned in and kissed her softly. "Merry Christmas."

"Buon Natale," answered Calli.

Dom raised a brow. "Joyeux Nöel."

"Feliz Navidad."

"Fröhliche Weihnachten."

Calli chewed the inside of her lip and looked around, searching with her eyes. A light went on. "Felicem natalem Christi."

Dom dropped back his head and laughed. Coming back face-to-face, he asked, "Latin?"

"What can I say, four years in high school and two in college. Oh, I have one more. Feliz Natal."

"Ah, yes. Portuguese. I only know two more, so you almost had me. God jul?" He phrased as a question to see if she could guess.

She pressed her lips together and shook her head.

"Norwegian. Come on, living in Minnesota, you never learned that one?"

"Nope, sorry."

"And . . . Glædelig Jul, Danish."

"I guess you win."

"But you have the romance languages, hands down. Speaking of . . . " He brushed her hair away from her neck, inhaled her floral-vanilla scent, and kissed under her ear.

"Dom." She tucked her head to the side, pushing his lips farther from that beautiful line. "Don't we have an appointment?"

Damn, she was right. They were scheduled for a sleigh ride before lunch. Maybe he should have planned for them to be somewhere private for the first part of the day . . . and the last part . . . hell, all day would have been good.

Apparently reading his intent, she said, "We're not going to make it if you keep that up."

"But that'll be cold. I'm sure it's warm inside." He jutted toward the door.

Calli rolled her eyes, shook her head, and released the embrace. "Let's go. We can have some winter fun first."

"First," he repeated. "I'll take that as a promise."

HOW IS THIS POSSIBLE? CALLI asked herself. I've been slogging through the days, reading nonstop, haven't really seen daylight except for what squeezed around the blinds, and didn't want to talk to anyone. She trailed behind Dom toward the idling SUV, his winter car, exhaust billowing from the tailpipe. *Now, he shows up and I'm schoolgirl giddy?* She watched him walk carefully to prevent slipping, still a graceful saunter. Calli couldn't figure out what this amazing man really saw in her. Obviously, it wasn't the past-her-prime woman, pathetic divorcée, and single mother of two that she saw in herself. She'd keep that to herself just a little longer too. She was beginning to feel like her old self when she was with this man, like the Calli who went away to college, knowing who she wanted to be and where she wanted to go, the pre-Bennett Calli. She hadn't realized how much she had missed that Calli.

Inside the toasty car, the seat warmers cocooned her in more heat. The clouds cleared and the sun sparkled on fresh snow. Today was the epitome of the beauty that winter in Minnesota held. Their plans for the day would take full advantage of the unspoiled snow that had blanketed the ground overnight. Not more than three sets of tire tracks marred her street, and it wasn't until they reached the highway that Dom could pick up any speed, then only to about forty. The normal ten- to fifteen-minute ride downtown took a half an hour, but Calli didn't complain. She was happy just being there, beside Dom. When he wasn't shifting, he'd drop his hand onto her knee or thigh and give a small satisfied smile. Maybe it was odd that they didn't speak about how they were both alone over the holidays, but Calli wanted to steer clear of anything that involved her ex-husband or that she had children nearing college age. She wondered briefly if he had reasons similar to her own but quickly dismissed that notion given that she'd seen his home and there had been no evidence of children of any age. Not wanting to spoil their companionable silence, she took a deep, cleansing breath and put such thoughts out of her mind, actively deciding to live in the moment.

Dom pulled off the highway and navigated the city streets to a garage near the river. They walked through the River Center to the cobblestone street that ran along the Mississippi on the Minneapolis side. Outside, a coach drawn by two Clydesdales was waiting. Calli looked up at Dom, surprised that it wasn't the standard white horses that littered the streets of downtown during the holiday season. The coach was a lacquered black sleigh with white furs piled on the benches.

"Where did you find this?" Calli asked, hugging closer to Dom's arm.

"I'll never give away my secrets. Come on."

The driver held open the door with a white-gloved hand. Dom helped Calli inside, then settled beside her and pulled the furs over them both.

"Mr. Moretti," the driver started, "there is an open bottle of champagne here, nicely chilled by Mother Nature." He gave a wide smile as he uncovered the bin on the side. "And glasses are there. I'm Chris. Call my name if you need anything at all." He closed the door.

The carriage lurched forward, jarring them both before smoothing out. They both laughed and readjusted in their seats. Dom angled his body, reached over, and pulled Calli's legs across his lap, then wrapped both arms around her waist. Curling into his embrace, she removed her mitten and slid one hand into his coat and under his shirt, craving the skin-to-skin contact. He braced himself but then relaxed.

Calli giggled. "It's not cold. I have hand warmers in my gloves." She hesitated, then added quietly, "I just wanted to be closer."

His arms flexed in response, hugging her tighter. In this carriage, beside the river, on a cold sleepy morning, warm under the covers and in the circle of Dom's arms, Calli felt at peace for the first time in more than twenty years.

"It's amazing how warm it is under the furs," she said by way of making small talk.

Dom blew out his breath, making fog in the air, and eyed her sideways.

"Well, I guess my nose is a little cold." She nuzzled it into his neck.

"Calli, tell me something about you that I don't know," he said.

Don't tense—don't tense—don't tense. Again, the topics she wanted to avoid popped into her mind. "Let me think," she said instead. Family was the obvious choice. "I grew up in the orchid business."

"Huh?" Dom's brow wrinkled.

"My father's grandfatherdiscovered an orchid called the Dendrobium lindleyi. His name was Charles Lindley."

"So, you're named after a flower?"

"Technically, the flower is named after my family if you're referring to Lindley. But I, along with my sister, am named after an orchid as well. Callista Linnea and Cattleya Linnea."

"You have a sister? And you have the same middle name? That's odd."

She made a small, affirmative noise.

"I'm jealous."

"A twin sister. Linnea means twin flower. My mother, though she married into the Lindley family, is a Southern belle and very obsessed."

"Really?" Dom pulled back to look at her face. "I can't imagine two of you in this world."

"There were many times growing up that I couldn't imagine it either. We were very close, and that has ups and downs. Sometimes, I think we're too much alike, except that she can be really direct. It's been hurtful in the past, but I've grown to accept it, even appreciate it at times . . . There was one time right after high school when we didn't talk for over a year, but we're better now." She gave him a tentative look. "Okay, your turn. What don't I know about the famous Dominic Moretti?"

"Hmm, that's a tough one. Most of my life revolves around the restaurant and my business. You know most of that. You also know Joe—he's really the only person I'd call a true friend in the world."

"Come on . . . there has to be something."

"I guess I come from a totally different background than you. I was an only child, and I often felt like I was a mistake in my parents' eyes." Dom rolled his lips between his teeth, biting, and looked down, then back. His eyes were glassy and bleak. "If I wanted to eat, I had to learn to cook early. I guess that's what started it all." He inhaled and pushed the air out, creating a cloud, then took her hand under the fur blanket. "They died in a car crash when I was only twelve. The police reports that I read many years later said they were both high at the time."

Calli's eyes burned and flooded. She gasped. "Oh, Dom, I'm so sorry."

"No, don't be." He hugged her and laughed without mirth, then said, "I've never really talked to anyone about it. Joe may know, but I have never really discussed it with even him, and I've known him since he first started his practice. God, that's been over twenty years."

They rode along in silence for several minutes. Calli looked out through the powder-dusted trees over the white-blanketed river and sank against Dom. After his story, she felt guilty over her cozy upbringing and family legacy. Guilty and a little reminiscent. She'd chosen to leave the legacy, as had her sister and brothers. Certainly, her father would allow her back in if she asked, but since she hadn't studied botany as he had wanted, it would be an uphill journey. She no longer felt qualified to pick up his research and didn't know how much she'd have to learn at this point.

"Well, my gorgeous orchid." Dom moved his shoulder and turned Calli to face him. "We're almost done, but I want to give you a Christmas present before this ride is finished." He reached into his coat pocket and pulled out a small black-velvet box.

Calli's hands flew from under the covers to her mouth, attempting to hide her shock. Her ungloved hand grew cold while the left remained warm inside the heated mitten. This wasn't happening. They barely knew each other. True, they had fabulous sex and a magnetism that was undeniable, but she hadn't even told him about Jax and Kent. There was absolutely no way she could say yes to a proposal. Oh-shit-oh-shit-oh-shit . . .

Dom looked deep into her eyes. They must have shown nothing but pure terror. Marriage had been the farthest thought from her mind. Hell, they hadn't even exchanged I love yous yet. Calli started shaking her head.

Dom's beautiful green eyes turned into a mask of confusion, his brows pinching, then he dropped his head back, laughing as realization apparently dawned. When he brought his gaze back to hers, he said, "Calli, no, it's not what you think."

"Really? Because it sure looks like a ring box."

Dom leaned in and kissed her ear. "Trust me, just a little," he whispered, warm, moist, and minty.

She nodded tightly.

He opened the box. Not one, but two diamonds sparkled back at her, picking up the light like the icicles hanging from the buildings they passed. Calli sighed her relief. "Earrings. I feel foolish."

Dom smiled. "You shouldn't. I didn't consider how the box would appear. Can we put these in?"

Calli smiled and removed the little silver studs already in her ears. "Yes." Then she laughed loudly into the sky, letting the hilarity fog the air.

He looked at her, again with confusion.

She answered his unspoken question, "I just find it funny that you opened a little black box, and my answer to your question is yes . . . after I nearly wet my pants with fear at the prospect of marriage." She wiped a tear from her eyes, coming off the high of laughter. Then she worried that she'd offended him and rushed to add, "I'm sorry, I, uh, it's not that, well—"

Dom smiled, leaned over, and kissed her with the sweetest kiss she could remember. "I'm not upset by your response." He brushed a brown curl away from her chin and over her shoulder to reveal her earlobe beneath the hat and held up the earrings.

She put them in and asked, "How do they look?"

"As beautiful as the orchid before me." Again, he kissed her, this time long and slow as the carriage came to a stop. Then he buried his head in her neck and breathed, "If you haven't figured out how much I love the curve of your neck yet, I'll be sure to show you later today. The earrings are more perfect on you than they could be anywhere else." He pulled back and placed his forehead against hers.

Vaguely, she realized the carriage had stopped and recognized the high squeal of the door to the carriage opening, but she didn't look away. She was melting here in this man's arms, falling.

"Callista, I've never before considered being with someone long-term. I am also not ready for marriage, but if there were anyone on earth who could change that, it would be you."

Twenty-Nine

AFTER THE CARRIAGE RIDE, THEY'D had lunch in a restaurant along the river—nothing fancy but a decent burger and beer. Dom had a light supper planned for the evening, so the hearty lunch was good and had prepared them for the afternoon ice skating. Even though they'd had an early onset of snow and ice, most of the true winter activities like the ice castles in Stillwater or St. Paul Winter Carnival didn't start until February, so the indoor ice rink was the best he could do.

Neither he nor Calli were skaters, something that became quite clear as each had stumbled into the other, then they'd both ended up with cold backsides. The entire episode had only taken about fifteen minutes before they had decided to pack it in and head over to the coffee shop down the road for something warm to drink.

"Snowshoeing next time." Dom laughed as he sipped the peppermint hot chocolate.

"You were quite a sight out there." Calli laughed too.

"I'm just thankful I avoided that little old couple."

"They were so adorable. You could just tell that they'd been doing that for years and years. I hope I'm in that good of shape when I'm eighty or so. Trisha's classes are helping with that endeavor." When she tipped her cocoa, she left a tiny dab of cream on her nose.

Dom captured her hands before she could wipe it off and kissed it away. The day had been nothing but companionship and sinking deeper and deeper into each other. A relationship, he thought, speculatively. Not something he'd ever believed he'd have. He'd never connected with anyone on this level, so this brown-eyed, brown-haired, five-foot-nothin' woman had taken him completely off guard.

Her smiling eyes met his over the rim of her cup. "What?" she asked.

Dom shrugged.

"Okay, what do you have planned for the remainder of today?"

"Light dinner at my place." He tapped his fingers on the side of his mug, watching for her reaction. "Then we can see where it goes from there."

She pulled her hair over one shoulder, exposing her exquisite neckline. Pressing forward onto her elbows, she came to about an inch from his nose, licked her lips, and lowered her voice. "Is there really any question about where it'll go if we're back at your place?"

"I'd hate to be presumptuous." He put on his best innocent look, no matter that he'd been anticipating having her back in his bed all day long . . . longer, truthfully. Probably since the last time they'd been together at the bar in his restaurant. Every time he'd walked by that spot or glanced over, he'd felt the corners of his mouth pulling into a knowing little smile.

$\mathcal{D}$OM STEPPED INTO HIS KITCHEN—HIS home—and opened a bottle of cabernet sauvignon and filled the bottom of a decanter. Calli took a seat in one of the two chairs at the island, and he set the decanter and two empty glasses near her. "We'll let that breathe for a few minutes while I get things ready."

From the refrigerator, he removed a tray of fruits, assorted bread cubes, and skewered cold cuts and slid the plate to the center of the granite-topped island. He placed a pan over the gas stovetop, dropped in the cheese, and poured in the crisp white wine, stirring until it formed just the right consistency. After lighting a can of jellied alcohol in the center of his island next to the platter, he placed the fondue bowl on top and poured in the cheese mixture.

He dropped the pan into the sink, went to the empty chair beside Calli, and poured their wine. Holding up his glass, he said, "To our first kind of Christmas."

"It's been the best day of my Christmas week." She clinked her glass to his.

"That, I'm happy to hear."

"Well, you're a little nicer than Jace Wayland . . . although, he's somewhat sexy in a smart-ass kind of way."

"Who?" Dom asked, shocked.

Calli laughed. "I read a series over the last three days. He's a character . . . in both the literal and figurative way."

"So, you think I'm a smart-ass? I guess that's a win." Dom said.

"Only a little." Calli took a bite of cheese fondue–covered bread, chewed, and chased it down with a sip of the cab. When she finished, she added, "But a hell of a lot sexier."

Dom turned her so her legs were between his, stabbed two grapes, dipped them in the cheese, and held them up between them. As the cheese ran down, Dom licked the drip from his side and Calli did the same from hers, their tongues meeting around the barrier. They each took one of the grapes in their mouths and chewed. A spark leapt between them as their eyes locked. Dom tossed the toothpick on the counter, grabbed her stool, and slid it along with Calli closer. Their lips met with fiery passion, devouring each other. Dom groaned. She tasted like his cheese fondue and wine, but he was no longer hungry for the food.

Calli kissed her way down his neck; he purred under the feel of her lips.

"The food will still be here later," he said on a gasp.

"Mmhmm," she answered.

At the sound, he growled and swept her from the stool. She wrapped her legs around his waist, and he carried her to his bedroom. Still kissing, tongues warring, Calli plunged her hands into Dom's hair. Dom held her with one hand around the waist and the other at the back of her neck.

As they arrived bedside, kissing slowed. Dom turned and sat on the bed with her still wrapped around him. Calli raised her hands to his face, fingers cold even through his trimmed beard. She searched his eyes and kissed him gently, then rubbed her thumb along each brow. As she finished tracing his nose with a finger, Dom caught it in his mouth and sucked, milking it with his tongue as he wished to do to other parts of her body. Her eyes widened.

"Hey," she said tentatively. Her hands fell between them and her eyes followed.

"Something wrong?"

"I didn't get you a Christmas gift," she said. In the dark, her worried frown was tinted in a bluish gray. Appropriate for how her words felt, Dom thought.

He lifted her chin to capture her warm brown eyes. "Calli, I'm not—"

She placed a finger over his lips. "Instead, I'd like to know if I can treat you to our next date?"

Dom smiled, still unsure why this seemed troublesome for her. "Sure. Next Saturday's all yours," he said jovially.

"On Tuesday . . . will you go out with me on Tuesday?" she asked with raised brows.

"Of course. I don't leave until Wednesday morning. We can absolutely move it up." He kissed her jawline. "Then I don't have to wait until after my trip next week. Though that just delays the week and a half gap between dates." Dom pouted.

Calli shook her head. "I want to go out with you on both Tuesday and Saturday."

Dom stopped breathing, eyes wide. "You mean . . . "

She grinned and nodded. "Yeah, I think it'd be okay to see each other a little more."

"Of course." He kissed her. "Yes. Of course."

She put a hand on his chest. "Let's try twice a week for now, then see how things are going after another few weeks."

He was high on this news—best Christmas present she could have given him. The earrings seemed cheap compared to her acceptance of him and their blooming relationship. As he kissed her long and hard, holding her head and willing his joy into her, he thought how odd that he'd be in such a state over being able to see the same woman more regularly. Then all rational thoughts evaporated as swelling need consumed him. His hands roamed from her tiny waist down around her curvy hips, then up over breasts and shoulders. Through the clothes, he felt every part of her that he longed to explore without that barrier.

Still engrossed in their kiss, he unzipped her vest and stretched it wide one way, then the other, while she freed her arms. She reached for the hem of his fleece hoodie, gripping the material. They broke apart while she pulled it over his head, leaving him in a thin T-shirt. He pushed hair out of his eyes as he leaned toward her. Forehead to forehead, they both paused to catch their breath, giggling slightly at their fervor.

Calli tugged her shirt over her head, her brown curls cascading over her bare shoulders. Dom lifted the thick curtain of hair and found the clasp to her bra, flipping it open with one hand. Her breasts fell free, heavy but not too large. He caressed each one with a hand, lifted one nipple to his mouth, and ran his tongue over it until it perked up in response. Calli watched, and he smiled up at her as he moved to the other, sucking it to attention.

"You, my little orchid, are stunning."

She reached down and tugged at his T-shirt, the only

remaining barrier between their chests. Dom answered the unspoken demand and ripped it from his torso, then he moved both hands to the waistline of her jeans. Calli stopped his working hands, placed both of hers on his chest, and pushed him back onto the bed.

Pleasantly surprised that she was taking the lead, he smiled broadly and watched as she went onto all fours, her breasts temptingly close between them. She kissed his mouth first, then ran one hand down his chest, following it with her delicate little flower kisses, stopping at each of his nipples to give him the same attention he had given her. Then she smiled up at him and crawled backward off the bed. Standing, she went to work removing his belt, then jeans, then boxers. He twisted to help in her efforts and was soon naked. While lying flat on his back, he was also standing at full attention, uncontrollably throbbing.

"Slide back," she said, her voice husky, "so that you're fully on the bed."

He did as she bid, grabbing a pillow for his head along the way. He'd been in control of the scene each time they'd played before. This was turning out to be an intense reversal of roles, and he was melting under her ministrations.

Calli smiled and worked the button on her jeans. She turned so her back was facing him and swept her hair over one shoulder, showing the line of her neck on the other side. Light glinted from the diamond he'd placed in her earlobe. Dom groaned.

She ran her hands down either side, watching Dom over her bare shoulder. Then she stopped, slid her fingers beneath the waistband, and swayed her hips side to side as she wiggled from the denim, revealing three little lines of fabric extending from a lacy triangle.

Dom's cock throbbed. He wanted to sink his teeth into one of those perfectly round cheeks. "Keep that up, and at this rate, you're not even going to have to touch me."

"Oh, but I want to touch you." She turned back to him, not removing the small swath of lace that covered the prize. "Then I'd like you to unwrap your other present for the evening."

He moaned and reached for her.

She stepped back, wagging a finger and giving him a warning look. "But not just yet. Lay back down . . . hands away."

With a long sigh, he did as she instructed, placing his hands on the pillow behind his head, watching.

She climbed over him, running her hands up his legs until she reached his cock. Then she put one knee between his legs, spreading them so she could rest back onto her heels between his legs—the prettiest little sphinx he could imagine. Continuing up his inner thighs with her hands— now warm—she took him into both her hands and leaned forward.

Be gentle, he thought. Or don't. He couldn't decide. Damn, I hope I can tend to her after this. He balled his fists under his head and tried for self-control as she lowered her pink lips to the head of his cock. Looking up and maintaining eye contact, she extended her tongue and ran it up the backside, then took the head into her mouth. That one spot on the back rested on her tongue as she held him in her mouth and stroked the shaft. As her hand stroked, she began slowly working her tongue. Dom's entire body tensed. Don't let it go, he coached himself. Oh. My. God. He gritted his teeth, first hissing through them, then calling, "Calli."

She released him and smiled wickedly. "Yeeesss?"

"You're going to end this before it begins."

She licked again. "You taste wonderful. And we have all night for you to recover." She wrapped her lips around his cock again and pushed him to the back of her throat before pulling out, then releasing him. Again, with the wicked smile, she said, "We can have dinner while you recover."

And again, he was buried inside her mouth, warm, wet, suckling erotically. He closed his eyes and gave up the fight. Behind his closed lids, he saw her hot brown eyes watching him as she attended to his every need. He held that vision as her hand worked the shaft up and down and her beautiful flower of a mouth accepted him deep, drawing him toward explosion. She massaged his sack, and his urgency grew, his hips joining the party. Her tempo increased. His breathing grew quick and shallow in contrast to how deeply he sank into her throat. Then every muscle in his body locked up tighter than ever. Jerking, he spilled into her, crying out again and again as she maintained steady suction until he was spent dry.

As the muscles in his body slowly relaxed into the bed, she crawled up toward him and draped her almost naked body over his, resting her cheek on his chest. When he came back to himself, he wrapped his arms around her and kissed her brow. She looked up and smiled like she'd just won a championship game.

"You're amazing," was all he could say as his body tingled in the aftermath. And as he kissed her, he tasted the salt of his own pleasure on her lips.

Thirty

CALLI POURED THREE GLASSES OF white wine and handed one to each of her parents, Richard and Isabelle Lindley. They'd arrived earlier in the day while Calli was finishing out her Friday at work and were now gathered around the peninsula in her kitchen before going to dinner. It was Bennett's weekend with Jax and Kent, so it would only be the three of them that evening. Calli asked, "Did you have anywhere specific you'd like to eat?"

"Oh, darling!" Isabelle exclaimed. "You know that man on the cooking show . . . The Dinner Shark? I hear he has a restaurant here in the Cities, and I hear the food is to die for."

Calli choked on her wine, coughing until she had tears in her eyes, and turned to grab a tissue. Dom would certainly be there tonight, and she was not ready to share him with her parents. It may have been selfish, but she'd been through so much with her ex that she just wanted it to be separate—hers alone. Plus, her mother would surely feel like she was cheating on Bennett, which was an absurd notion given that he'd been cheating on her for so many years before they'd split. But that didn't matter to her mother—a woman who'd never experienced anything but loyalty, yet firmly held to her opinion that you had to work through infidelity issues.

"Belle," Richard chided, "I'm sure we need reservations for such a famous place. Maybe we should just go somewhere more casual." He paused, then asked Calli, "Are you okay, honey?"

"Yeah, just went down the wrong pipe." Calli filled a glass of water and guzzled it as she considered her mom's request. Despite her own desires and that she constantly felt scrutinized by her mom, she still wanted to make her happy. They came to the Cities so infrequently that she felt a need to make it work. "I think I can get us reservations if that's where you really want to go."

"Oh, darling, yes. Could you?" She reached across the counter toward her daughter.

Calli took her hand and smiled. "Let me make a call. I'll be right back." She grabbed her phone, then walked out of the kitchen and to the front window. Scrolling through her favorites, she selected the selfie Dom had taken and set as his contact picture in her phone on the day after Christmas—the day when their relationship had taken a deeper turn. She sighed and hit send.

"Hi, beautiful," he answered on the first ring.

"Hi," she breathed, happy to hear his voice after three days.

"I can't wait for tomorrow night. I can't think of a better Broadway show for a date night."

She couldn't either. She'd seen Beauty and the Beast, West Side Story, Les Misérables, and Wicked all before, and Phantom twice, but she'd never seen the Broadway production of Cinderella. And the fact that she was falling so hard for her Prince Charming only added to the magic and anticipation.

She shook her head. "That's not the reason for my call though."

"Oh. Is everything all right? We're still on for tomorrow, yes?"

"Yes, absolutely!" she said. "I just need to see if I can ask a favor for tonight."

"You name it," he answered enthusiastically.

Calli chewed on a cuticle. "You know my parents are in town."

"Yes."

"Well, my mother has asked to go to dinner at Moretti's."

"Calli," he said a bit regretfully. "You know my tables fill up months in advance. I don't have anything outside the bar for tonight."

"Yeah." Her stomach sank. No matter what she thought of her mother, she still wanted to impress her. "I understand."

"Wait," Dom barked. "Let me make a phone call. I'll phone you right back."

"What? Why?"

"Trust, Calli?" he pleaded.

"Okay," she said and ended the call.

She didn't return to the kitchen but stared out the window, considering his words. Trust, Calli? had become something he'd learned to ask when he sensed her doubting his intentions. He hadn't let her down yet, so every time he asked, she relented. She still hadn't told him about Bennett and the boys, but she would . . . probably after tomorrow. They were getting serious enough that she found herself giving in to that trust. She just hoped that coming clean about the divorce and kids after two months wouldn't drive a wedge between them. If it did, there wasn't much she could do except apologize and hope for his acceptance. And if he didn't accept her sons, she'd be forced to understand and let go. Bennett wasn't important; he was the past. Her ex-baggage could go to hell, but Jax and Kent came first.

Precisely three minutes later, Calli's phone buzzed in her hand. She swiped and said, "Dom?"

"Yes, beautiful. Good news. I have a table for you."

"Really?"

"Yeah, when you arrive, have Anton show you to the chef's table."

"Oh—" Calli's stomach flopped. "I don't think it's a good idea for you to cook for me and my parents yet." She lowered her voice. "My mother can be moody . . . judgmental. I'd really like to save introducing you as my boyfriend."

"I wasn't planning to cook for you unless you're making a personal request."

"Oh, heavens, no. I can't do that to you yet."

"I needed to call my second chef to make sure he was

available. He'll prepare your meal. I'll drop in and say hi, but I'll introduce myself as Nic, like I do to the rest of the patrons. Only you and I will know about us. I promise."

"Smooth faced today?"

"Yes, but I'll rock the stubble for you tomorrow night."

"Mmm," Calli said. "Can't wait. Gotta run. Kisses."

"Is that a promise?"

She grinned. "Yes." Then clicked off the phone. She made one more call before returning to the kitchen. Once there, she said to her mom and dad, "We need to get dressed up. We have a reservation in an hour at Moretti's, and the car will be here in forty-five minutes."

$\mathcal{N}$IC MOORE STUDIED THE EVENING'S schedule and looked up as he felt a hand land on the back of his shoulder.

Moretti's maggiordomo stood close and said, "Mr. Moore, your table is seated and they are enjoying their first course."

"Very well, Anton. Thank you."

Anton turned to attend to the next couple, and Nic finished reviewing the evening before he walked the dining floor one more time. As he went, he smiled and asked one couple how their meal was, asked the next family if he could get them anything, asked how a third's evening had been so far, and so on and so forth until he had made his way to the kitchen doors at the far end. Nic pushed into the hustling and bustling kitchen and noted that his chefs and sous chefs had everything under control—a well-olive-oiled culinary machine. His chest swelled on a sigh as he passed the sinks, the long stainless islands, the roasting hearth, and the bank of refrigerators. Through the door and down the hall he walked to the second, private chef's kitchen and dining room where Calli and her parents dined. Before pushing through that door, he stroked his smooth chin and slicked back hair. Nothing rough or out of place for Nic Moore—unlike his full-time, more famous and more rugged persona, Dominic Moretti.

He cracked the door just enough to see the guests at his chef's table. His radiant, most beautiful orchid, Calli, laughed at some story her father, a lanky man with a hooked nose and salt-and-pepper-colored hair, was telling. He really couldn't believe how hard he'd fallen for the woman. On her other side sat a woman who was an older version of Calli's perfection, hair a gorgeous shade of silver hanging heavy to her shoulders. Many years of smiles and happiness pinched at the skin around her eyes, but her heart-shaped face was every bit the source of Calli's. He wanted to pull up a chair and join them, but he'd give her the space she'd requested and let her do that on her own time. Meanwhile, Nic Moore pushed into the room, smiling professionally. He crossed to tableside, lifted the bottle of wine from the wine bucket, and refilled glasses.

"Good evening, Mr. and Mrs. Lindley, and Miss Lindley," he said as he poured. "I'm the manager this evening at Moretti's, Nic. How are you finding the first bites of your meal?" He turned to Calli and her milk-chocolate eyes sparkled up at him.

"Good evening, Nic," said Mrs. Lindley. "The rosemary

shrimp crostini are delightful."

"Those are one of my favorites as well."

"Please, do call me Isabelle, Nic."

"Yes, ma'am, Isabelle."

She glowed almost as much as her daughter.

Nic turned to the quiet Mr. Lindley. "Is there anything I can get for you, sir?"

"Nic, this is just fabulous. I can't think of anything that your chef here, Marco, hasn't already considered."

Marco approached with a platter—an assortment of thinly sliced melon layered with prosciutto, and for the garnish, mozzarella balls and three varieties of orchid. Nic appraised the tray, then exchanged a look with Calli. She smiled widely, knowingly. A pink blush danced across her cheeks as she lowered her gaze. He'd done well.

Placing a hand on Mr. Lindley's shoulder, Nic said, "Well, do enjoy your meal. You're in good hands with Marco here." He walked over to inspect the private kitchen adjacent to the chef's table. Seeing that it was indeed immaculate, he answered a few of Marco's whispered questions and retreated from the room.

Outside and already to the end of the hall, he'd just placed a hand on the door to the larger kitchen when he heard whispered behind him, "Dom?" Calli rushed to him, grinning.

When they met, she pressed her body into his and leaned up toward his face. He backed her up against the wall and kissed her long and languorously.

"Thank you so much for this," she said.

"This is my pleasure. Especially when the repayment is so delicious." He kissed her again.

"Would you like to have lunch with my parents on Sunday before they return to Lindleyi Manor? As Dom . . . my, um, boyfriend?"

His heart double-timed. "Only if you're sure you're ready," he said, stroking her chin with a thumb as he searched for answers in her eyes.

"I can barely stand being in there, knowing you're out here working." She stepped back, grasping his hands and looking down to where they were joined. "I'm sure if you are."

Dom lifted her chin. "I don't think you have anything to worry about. I'd love to." He kissed her wine-sweetened lips lightly and added, "My beautiful orchid."

Thirty-One

THE CAST OF CINDERELLA SANG the final lines of "There's music in you," the words perfectly fitting Calli's mood and thoughts after the romantic play. Moving mountains and lighting her section of the sky, Dom had made all her wishes come true as well. During the final notes, Calli wiped away a happy tear. The music died down, and the applause erupted in the Orpheum. As the "Cinderella March" started and the cast scurried to center stage to take their bows, the audience came to their feet. Calli and Dom joined in the ovation, smiling at one another as they clapped. Dom put an arm around Calli and kissed her lightly. Romantic indeed—she didn't care if it was a story saying how a woman needed a prince to rescue her. That was simply true sometimes. Princes took all forms, and Dom had become hers.

In the balcony's front row and center, she turned into his arm, wrapping her own arms around his waist and resting her chin on his chest. "Can I say something way girly?"

Dom chuckled. "Of course."

She giggled too. "No, never mind."

"Hey, don't hide." He looked up, then back at her. "Fine, at the risk of losing my guy card, I'll go first . . . That wedding scene was more touching than the romance number in the last third of Tangled."

Calli's jaw dropped, and she barked a laugh. "You watched Tangled? No, wait, you liked Tangled?"

"Of course. Show me someone who doesn't!" They both laughed, then he added, "Okay, your turn."

"All right." She looked up at him with suspicion, then said, "I love the costumes. If I ever . . . Well, the prince in all white next to Ella's flowing and glittering dress . . . Well, it gave me the feels." She shrugged. She'd almost said if she ever married again but decided to leave that one alone.

Dom hugged her. "See, that wasn't so hard." He looked around at the nearly empty auditorium and added, "We should probably go."

"Yeah," she answered. Reaching down to grab her purse, she noticed the light on her phone blinking inside.

Dom started walking toward the aisle as she pulled out the phone and looked at the notifications. Four missed calls, two voice messages.

"Shit," she said and dismissed the lock screen as she moved to the aisle. Nine text messages.

"What's wrong?" Dom asked.

Calli didn't answer, but opened the messaging app. All nine messages were from Jax. She scrolled to the first.

JAX:	MOM, KENT AND I NEED YOU TO PICK US UP.

8:46 P.M.

Calli's brows dropped. They were with their father this weekend. He'd never give up his time. She kept reading.

JAX:	MOM?

JAX:	MOM?!?

8:58 P.M.

Oh no, she thought. Jax never bugs me like that when I don't answer right away.

JAX:	MOM, I JUST CALLED, BUT NO ANSWER. I DON'T WANT TO TELL YOU THIS OVER TEXT. PLEASE CALL.

9:05 P.M.

Oh shit! Her mind raced with the worst possibilities. She kept scrolling.

JAX:	I CALLED AGAIN. KENT AND I REALLY NEED YOU RIGHT NOW.

JAX:	MOM?!?

9:08 P.M.

"Calli, what's up?" she heard Dom ask, but it sounded distant.

JAX: OK. WE'RE AT THE MINNEAPOLIS PD. I DON'T KNOW WHERE YOU ARE, BUT YOU NEED TO COME GET US.

JAX: DAD GOT ARRESTED.

JAX: KENT IS FREAKING OUT! PLEASE HURRY.

9:19 P.M.

Calli looked at the time: 9:36 p.m. She immediately pressed the phone in the corner of the message window and looked up at Dom. This wasn't how she wanted to tell him, but it appeared she had no choice. As the phone rang, she said, "We have to go to the police department. Now."

"Calli? What's happening? Are your parents okay?"

"Yeah . . . " She held up a hand as Jax answered. "Jax, what's going on?"

"Mom," he breathed as if overly relieved. Then he rushed his explanation, "Dad got pulled over. He had a couple of drinks at dinner. They made him do a bunch of things on the side of the road, then cuffed him and loaded him into the back of a car. Detective Harris told me to follow him to the police department in Dad's car, but they won't let me take it. Something about impounding."

"It's okay, honey. I'll be there soon. How's Kent?"

Dom looked at her worried, but wearily, and seemed to be backing away as if she'd slapped him.

"Hang on, Jax." She covered her mobile and asked Dom,

"Can you take me over there, please? I'll explain on the way."

"Yeah." He turned and climbed the stairs toward the doors.

She followed but turned her attention to her son on the phone. "I'm back." They'd dallied long enough that the crowds leaving the Orpheum had thinned. They rushed past the upstairs concession, jogged down the stairs, and speed walked through the lobby to the street. Outside, they stopped at the crosswalk to wait for the light.

"Yeah, Mom, he's gone kinda silent. Just locked up, like he totally forgot how to talk. I think he's freaked out. He wouldn't answer any of the questions Detective Harris was asking. I got a pop from the machine, and he won't touch that either."

That was strange. Kent consumed sodas like they were water. She couldn't keep them in the house if she bought them. Calli squeezed her eyes shut and pinched the bridge of her nose against the immediate headache that had formed behind her eyes. When she opened them again, the light switched to walk. They did. "Okay, okay, I'm on my way." She ended the call.

Dom led the way silently, and Calli nearly had to jog to keep up with his long strides—not that she minded presently. How the fuck could Bennett drink and drive with her boys in the car. How the fuck could he be so careless. How the fuck could he—Mr. Prestige himself—expose them to the Minneapolis PD. Where the fuck was his little trollop, Zoe? Before ducking into Dom's car, Calli yelled her frustration at the garage, and it echoed back to her from the cement walls.

Inside the car, Dom eyed her sideways with his mouth pursed. "Doin' all right there?"

"Yeah . . . I mean, NO!" Her nails dug into her palms.

Dom backed out, not asking more.

At length, Calli sighed out loud, then shifted in her seat to face Dom, tucking the seatbelt under her arm. "I am so very sorry about this," she said.

He listened as he pulled onto Hennepin toward the police department.

"I was almost ready to share all this with you, but it seems I don't have a choice now." She laughed without humor. "Not exactly how you should hear all of this."

"Calli, I'm confused. Just tell me what's going on." His voice was short, like he was exasperated or had simply lost interest. It wasn't the concern he'd first shown when she was reading the texts. What conclusions had he already drawn?

She fidgeted with her hands, and not looking at him, she said, "You know I told you I'd been burned and had trouble trusting?"

"Mmm," he said.

"Well, I was married . . . for a long time."

She saw a piece fall into place for him. "That's why your card said Callista Stockton originally. I guess I should have seen that coming. So why are we going to MPD?"

"Well, my ex-asshole got arrested for drunk driving tonight." Calli chewed her lip.

"Why did he call you?"

"He didn't. My oldest son did. My boys were in the car." Calli watched for his reaction.

Nothing. His face was as blank as a freshly cleaned

whiteboard. "Say something?" she asked weakly.

His Adam's apple worked. "There's nothing to say. Let's just get there so you can take care of your kids." He looked away, out the window.

aFTER DOM DROPPED CALLI OFF at the front door, she ran inside and to the reception desk. "I'm looking for Officer Harris. My ex was arrested. I'm here to get my sons."

"One second," the young uniformed woman said and picked up the phone. "Yeah, Dave. The mom's here." She hung up. "He'll be right up."

As she waited, Calli watched the door for Dom. She moved out of the way as a pair of policemen led a blond boy, couldn't have been much older than Jax, by in cuffs. Blood ran from his soon-to-be black-and-blue nose. Calli shivered.

"Mrs. Stockton?" Officer Harris's voice called.

"No. I mean, I was." She stopped, then said. "I'm Callista Lindley, Bennett Stockton is my ex-husband. Where are my sons? Jackson and Kent?"

"Right this way." He held out an arm.

Calli looked toward the door one more time before heading in to rescue her boys.

Jax ran into her arms, but Kent didn't even look up. Calli examined Jax's face. His eyes were rimmed red, but he was holding it together. "Thank you for being so strong," she whispered and nodded toward Kent who sat in the chair with his knees hugged under his chin. She held Jax's hand as she walked to her other son and took a seat. Wrapping her arm around his broadening shoulders, she said his name softly. He didn't look up but teetered, fell into her arms, and cried.

Calli cried too.

Thirty-Two

THIS SORT OF FAMILY MATTER being none of his business, Dom had sat in his car for a good ten minutes, had considered driving home, but eventually he decided that she didn't need the added stress of having to find a ride home. He pushed open the door to the police department. He'd get Calli and her sons home to safety, serving as their driver this evening. He hated to add to her turmoil, but this was beyond what he believed he could accept. They'd been together for almost two months now. How could she hide such important details about her life?

Shit, Dom! And to think, you thought she was the one . . .

He'd begged time and time again for her trust, yet she hadn't trusted him to know this about her. As he'd always believed, this proved that relationships were too complex, too much to worry over. He wasn't a man meant to be a father— even a stand-in—and no way could he bear being with a woman who was so damaged that she couldn't be real with him. That was the thing he'd sensed with most women—other than Calli, he'd thought—that they were somehow putting up pretenses. Yeah, he'd done that at his restaurant, but weren't they past that as a couple? He'd play chauffeur and see them safely to her ultra-suburban home.

Yeah, Dom! That should have been a clue as well.

Before he left her, he'd have to let her know that things weren't going to work out. Maybe she was right to hold off on having him meet her parents—they weren't the most important people in her life anyway.

How much more is she hiding?

Dom shook his head as he approached the young woman staffing the front desk, her sandy-blonde hair pulled into a low, severe bun that made her blue eyes look too large for her face. They widened even more as she looked up. Then her mouth broke into a grin as her head tilted. "How can I help you?" she asked and leaned onto the desk toward him.

"I'm with Callista Lindley."

"Aahhh, yes." Her shoulders slouched, just slightly but noticeably. "Hey, Curt,"—she flagged over another officer—"can you show this gentleman back to Detective Harris?"

"Thank you," said Dom.

He slowly followed Curt with his hands shoved into his coat pockets and his head down. They made several turns before coming to a bustling office with a handful of cluttered desks. Two more officers huddled around one in the far corner, and Calli sat in a row of chairs between two teen boys, her arm around one. Even from across the room, the tear trails on her cheeks were apparent. Dom inhaled and rubbed his eyes. A sense of guilt gathered in his stomach over the hurt he was about to add.

Be strong here, he told himself. Let her get them home first.

As her beautiful, sad brown eyes met his, he forced a smile.

An older officer, white at the temples and mostly thin save a small donut around his midsection, approached. "May I help you, sir?"

Dom swallowed and motioned toward the mother and her traumatized sons. "Are they ready to go?"

His formal, questioning gaze relaxed. "Oh, yeah. Those boys have had quite an evening. The dad's in lockup, sobering up." He shook his head. "I see far too many of these situations. It'll be good for the family to go somewhere they can feel safe and comfortable." He looked Dom up and down.

"I'll get them home safely. Thank you, Officer."

He handed Dom a card. "My name is Dave Harris. You seem the most put together, and obviously you were with Ms. Lindley. If they need anything, have her give me a call."

Dom accepted the card and walked over to the trio. "Calli, Detective Harris said you can go. Should I get you home?"

Calli looked between her boys. The one with long, multi-colored hair nodded, and Calli urged the other to standing. Dom worried that there was more wrong with him than a little trauma but shoved his hands deeper into his pockets.

You're not welcome with them, remember, Dom? He turned and led the way to the front door, onto the street, and to his car parked in the guest area.

Clicking the button to open the doors, he pulled on the back passenger handle. The older boy got in behind the driver seat, and Calli helped her younger son into his seat. "Kent, can you buckle up," she said gently.

The boy complied, and she stepped back. Dom gave her a tight smile and went to the driver's door. Inside, he pressed the ignition button and turned the radio down as the SUV fired up.

Calli got into the passenger seat. "Dom?"

He held up a hand and pressed his lips together, shaking his head. Dropping into reverse, he checked his mirrors and backed out, then drove toward the suburbs in tense silence.

CALLI LEFT DOM SITTING IN her kitchen and went upstairs with the boys. She tucked Kent into bed, wrapping the blanket tight around him—being tightly wrapped up was a sensation that had always given him comfort. She leaned over and kissed his forehead. "You're going to be okay. We all are." She gave him a small smile.

"Mom, why is Dad being like this? He never acted this way when he lived here."

She dropped her chin, then looked back into her superman's brown eyes, a mirror of her own. "I don't know, kiddo. But it's not your fault."

"I don't want to go back to his new house."

She pinched her eyes shut, fighting a tightness behind her eyes, then reopened them. "Kent, baby." She smoothed his hair away from his eyes. "You don't know how much I want to say you don't have to. Unfortunately, I don't get much choice in that. The divorce agreement says that he has certain rights to see you guys."

"Mom?"

Calli looked up to see Jax in the door. "Yeah, honey?"

"Aren't we old enough to ask the courts ourselves?"

She dropped her head. She'd worked so hard to get four out of seven days in the custody arrangements. Dom's lawyers had been brutal in that battle. She simply wanted things to get to some level of normal now, and she did believe that she really couldn't stand in the way of their relationship with their father. "Come here." She patted the bed. "Sit with us for a minute."

Jax sat on the bed on the other side of Kent.

Calli grabbed his hand so she was in contact with both of her sons and took a deep breath. "Listen, your father and I have had our disagreements. We weren't really partners in our marriage for many years. I'm sure you've been able to see that."

"Why did you stay?" Kent blurted.

She smiled ruefully, squeezing their hands. That was her mistake that she didn't want to share. She'd let the bum relationship go on because it had seemed easier to keep going on. She'd partly stayed because of her mother's emphasis throughout her life on being a "good wife." She didn't want to say that it was for them, though that too was part of the truth. Instead of all this, she focused on him. "Someday, you will want to have a relationship with your father. Family is important." She swallowed, thinking of her own and how she'd walked away from a family business she'd loved as a young girl. In essence, she'd also turned away from her father through her actions. Her eyes watered again. "And he is your family. Families stick together." These words, she said to herself as much as to him. Heaven forbid her children make her mistakes too.

They both stared at her. It was probably her imagination, but she thought their gazes were accusatory. Guilt throbbed in her chest—guilt that she hadn't stuck with Bennett—though the affairs had been his choice and had driven her away. Then there was the guilt that she'd left her parents. "I know I may sound hypocritical, but even mothers make mistakes. Fathers do too. It is a sign of maturity when you're able to accept someone's mistakes and love them anyway."

Jax nodded. Kent sat up and hugged his mom. Calli's heart was so full, she thought her chest might explode.

"Okay, boys. It's been a long night." She thought about Dom waiting for her downstairs and how much explaining she had left to do. Wiping away a stray tear, she added, "Let's get a good night's sleep, and we can talk more about all this stuff tomorrow."

In the hall, after she closed Kent's door, Jax fell into her arms, letting himself go as well.

She squeezed him tight and whispered, "You're such a strong young man. I am so very proud of you. We'll get through this. Together."

He turned, went into his room, and closed the door without turning on the lights or looking back.

$\mathcal{C}$ALLI STEPPED INTO THE BATHROOM and cleaned up under her eyes before heading downstairs to face her next problem of the evening. Hopefully he'd understand. Slowly, she walked down the stairs and turned the corner to where Dom sat at her peninsula, leaning forward on propped elbows, forehead resting on folded hands, eyes closed.

"Hi." Her voice cracked.

When he looked up, she saw goodbye in his amazing but sad sage-colored eyes.

"Can I even explain?"

"Calli." He stood and came to her, grabbed both her hands, and said, "I hate the man I am about to be right now. I hate to do this after all you've been through tonight."

She held her breath, searching his face.

"I'm going to go. You take care of you and yours. Kids, ex, all this . . . It's not a place I can be. I'm sorry."

Tears dripped and she sniffed. "That easy, huh?" So much for trust.

"No," was all he said. He wiped away a tear and leaned down. Dom kissed her gently, leaving mint lingering on her lips, and walked out her front door.

At the foot of her stairs, Calli melted to the floor.

Thirty-Three

$\mathcal{F}$OCUS WAS IMPOSSIBLE. CALLI SAT with her chin propped on one hand and stared in the general direction of her double monitors, the words and numbers blurry. She had told herself that she wasn't ready for a relationship, had tried to take it slow and be certain that it would be worth allowing him inside her world. She had been right to doubt. Why couldn't she have been stronger and resisted that amazing, beautiful man? Her gaze drifted to the folder beside the keyboard: Moretti, Dominic A. She flipped it over, scolding herself again for wondering what the L stood for. He'd taken residence in some corner of her heart and mind and . . . life, and he wouldn't leave.

She heard a rustle behind her and turned as Jordan plopped down in her guest chair.

"Where were you? I texted like a hundred times."

"Good morning to you, too."

"I thought we were past me having to pick you up for the gym." Jordan side-eyed her. "Were you sick yesterday?"

Calli wrung her hands in her lap. "I'm not going back to Trisha's class."

"What? We just paid for the new session. It's only the second week."

She didn't reply.

Jordan pursed her lips, pulled the small table forward, and leaned in. "Dom wasn't there either. Something went wrong."

"You could say that." Calli turned to grab a tissue and wipe away the tears before they fell. She took a deep breath, sighed it out, and said, "Bennett got a DUI Saturday night. Dom and I had to go pick up the boys at MPD after Cinderella."

"He had the boys in the car?" Her eyes widened with shock.

Calli nodded.

"What an ass! How are Jax and Kent?"

"They were pretty torn up over it. I can't understand why he'd put them through something like that. Bright side . . . the shared custody thing is on hold for now. They get to stay with me while he works it all out. They were freaked out at the precinct, but they're not terribly upset over not having to go to his new house."

"Shit. Bet that killed the mood for your hot date. And after a play as romantic as that, I'll bet the night would have been ahh-ma-zing."

Calli chuckled dryly. "Would have been is right. Dom

couldn't deal with me having an ex and kids. Too much drama, I guess." She wiped her eyes again, wishing she could hold the tears at bay. Somehow, she couldn't seem to control them, and her face already felt swollen from the ones that had leaked out over the last couple of days.

Jordan's jaw fell, and her brows peaked. "Oh no, but things were going so well with you two."

Sniffling, Calli said, "Guess I should have told him about Bennett and the boys before."

Her friend nearly fell out of the chair. "Calli? You didn't tell him? How could you not tell him?"

"I was being careful." She shrugged one shoulder. "I was afraid to tell him how weak I was in my marriage, what a failure I was. It's embarrassing."

"That's your mother speaking. Divorce happens these days, and it was him anyway. You didn't ask for that."

"Doesn't really matter now, does it? Anyway, it seems I was right to keep it from him." She reconsidered. "Or maybe I was wrong. Had I told him, maybe he wouldn't have kept asking me out."

"Quit beating yourself up."

"I'm really not."

"You are absolutely too hard on yourself. You've overcome so much. If he can't deal with that, you can find someone better."

Calli pressed her lips into a tight line and nodded. There would be no finding someone. She was going to work hard to find happiness within herself and her boys right now. That's all there was to the matter. Time for a subject change.

"Enough about me. You had a date Saturday too. How was that? And who is this mystery man?"

Jordan stuttered, looked around, and fidgeted. "Er . . . you know. It was all right. Nothing to talk about." She stood and leaned on the cube wall. "I'd better get back. Is there anything I can help you with?"

Calli drew her brows together in confusion. "Nah, I'm all right, or I will be."

Jordan nodded and started to leave.

"Jordan, wait," Calli called. "Do you have an account you can trade for Dom's? I don't think we can work together anymore. Hell, I don't think he'll want to work with me."

"I think so. Let me look through my files." She held out a hand for the one Calli had picked up.

Calli started to hand it over, then hesitated, not wanting to let it go. Again, that place in her life he'd moved into wouldn't let her give it away so easily. "Let me call and tell him that you'll be contacting him."

Jordan gave a small nod and walked away. Calli likely wasn't hiding much from her oldest friend, but what did it matter? She was torn apart again after the events of the last few days. Being a little scattered wasn't that bad. She picked up the phone to dial Dom's personal number.

After three rings, the line clicked and a very feminine voice said, "Good morning, Dominic Moretti's phone, this is Pauline."

Everything stopped—breathing, blinking, her heart, her ability to speak. Calli sat there at her desk, numb. His assistant was answering his personal phone. What had he done, gone straight to her place last night? Wow, Calli. Maybe this relationship was indeed too soon. Or maybe all men are like Bennett.

Recovering, she stammered, "H-hi." Pause. "This is Callista Lindley, is Dom available?"

The sound of water running trickled through the line, and a door—a shower door by the sounds of it—closed.

Sweetly, Pauline answered, "I'm afraid he's a little indisposed right now. Is there something I can do for you? Oh—oh, hang on one sec." The creaky glass shower door sounded again, then she was back. "I'm sorry, you were saying?"

Calli gasped, throwing a hand over her mouth. Had they really meant that little? "Can you just tell . . . Mr. Moretti"— she swallowed, no, choked on the name—"that his account has been reassigned and Jordan Shuler will be in contact to reschedule his appointments?"

"Of course." The sound of running water faded.

Calli tapped the end button and stared at the dead phone, then threw it onto her desk, disgusted. He was showering. And Pauline answered his phone. He certainly didn't waste any time with moving on—or maybe back—to the next piece of ass. She dropped her face into her hands. How could she have been so stupid to have fallen for a player like that?

When she had recovered from her moment of shock, she switched to the browser and pulled up a travel site to look for deals. She needed to get away. She had her sons right now, free and clear. Scrolling through, she found flights to Orlando for two hundred each. She moved the pointer to the Book Now button. Her finger hesitated over the mouse button for a second, then clicked and booked flights leaving Friday and returning in a week. Then she went to the company vacation calendar and sent a request for six days off. Two more tasks, and she'd be all set. She booked a room at the Hilton right outside of Disney, then walked down to Jordan's, threw Dom's folder on the desk, and recapped her conversation with the harlot Pauline.

ON THURSDAY'S CLASS, JORDAN FINISHED the warm-up run—alone, without her gym partner. She picked up the workout list from Trisha's pile and read through the partnered exercises. Dom wasn't there either, but his friend, Joe, appeared at her side.

"Looks like we're both partnerless today," he said.

"It might be a good idea if we found other partners," Jordan replied.

He motioned to the rest of the class. "I think everyone else is already paired up. Looks like you and me."

Reluctantly, Jordan went to the equipment room and grabbed kettlebells for the work Trisha had prescribed. She started at the top of the list.

"Where's Calli?" Joe asked.

Jordan glared at him. "After what your friend"—he didn't deserve to be called by name—"did, she won't be coming back to class."

294

Joe's brows dropped. How incredulous, Jordan thought. He didn't know or didn't understand, she couldn't be sure which.

"Where is he, by the way?" she asked.

"He took an unexpected business trip. What did he do?" Joe air-quoted.

"He dumped her in the middle of her having to deal with her ex endangering her kids' lives."

"No way?!" He looked genuinely shocked.

"You didn't know? Then he had the nerve to shack up with his admin assistant."

"What?! Not a chance." Joe shook his head.

"Well, when Calli called his personal phone, Pauline answered, and someone was showering in the background. You're a lawyer, right? I think you can put two and two together." Jordan rolled her eyes. "Let's just work out, can we?"

Thirty-Four

CALLI STEPPED OFF THE SHUTTLE at the Hilton into the hot, sticky air. It felt wonderful to be in shorts at the end of January and away from all the stress she'd been under. This was her leaving it behind, her chance to not be with a man, the start of finding her new identity as a single woman and mother. Seeing her boys so happy after the stress of their father's DUI was likewise refreshing.

Jax stopped and waited at the door, two plastic Universal Studios bags in hand, and Kent came running off the shuttle after her, carrying his wand and still wearing the Hogwarts robe that she'd splurged on for him. She still couldn't believe she'd forked over more than two hundred dollars for a souvenir, but she would've paid double to see her youngest in a state this happy. It probably also helped that she'd pulled him out of school to come on this trip.

Inside, they went to the glass elevators, passing all the gardens that spilled into the lobby from the outdoors, and up to the ninth floor. Jax swiped the card to unlock the room and held the door while they entered, Kent first.

Kent hung up his new wizard's robe—probably the only piece of clothing he'd hung up in months. Calli hid a smile. Maybe one day, he'd learn to care for all his things better. Maybe this was a sign. She could hope. Back in modern-day shorts and T-shirt, he threw himself down onto the bed and grabbed the remote. "Hey, Mom," he called. "There's a red light blinking on the phone."

Calli picked it up and pressed the message button.

"Good afternoon. This is Sal from the concierge desk. Your limo to dinner will be waiting at the front door at seven for your seven-thirty reservation at Moonfish."

The message beeped to an end, and Calli stared at the dead phone. "But we don't have a reservation?" she questioned, confused.

Her boys also gave her a pair of puzzled looks.

"I'll be right back." She grabbed the room key and headed down to the concierge's desk where she waited in line behind an older couple wearing matching white and yellow golfing attire. She smiled at the sight; it would have been so nice to have grown old with someone. At the thought, she turned and chewed on a nail, scanning the lobby that bustled with tourists returning from one amusement park or another.

"May I help you?" the gentleman behind the desk asked.

Calli whirled around. "Oh, yes." She read the nametag. "Sal. I am in room 938, you left a message on my room phone about a limo that would be here to pick me up for a dinner reservation."

Sal scrolled through something on his tablet, then apparently finding what he was looking for, smiled. "Yes, your driver will be waiting at 7:00 p.m. Did you need to change the time?"

She shook her head. "No. I think you may have called the wrong room. I didn't order a limo, and I don't have reservations."

The concierge dropped his brow, scratching his goatee. "Funny, it says here that we have a reservation for three at Moonfish—quite a lovely seafood restaurant, might I add—at seven-thirty. And the notes say that the restaurant called to confirm it this morning around ten. The names on the reservation are Callista, Jackson, and Kent Lindley. That is your party, correct?"

Calli pursed her lips and said softly, "Stockton. Jackson and Kent Stockton. I'm Lindley. But I didn't book that. And I didn't order a car."

"If you'd like, Ms. Lindley, I can call and cancel the reservation and the driver?" Sal offered.

She shook her head, still confused.

"We see this sometimes as a gift from the travel agency," Sal offered, but that didn't sound very likely either.

"Okay. Well, we didn't have plans other than pizza or room service." Maybe this would be okay. Seafood, she contemplated. "Do they have sushi?"

"Oh, yes. You'll definitely enjoy Moonfish. It's one of my favorites. They have the best lobster bisque in Florida, and their sushi is to die for."

"Hmm." Calli raised her brows. "That'll seal the deal for

Jax. I guess we'll be down at seven. How should we dress?"

"The upper end of casual. Slacks or a sundress would be nice for you. No ties required for the boys." The corners of Sal's eyes crinkled as he smiled. "Do let me know if you need anything else, Ms. Lindley."

Somehow he reminded Calli of her father, so she returned the buoyant smile. "Thank you, Sal."

Back up the elevator and to her room, Calli swiped the card and went inside. "Let's get ready for dinner. Apparently, there will be a limo here in an hour to take us for seafood and sushi." Jax hopped up from the bed and headed to the bathroom. The door clicked shut and the spray of the shower began. Calli grinned.

Kent went to the dresser where he'd stowed his clothes.

"You need a shower, too," she said, infusing that motherly warning tone into her voice. "It's somewhat upscale, so get your dress pants from the closet. The polo shirt should be okay." She pulled out a shirt for Jax and laid it on the bed, then went to the closet and pulled a floor-length sundress for herself. The boys had been watching anime again—something she simply couldn't find an interest in, so she grabbed her book and sat in a chair to wait her turn in the shower.

Thirty-Five

ON THE TRIP TO MOONFISH, Calli had peppered the driver with questions about who'd arranged the ride and who was paying, but he was tight-lipped to the point that she wondered if he spoke English. The only thing he said was a heavily accented, "Paid in full." Calli looked at him funny in the rear-view mirror. Russian, she wondered briefly.

Under the backlit Moonfish sign, the stained-glass doors boasted a huge metal sculpture of a tropical fish in a wooden circle. The sculpture and the circle were split in half and served as the handles. Calli heaved the door open. Surprised at how easily and quickly it swung outward, she let out a little embarrassed giggle.

"Whoa there, muscles," Jax said with a glint in his eye.

The hostess stand was staffed with two young women managing the floor. Both disappeared with the two parties who'd arrived before them, leaving them waiting. In the dining room to one side, on the far wall, was a long sushi bar where three chefs were chopping and artfully decorating plates. To the other side, an open-air kitchen behind a stone counter and staff in white manned the grill and prep areas. The steak and seafood scents mingled in the air and made Calli's mouth water. She supposed that walking around an amusement park for hours on end stirred up quite the appetite.

When one of the hostesses returned, Calli approached the stand. "I believe there is a reservation for three under Lindley?"

She scanned the screen, tapped, then grabbed three menus. "Right this way." The hostess led the way toward the booths at the far end of the grill room.

Her boys went first, and Calli pulled up the rear. She checked her phone for the time, then stowed it in her purse as they walked. When they arrived at the table, her boys both turned to her abruptly, then looked with twin raised brows between her and the booth.

Calli gasped, a hand flying to her mouth. "Dom?"

He slid from the booth and reached for her.

She backed away. "What are you doing here?"

He dropped his eyes and hands. "Will you . . . all three of you . . . have dinner with me? And I'll explain." He held out a hand for the boys to take a seat, but they looked to her for permission.

Calli nodded once, and they both slid into one side of the booth.

Dom whispered, "Calli, I was wrong—in so many ways,

I was wrong."

Her eyes prickled.

Dom shook his head. "Don't." He swept a tear away as it leaked from her eye, then held out his arms.

She hesitated but then went to him, not strong enough to resist. After a minute, she pulled back and wiped her eyes, then took the inside of the booth, Dom sitting down beside her. His hand landed on her knee under the table, and he gave her his heart-melting crooked grin. Calli's cheeks felt warm as she looked between her awestruck boys and the man who'd followed her to Florida.

Dom followed her gaze toward Jax and Kent. "We should do this properly." He stretched a hand across the table. "My name is Dominic Moretti."

Jax's eyes flicked to Calli, and he took Dom's hand when she nodded her approval. "I'm Jax."

Dom reached across to Kent.

Calli's younger son reached over. "Uh, Kent," he said, then retracted his hand quickly as if discomfited.

"It's very nice to meet you both. I've been seeing your mother for the last couple of months. I must apologize for not greeting you properly that night when we first met. I wasn't quite feeling like myself." He squeezed Calli's knee under the table. "Do you like seafood? Or sushi?" he asked.

Jax beamed. "Sushi is my absolute favorite!"

Kent showed less enthusiasm. "I'll probably just get a California Roll."

Dom pursed his lips, nodding. "The Cali Roll is very good, but I recommend the Rainbow Dragon."

Jax flipped through the menu and quickly read the description. "Holy shit! That has like everything," he said without looking up. "Yeah, I'm in!"

When he did pull his nose out of the menu, Calli glared at him. He was always so raw and honest, but did he really have to swear when he first met people?

Dom must've seen her worry, because he squeezed her knee again and smiled. "So, Kent . . . you're not a sushi fan, what do you like?"

He shrugged. "A lot of things."

"Pizza," Jax scoffed, "and bread, and anything full of sugar."

Kent backhanded his brother. "I like more than that."

Calli ducked her head to hide a smirk. Kent really didn't eat much. She usually had to force him to eat protein of any kind, and it always surprised her when he tried new things. He was a creature of habit, hated change, and steered toward anything bland or sweet.

Dom jumped in. "There's a roll here called the Sweet and Sassy. It's a lot like a Cali but has crunchies on top and is doused with eel sauce. I'll order it, and you can give it a try. If you like it, we can order some more."

Calli's heart swelled. That was precisely the way to win over Kent, and she loved the fact that Dom naturally encouraged him while not belittling or perpetuating conflict between the boys.

He turned back to Jax. "And you're an artist?"

Jax had taken a drink of water, so it gave Calli a moment to jump in before he could answer. She was puzzled as they'd never talked about her boys. "How'd you know that?"

"When I was waiting for you that night after . . . well, you know . . . I noticed a couple of paintings in your hall signed Jax."

Running his fingers through the sweat dripping from the water glass, Jax said, "I guess. At least I hope to be one day."

"Nonsense," said Calli. "You're super-talented. He won three prizes in the school art expo and has published two graphic novels with a third in the works. Modest is what he really is."

Jax tucked his hair behind an ear as his cheeks pinkened.

"That is impressive. I'll have to see the graphic novels, but the paintings were very good," said Dom. "What are you planning to do after school?"

"I'm going to study graphic design," Jax answered. "But it'd be awesome if I could do something like movie special effects."

"That sounds like tons of fun!" Dom turned his attention to Kent. "What do you like to do?"

Calli caught the flick of Kent's eyes toward her and hoped he wouldn't say what she thought he would. The kid was dead set on being a professional video gamer—yeah, he said he wanted to develop video games, but he'd never taken any initiative to start learning how. Calli had had conversations with many other parents over the years, and so many of them had children who wanted to be in the gaming industry. So many of them had kids who found ways to learn how to code on their own. So many of them had kids who'd received scholarships to colleges in Washington or California to focus on various aspects of gaming. Kent only played, and he'd play for hours without eating and only rushing to the bathroom at the last possible minute before losing control. She hoped desperately that he'd show some interest outside of playing, had worked with his school social worker to develop his career goals, had urged him to look at something a bit less competitive, but he kept coming back to the same thing.

"I want to be a game tester or programmer," he mumbled.

Calli remained silent.

"That sounds like fun, too," said Dom.

The waitress stopped by and took their drink orders, then they all opened their menus and read quietly. Calli's stomach growled, and they shared a small giggle over the sound. Dinner, no matter what it was, would taste like heaven.

$\mathcal{D}$OM PAID FOR THE MEAL, and as they were leaving, he called the boys aside. "Would the two of you mind terribly if I were to send you back to the hotel and take your mother out for dessert? I have some explaining—and quite a bit of apologizing—to do."

Kent said hesitantly, "Suuure."

Jax turned so his back was to his mother and said, "She's been really down since Dad got the DUI. She's also been really quiet, and I'm guessing that has something to do with you." He crossed his arms over his chest.

Dom pressed his lips into a tight line, guilt curdling in his gut. But at the same time, he was impressed with the young man who stood before him, trying to protect such a wonderful woman. "I was wrong in not being there for her. I won't give you any excuses, but I will vow that it won't happen again."

Jax seemed reluctant to let them go, but he nodded and went to Calli. Dom didn't hear what he asked but assumed he was making sure it was what she wanted too. They hugged, Calli wrapping her arms around Jax's waist and resting her head in the curve of his shoulder. Dom wished he had a camera at the ready to take a picture . . . the image would surely be memorable, perhaps even iconic. It reminded him of the better times with his own mother before . . . He shoved his hands into his pockets. He'd have to settle for the memory.

As the boys settled into the limo, Dom watched Calli in the soft cream-colored sundress with blue flowers from her knees to the ground. The lines of the dress hugged her curves just perfectly, and he yearned to pull her into his arms. But he would wait. He went to the valet desk and asked the attendant to call another limo. Once settled inside, he instructed the driver to Disney's Polynesian Village Resort.

As they exited the limo, Dom tipped the driver, smiled, and took Calli's hand. She looked at him with puzzled, raised brows. "When are we going to sit and talk?"

He turned back to her, pressing his body to hers, and put a finger over her mouth. "Shortly." Removing his hand, he leaned down and placed a light kiss where his finger had been. He led the way to the walk at the end of the parking area, then turned between the Tonga and Aotearoa buildings, heading for the marina and the beach beyond. When he reached the sand, he removed his shoes and had Calli do the same. Holding his shoes in one hand, he took hers with the other, and they walked along the sandy beach toward his bungalow. He crossed the first walkway and continued on the sand to the second where he lifted Calli onto the walk and lingered, holding her around the hips as she looked down on him with her rich chocolaty eyes. Reluctantly, he pulled away and climbed onto the walk himself, then pointed to the bungalow furthest out over the lake.

He entered first and turned to watch Calli's awe and small gasp as she entered behind him with wide eyes.

"This place is amazing," she said. "It must cost a fortune."

"It's quiet and private. My favorite place here at Disney."

"And you come here so often?"

He quirked a brow. "I've been here a time or two. It's not quite Tahiti or Fiji but has a similar feel. Come on." He led the way through the bungalow to the patio over the lake. Lights shone from the resort across the lake, and he could just make out the glow of Magic Kingdom beyond. The night was filled with cicadas and frogs singing to the stars. He indicated the hanging chairs, and Calli took a seat. He took the other and faced her, bringing them as close together as possible. "Now, we can talk."

Calli held up a hand to his cheek, searching his face. He couldn't resist the temptation and leaned forward, tasting her sweet lips. But he fought his urges and pulled away, resting his forehead against hers.

"I'm sorry," he said, then laughed. "I sound like a broken record, but I am so very sorry."

"I am too," she answered softly.

He snapped his eyes to hers—questioning. What could she have to be sorry for? He was the one who'd run like a scared child. "You didn't do anything to apologize for."

"I did. You kept begging me to trust you, and I didn't. Had I told you about my divorce and the boys before, this may not have happened."

Dom smiled. "You don't need to be sorry for that. I can understand why you didn't tell me about what must have been a very painful experience. And I did run after all, right?"

Calli dropped her hand. "I have to ask, though . . . Pauline?"

Dom growled in frustration. "Yeah, I need to apologize for that. I guess I led her on a little."

Calli pulled back, face wide with shock.

"Oh, not like that. I invited her to Thanksgiving at Moretti's with Joe and his wife, and she thought it meant more than friends."

She folded her hands in her lap. "But what about the other day? She said you were in the shower?"

"Calli, I had lunch with Jordan and Joe yesterday. They told me what Pauline did to you." He hesitated, grinding his teeth in lingering anger. "I went on a business trip the day after your ex's DUI. I forwarded all my business and personal lines to Pauline. She knew that we'd started dating and took advantage of the opportunity. I was in Montreal at the time."

"Oh," was all Calli said.

"I promptly fired her and booked the next flight to Orlando to explain. Jordan told me where you were. I think she's rooting for us." He shot her a wide smile. "What else do

I need to make up for?"

She shook her head, her eyes glistening with unshed tears.

𝒞ALLI COULDN'T BELIEVE WHAT SHE was hearing, or for that matter, experiencing. Her chest was so tight with hope, she couldn't speak. The knot in her throat and the watering eyes didn't help either. Dom was here. He'd actually come after her. The tears fell, and Calli laughed through the waterworks. "Where's your white horse?"

"If you want me to get one, I surely will." His green-gray eyes sparkled like the moon that reflected over the lake. They both laughed, and his eyes leaked a little too. Then he asked, "So, am I forgiven?"

Calli kissed him. "Only if I am."

"You, my beautiful orchid, are." He pushed her curls over a shoulder and dropped his lips to the curve of her neck. Chills ran up her spine, and she melted for him once again. As he trailed up her neck and reached her ear, his other hand slid under her hair. "Callista Linnea, I'm falling for you like I never have before, and I'm scared."

She pulled back so that they were face-to-face. "I'm scared, too, but I've already fallen. I realized that when you walked out my front door last weekend. It was what I asked for by not sharing with you, but I broke when you left."

Dom pulled her from the chair and into his arms. He kissed her slowly, lovingly, over and over and over again. The tears on her cheeks mingled with his—regardless of how happy she was to be back in his arms. At length, he slowed, then led her to the bedroom, lowering her onto the king-sized bed. Tenderly, they undressed one another. He settled beside her, their naked bodies just touching, and roamed his hand over her hip and waist and stopped to give attention to an aching nipple. Soon, the hand was replaced by his warm, wet tongue. Calli whimpered, and when he pulled away and smiled, the air was cold on her exposed wet skin. She let her hands wander over his chest and hard abs, then lower to where he was ready and patiently waiting for her ministrations. They explored each other with touch and tongue for some time before he laid back and pulled her on top of him.

She sat up with a sigh, pulling her hair to one side. His hands found her breasts as she found his length and settled onto him. They both exhaled heavily, and as her body adjusted once again to his size, she began small, slow movements, then circled. There was no immediate urgency, the feel of him was enough, and she sensed the same in him. He ran his hands from her breasts down her waist and settled them on her hips as she rocked. She stared deeply into his green-gray eyes and felt a connection she only vaguely recalled. Then, on the heels of that thought, the need built and bloomed around the word she wouldn't yet acknowledge, the name she was reluctant to give to her emotion. The tempo sped up, and Dom sat to meet her. Face-to-face, breath-to-breath, they rocked, matching one another's movements in a perfect dance, pressing closer and closer and closer until Calli threw her head back and screamed his name. He did the same, and their bodies froze in shared orgasmic embrace. As she surfed the rolling and cresting waves, her head fell forward onto his shoulder, and they panted.

c*A*N HOUR LATER, CALLI ROSE and dressed to return to the Hilton. She would have loved nothing more than to stay warm in Dom's arms, but her boys would be waiting. Dom pulled her back and stared at her with an urgent and frightened look.

"Calli, we didn't use protection. I d-don't want children."

Calli placed a hand on his chest. "You don't have to worry about that. I had some complications after Kent and ended up with a hysterectomy." She smiled. His concern didn't worry her. She'd almost finished raising her children and wasn't about to start over. "We're in solid agreement on the not getting pregnant thing."

Dom breathed a sigh of relief and grabbed a T-shirt. "I'll see you back to your hotel. Do you think your sons would be willing to move over here for the remainder of your trip? I'd like to spend more time with you and get to know them a little."

"Are you certain? I'm not asking you to be a part of their lives."

"I want to be a part of yours, and they are a big part of you." He rubbed a thumb over her cheek.

"Very well, I'll ask. I'm sure they will. This is a hell of a lot nicer place than the room we have."

Thirty-Six

THE DAYS FOLLOWING WERE SOMETHING Calli had never expected. She'd thought that dating with kids would be the hardest part, but the boys and Dom took to one another and bonded quickly. It was as if they were old friends and had known each other for the last decade. At one point, Dom even mentioned to her that he was surprised himself about how much he enjoyed their company. They'd gone together to Magic Kingdom and Disney's Animal Kingdom, and it was the best vacation she could recall.

For the plane ride home, Dom had upgraded them all to first class, and they had commandeered the second row of the plane—Dom stating that he hated the first row because you didn't have the tray in front of you. The boys played Magic: The Gathering the whole way home with the extra room they had. Calli cuddled with Dom, and they'd whispered about the fun they'd had over the last few days.

After the plane landed, Dom took Calli's hands and

turned to face her so that the boys couldn't see or hear their conversation. "Before we get off this plane, I want you to know that the last three days have been the most fun I've had in I can't remember how long. I want you to know that the last couple of months, and our dates and relationship, have been the best things to happen to me in, I think, ever." He swallowed, and Calli chewed her lip in worry for a minute. Her old, scared friend crept up as she waited nervously for him to finish. "Anyway, I just wanted to tell you . . . I think . . . no, that's not right. I love you." He dropped his eyes.

Calli exhaled and grinned, then reached over and raised his chin. "It's fast, but I love you too."

They kissed just as the seat belt sign dinged and chaos broke loose with people trying to get off the plane.

"Mom! Let's go," said Kent with an eye roll, then she heard him murmur to Jax, "Gross."

OFF THE PLANE AND AT the baggage claim, Calli, Dom, Jax, and Kent waited. The belt hadn't started when Calli felt a hand tap her on the shoulder. She turned to a police officer.

"Are you Callista Lindley, ma'am?" he said.

"I am," she replied.

"My name is Officer Thomas Washington. I need you to come with me."

"What? Why?" Calli asked.

Dom stepped in front of her.

The officer looked toward the doors. Bennett Stockton

with his now live-in girlfriend, Zoe, were standing by one of the benches.

Officer Washington said, "Mr. Stockton has filed charges against you for kidnapping." The officer looked the nearly full-grown boys doubtfully up and down. "I'm sorry but just doing my job. According to the legal papers, you're not allowed to take them across state lines without permission from their father." He pulled out the cuffs.

Dom held out a hand. "I don't think you'll need those. We don't need to make a scene."

Calli said weakly, "Yeah, I'll come."

"Mom?" Kent threw his arms around her.

She hugged him back. "It'll be all right," she said and smoothed his hair. "You're going to have to go with your dad though. Jax?" She held out her arm for him. When he hugged her, she whispered, "Please take care of him."

Jax nodded.

Calli turned to Dom. "You should probably go. I think you were right to not want to be tangled up with me and this mess. It seems to be getting nastier and nastier. You move on. I'll call you when I have some normalcy in my life, and maybe we can try again." She ducked her head and went with the officer. It would only be three years or so, right?

Bennett passed her without meeting her eyes as he walked toward her sons. Fucking asshole, she thought. Zoe, on the other hand, met her gaze and smirked radiantly on Bennett's behalf. It was all Calli could do to not lunge for the trollop, but she took a little satisfaction in knowing that she'd get a dose of her own medicine when Bennett turned the tables on her just as soon as things started to fall from their perky places. She was only eight years older than their son, for Christ's sake. Maybe she'd have a kid too. The next one in Bennett's long line would probably be even younger than Jax. Calli shook her head and walked through the sliding glass doors into the cold Minnesota air and allowed the officer to help her into the back of the car. Lights danced on the concrete pillars and walls as Officer Washington drove her away.

$\mathcal{D}$OMINIC PULLED OUT HIS PHONE and called his lawyer. "Joe, can you get me a defense attorney for Calli? Her ex is a real piece of work."

Joe answered, "Yeah, I have a good friend. What are the charges?"

"He filed kidnapping charges against her for taking the boys out of state without his permission."

"Wow, what a dick move."

"Yeah, I think he's just trying to make a show of her being arrested too. He had cops waiting at the airport."

"Okay, I'll call Karl."

"Thanks." Dom hung up the phone and took a long cleansing breath, blowing out deliberately.

Bennett Stockton approached wearing the most superior grin he'd ever seen. Narcissist, thought Dom as he stepped between the boys and their father. He probably shouldn't, but that man needed a lesson in morality, or at the very least reality.

"What are you doing? How could you have their mother arrested in front of them? Don't you think that might be a little damaging?"

Bennett looked at Dom from head to toe. "And you are?"

"That's beside the point."

"Well, since those are my sons behind you, you'd best step aside before I have you arrested as her accomplice. She knew not to take them out of state, and she took the opportunity while I was taking care of legal matters of my own."

"Yeah, you drove drunk. With your children in the car. What's the matter with you?"

"This is none of your business, and I wasn't drunk."

"Apparently the breathalyzer said you were."

"Again, you are a perfect stranger, and this matter is none of your business." Bennett looked around, presumably for another police officer.

Dom felt a nudge on his shoulder. Jax stepped forward. "No, Dad. This is insane. You know that Mom didn't kidnap us, and you knew that she was bringing us back. Otherwise you wouldn't be here."

"Jackson," said Bennett.

Jax held up his hand. "I go by Jax. That is not changing no matter how much you want it to. I'm going to a school for arts. That, too, is not changing."

Bennett moved around toward Kent. "Let's discuss this at home."

"That's not our home." Kent backed away and hid

behind Jax.

Jax said, "You should know that Mom has been the biggest reason why we haven't asked the judge to let us live with her full time. She's defended you all the way while you hooked up with . . . with . . . her." Jax pointed at the woman by the bench.

Bennett's girlfriend was precisely the kind of woman who had always made Dom want to remain single. So different from Calli, this person, who could barely be called a woman at her young age, who wore too much makeup, and who strutted around in clothes a size too small, reminded him a little of Pauline.

Jax put an arm around his brother. "We're not going with you. We're going with Dom. We're going to meet the lawyer he just called. We're going to get our mother out of jail. And, we are going to petition the judge to have the custody order revoked. We are both over fifteen, and that's the legal age."

The carousel whirred to life, but the silence was otherwise thick as the crowd had stopped to stare.

*C*ALLI SAT IN THE COLD cell with only a scratchy blanket for warmth and cried. She kept trying to get her life on a happy path, but the results always ended up the same—her landing some form of disaster. This was the first time in her life she'd ever been arrested. The booking, strip search, observed shower, and dingy gray clothes were only the surface humiliation. Wait until she had to tell her mother what had happened. That would be the worst kind of torment she could imagine.

Thinking of her mother and father reminded her . . . she wondered how their trip home had been. She wondered how her father's speech on the latest in orchid genetics had gone. Her stomach knotted with guilt. She should have gone to the speech rather than work that day. She wondered, not for the first time, what she was doing in financial services. The pay was decent, but it was nothing special. She was good at her job, but again, it was nothing special. She'd made friends, and they were dear to her, but it didn't require she stay in the Cities. She missed the perfumed and humid greenhouses. She missed seeing her father's face alight with pleasure when she learned something new about the orchids or when she brought a new plant into bloom. Why hadn't she followed what she loved as a child?

Instead, she'd married a suave and charming man. Sure, they'd been happy during the first years, but what she predicted would happen to Zoe was exactly what had happened to her—she'd started to age. Bennett liked young and tight bodies. In relationships, that's the only thing he really prized. She'd seen it time and time again in the second decade of their so-called marriage. He was dead set on climbing the corporate ladder, and he took his pleasure wherever he traveled and with whomever he pleased. When they were both in college, Bennett's enthusiasm about the corporate life was contagious, and Calli had chosen to follow that thirst—had thought it was her own. But it wasn't hers, and she knew that now.

In the lonely and cold, dark, and damp cell, she decided that when she was out of here and through this mess, she'd move closer to home and begin taking botany classes. Online if she could, because she had the best lab imaginable at

Lindleyi Manor. She'd obviously stay on the Minnesota side of the Mississippi, she didn't want to land in jail again for taking Jax and Kent across state lines.

Ha! What an effin' joke!

Working out the custody thing would be challenging, but she thought they could figure something out. Maybe they'd alternate full weeks instead of split weeks. She had some money saved, and the proceeds from the house would get her started. She was certain she could work in the family business and make ends meet. She must have just had to hit rock bottom before realizing that she needed to go home.

Maybe after she discovered herself—who she really should have been—she could reach out to Dom. It was doubtful but she could hope that such a wonderful man would then still be available and want her. Calli sighed and curled up on the hard bench—exhausted from everything but somehow feeling better about the forward direction. Hopefully, Jax and Kent would be okay with the decision. She'd wait until summer so Jax could graduate first, but she thought Kent would like it better there—being around the greenhouses and the science. Just like her father, he'd always loved the science behind the family business.

She'd just dozed off when the clattering slide of the metal bars brought her rudely awake, and she sat up straight. A female officer, she thought the one she'd met at reception the night of Bennett's DUI, motioned a stranger dressed in a navy-blue suit into the cell. The young officer with the severely tight bun left without a word and without closing the door, but the man came in and sat on the bench beside Calli.

"Calli, my name is Karl Gordon." He was tall with sandy

hair and a long face. "You may know my friend and colleague, Joe Cates."

Recognition hit her. Lawyer Joe. Dom's lawyer. "Yes. But that doesn't explain why you're here."

"Joe called in a favor. If you're okay with it, I'll be your lawyer in the matter. I'll just need you to sign a client-attorney agreement." He dug in his bag. "I have it here."

"Mr. Larson, I appreciate you coming down here and all, but this matter is just petty. The DA should be here in the morning. I'm sure they'll take care of it without me having to hire a big defense lawyer."

"My fees are already paid. So the hiring has already been done. I just need you to sign here." He cocked a half smile while holding the paper to his bag and handing over a pen.

Puzzled, but too tired to worry over it, Calli signed. She'd figure out how to pay him back tomorrow.

"Great," said the lawyer. "Let's get you out of here so you can sleep in your own bed tonight."

Just then, the severe young officer returned with Calli's purse and clothes. "There's a toilet there." She pointed to a door right outside the opening.

Calli ducked inside and changed quickly, leaving the gray clothes in a pile on the floor. Rejoining the lawyer, they walked through the same room where she'd met the boys the night after Cinderella and toward the lobby of the Minneapolis Police Department. She dug in her bag for her phone so she could call for a Ryde and was watching the cars drive around the screen as they made it into the waiting area.

"Mom!" Kent called her attention from the phone.

Standing in a huddle were her two boys and Dom. She dropped the phone and ran into their collective waiting arms. Dom—her Dom—wrapped his arms around all three of them. Calli looked up at his piercing, light-green eyes, once again fighting back tears.

Thirty-Seven

CALLISTA LINNEA LINDLEY STOOD ON the balcony of her bridal rooms in Neuschwanstein Castle overlooking the Alps. The dress she wore looked every bit like Ella's in the final scenes of the Broadway production of Cinderella. Yes, it was her second wedding, but in this one, she was having the wedding she'd imagined when she was a child. Dom would be in a white tux with a gray vest that matched his eyes. She couldn't wait to see him dressed for the role of Prince Charming.

Neuschwanstein castle, the inspiration for Disney's Sleeping Beauty, was also one of the many that inspired Cinderella. It felt ideal for her own personal fairy tale, and the fact that the name of the castle meant "New Swan Stone" was just magical. King Ludwig II's dressing room on the third floor had been appropriated as Calli's bridal room.

Of course, she wasn't allowed to use the historic furniture, but the wedding planners brought in a temporary vanity that melded with the décor beautifully. The artwork on the ceiling depicted a garden bower with vines climbing a trellis to an open sky. Seats were covered in violet silk and embroidered with gold, and the view over the valley was simply magnificent.

Cat, Calli's sister, came in and pinned her hair with the heirloom sapphires handed down in their mother's family for six generations. Their mother was at her side wearing lacy midnight blue.

"Calli, darling." Isabelle held out her arms with a wide smile on her face. As she came closer, her eyes lowered shamefully. She took her daughter in her arms and whispered, "I was wrong to have pressured you so hard to stay with— well, you know. We don't need to soil this day with ghosts from the past."

Calli melted at her mother's long-awaited acknowledgement and admission. She came away from her mother, shifting the layers upon layers of white tulle as she did so, and held her mother's hands.

"You are the epitome of sophisticated beauty," said Isabelle. "You were pretty on your wedding day all those years ago, but I don't think you could have looked this radiant when you married before. Today, darling, you are the woman you were meant to be. And Dom is who you are meant to be with."

Calli's heart was full. She'd been elated when her family accepted him with open arms as if he'd been a part of them for as long as they could remember. Alder and Dom had talked cars like they were old friends. Jon had given him all sorts of marital advice, whatever that meant. And to hear her mother—though not quite apologizing—admitting her errors in how she'd considered Bennett was music to her ears. She looked deep into her mother's glistening brown eyes, the ones she and Cat had inherited. "Mom, thank you. Everything about this day is ideal. I love you and Dad, and I am so elated that Dad has accepted me back into the business."

"He was waiting for you, darling. He has been waiting for you for twenty-something years."

Cat joined in the hugfest. "Calli, Mom's right. You're radiant. And you were always meant to follow in the family business. You were the one who hung on his every word as a child. It's just right."

Jon's wife, Meg, carrying their baby in her arms, poked her head into the room. "The boys are ready and heading up to Singers' Hall."

Calli took a deep breath and let it go loudly as her best friend, Jordan, came into the room behind Meg. Her friends Tory and Trina trailed. All three wore the silver empire-waisted dresses Calli had chosen for the bridesmaids. Chiffon flowed around the three women as they came to Calli's side.

Jordan handed Calli a bouquet full of none other than amazing yellow-gold lindleyi orchids. With a smile, she asked, "Are you ready?"

AS CALLI ENTERED SINGERS' HALL, her breath was once again stolen by the beauty of her surroundings. She couldn't imagine the favors Dom must have had to call in to secure the famous hall in the eastern section on the fourth floor of a castle that averaged six thousand tourists per day in the summer. She looked up at the intricate golden chandeliers, then back to the small crowd lining the aisle. Family and close friends only, there were still more than twenty in attendance. Tory went first on Kent's arm, then Trina on Jax's, and Jordan as the maid of honor took Joe's arm. Then Calli's father stepped forward wearing the most amazing smile.

"My dearest daughter. I couldn't be happier and prouder for you," said Richard Lindley, and lifted the lip of a lindleyi orchid in her bouquet before extending his elbow.

She took the arm. "Thank you, Dad. I love you."

"I love you, honey."

Together, they took the first steps down the aisle.

*F*RUSTRATED AND IMPATIENT, DOM STRETCHED his neck one way, then the other. He could see the edges of the white dress, but the procession blocked his view of his bride. Joe grinned as he came down the aisle. As he and Jordan parted, Dom knew he'd never seen a princess in more grandeur than his orchid, Callista soon-to-be Moretti. The pitched ceilings, murals, inlaid flooring, their friends and family all fell away when the most splendid woman in the world stepped toward him. The dress was more magical than any he'd seen in a fairy tale, but his gaze traced the bared line of her neck, revealed perfectly by the updo. On her lips, she wore a shy but joyful smile.

326

Calli handed her bouquet of orchids to Jordan and reached for him.

Dom's hands shook as Richard Lindley took them and placed Calli's hands in Dom's. Hopefully they weren't sweaty with anticipation, but if they were, she didn't seem to mind. In the moments before the minister stepped forward to begin the ceremony, a full but silent conversation leapt between their gazes, but he could only manage a few small words—inadequate though they were. "I am the luckiest man on earth." He lifted her hands and kissed her left ring finger on the spot where he would soon place the ring.

The minister began the ceremony by asking who gave this woman away, and Calli's father responded, "Her mother and I."

"Thank you," replied the priest formally.

The ceremony continued with minimal fanfare, and he turned the floor over to the couple for their custom vows. Dom shifted his stance as he began. "Callista Linnea Lindley, you are the half of me that I never knew. You brought out who I needed to become. You showed me beauty in things I feared, and I am a better man today because I have had the pleasure of knowing you." He squeezed her hands.

Calli gave a small nervous laugh, bit her lip, and started with her own vows. "Dominic Andre Moretti, I never thought to love again, and today, I stand here before you and everyone I care about wholeheartedly in love with the most wonderful man alive. You are the other half of me, and you were absent for far too long. Your persistence and patience are the reasons why we are standing here today, loving each other for all to see."

Dom said, "Will you be my wife . . . for today, tomorrow,

and forever more?"

"I will," answered Calli. "And will you be my husband . . . for this moment, this month, and until the end of time?"

Dom grinned. "Happily, I will." He took the ring from his pocket. "I give this ring to you as an endless circle symbolizing my love for you."

Calli turned to Jordan who placed a ring in her hand. "Two circles entwined, symbolizing infinity and my love for you."

The minister stepped forward and gave the cue for Dom to kiss his bride, and he did so with more enthusiasm than anything he'd done before. Her lips were honey sweet and she smelled like the orchids of her father's greenhouse, and when Dom finished kissing her, he held her for a long time and she held him. They were alone in the crowd until the priest's announcement came.

"I present to you . . . Mister and Missus Moretti. May the Lord bless and watch over their union."

Thirty-Eight

THE COMMOTION THAT FOLLOWED THE announcement of the newly married couple turned into melodies and harmonies as the family and friends broke into cheers. A murmur of conversation unfolded as hugs were shared by all, beginning with Richard and Isabelle, who looked lovingly into each other's eyes and shared a sweet kiss that rejoiced in the happiness of their family inside the fairy tale castle. Jon and Meg stood side-by-side with his arm around her shoulder. She held their child, and they both gave the newlyweds a nod of congratulations. As for Tory and Steve, one would think they had just renewed their vows as they embraced in a kiss almost as epic as Dom and Calli's.

Jax wrapped his mother in a hug that bespoke of pride he seemed too young to possess. Kent gave Dom a slightly awkward embrace, but Superman wore a smile as he did so. Toward the back of the crowd, one unexpected hug lingered a little longer than anyone had anticipated. Nudges and head nods were shared all around as one-by-one the family turned all attention in their direction.

Realizing they had an audience, they separated, cheeks aglow. Shifting his weight from one foot to the other, Alder glanced sidelong at Jordan, who tucked a blonde curl behind her ear and smiled shyly at the floor.

Isabelle leaned over to Richard and stage-whispered, "Looks like we'll be planning another wedding before long."

He turned to his wife and took her into his arms. "I can't imagine anything better."

Epilogue

IN THEIR HONEYMOON SUITE, CALLI propped her elbow on the pillow and gazed at her new husband stretched out beside her on their marital bed. She couldn't banish the smile from her face, and it seemed Dom was having the same problem. "Neuschwanstein was a spectacular choice. You'll still have to tell me how you called in such a favor."

"Nothing but the best for my beautiful orchid."

Calli worried at her lip, then said, "Thank you for everything. Now and then. You truly saved my life, I think."

"I could say the same." He reached up and pushed her hair away from her eyes.

"It's still so hard for me to believe you were never in love before me."

"Calli, I think this was a true destiny. Our destiny. I'm just sorry you had to go through so much pain to receive this much happiness."

She smiled and kissed him lightly on the lips. "Could you be any more perfect?"

He shrugged, "Probably not."

"Or modest?" She laughed, then turned serious. "Are you certain about moving? You've never lived away from the city."

"We'll keep the loft above Moretti's, but you need to be close to your family. You need to be involved with the business. It's a part of you, and therefore, it's a part of us and me."

"Again, thank you. I'm just so relieved that Bennett gave up the battle to keep the boys in the city."

"It was a little hard after Jax turned eighteen, don't you think? And with both boys demanding to live with you, it really made his points invalid."

"You're right. I'm also happy the boys have agreed to keep trying with him. Family is family and walking away is something they'd certainly regret."

Dom rolled her over and kissed her until they were both breathless. When he pulled back, he said, "This is why we need to be near Lindleyi. You know this family thing from firsthand experience, and I'll not have you walking away from yours again." He kissed down her chin. "Besides, I think you should try to get Kent into the family business. The kid's smart beyond belief. School's just not his thing."

Calli raised a brow. "For not wanting a family, you fit tightly into mine."

They kissed again, and Mr. and Mrs. Moretti enjoyed each other well into the night.

The End

Book reviews

are the best way

to support an author!

If you enjoyed this story, please leave a review anywhere you can give a shout out! Access Susan's Portfolio

https://susanstradiotto.com/susansportfolio/

Order the next in series: *Midnight Orchid*

https://books2read/midnightorchid

9 781949 357394